## "Dance with me," insisted Betsy

Drew looked pleasantly surprised, but Betsy said, "Please, I've just spotted that nosy reporter. I don't want publicity any more than you do, and I don't trust him."

As they moved around the floor, Betsy said, "Thanks. You're a good dancer, you know that?" She hadn't planned on being so close to him. She wished her pulse would stop hammering.

"I've never taken lessons," Drew replied, moving his palm across her back, "but no one's ever complained."

"I can see why," she murmured. His eyes caught hers and held. She was intoxicated, but not with wine.

Just then their dance was interrupted. Betsy was needed by her kitchen staff, so with an apology she hurried off the floor. Before disappearing into the kitchen she glanced back longingly at Drew...

...and saw him walk over to the reporter, whom Drew, too, had supposedly wanted to avoid, and greet him like a long-lost friend.

So, thought Betsy, she had been deceived....

# ABOUT THE AUTHOR

Linda and Walter Rice, the husband and wife writing team who publish under the pseudonym Linda Walters, thought the Yukon would make an ideal setting for their second Intrigue. Having been there herself, Linda says the spell of the Yukon is unforgettable. Also unforgettable was their first Intrigue, *Dragon's Eye*, set in North Wales, where they had their honeymoon. Prior to writing with her husband, Linda wrote with Stella Cameron under the pseudonym Alicia Brandon. Together they produced *Love Beyond Question*, an American Romance, and *Full Circle*, an Intrigue. Linda and Walter live in a suburb of Seattle, Washington, with their one son, one dog and one cat.

## Books by Linda Walters

HARLEQUIN INTRIGUE
60–DRAGON'S EYE

## Books by Alicia Brandon

HARLEQUIN AMERICAN ROMANCE
121–LOVE BEYOND QUESTION

HARLEQUIN INTRIGUE
40–FULL CIRCLE

# Dead Reckoning

**Linda Walters**

## *Harlequin Books*

TORONTO • NEW YORK • LONDON
AMSTERDAM • PARIS • SYDNEY • HAMBURG
STOCKHOLM • ATHENS • TOKYO • MILAN

For Linda's parents, Lester and Goldie Mally—

You loved and encouraged us—
your love of the Yukon inspired us.

Harlequin Intrigue edition published January 1988

ISBN 0-373-22082-0

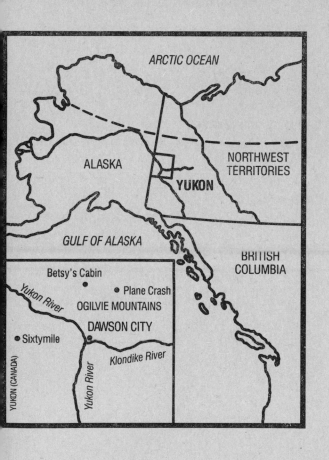

# CAST OF CHARACTERS

*Betsy Archer*—She was ready for love . . . but not the dangers that came with it.

*Drew McKay*—He was a man with a mission. Nothing would stand in his way.

*Sam McKay*—Devoted father? Or a man his son never really knew.

*Jacob Talbot*—He was an old friend. Might he be even more?

*Greg Harsted*—A nosy reporter driven beyond the call of duty.

*Evie Saunders*—What secrets was she hiding?

*Conrad Parks*—He'd willed his granddaughter much more than land.

# Chapter One

Betsy Archer knew something was wrong when she crested the hill. Metallic blue and white showed stark and incongruous a few hundred yards away, surrounded by the wind-torn trees of the Yukon forest. A mixture of dread and curiosity pushed her on and she scrambled over the fallen birch branches brought down by yesterday's violent windstorm, hardly daring to shift her gaze from the object below her, both fearing and hoping she'd been mistaken.

She wasn't even halfway down the hill when the danger and the urgency became clear to her. As she got closer, the blue lines and white contours between the ragged trees began to take on a distinctive, familiar form. She knew little about first aid but if she didn't help, nobody would. Out here in the Ogilvie Mountains, she was probably the only able-bodied person within miles.

Betsy broke into a run, fear fueling her pace. There was no time to waste. The plane probably had crashed during the storm, she thought. Way out here, the passengers wouldn't have had much hope of getting help unless somebody just stumbled across them.

*Assuming there were survivors.*

Betsy shook off the negative thought and charged ahead. Fate seemed to have had a hand in all this, so there was no turning back now. If she hadn't taken a break from panning for gold in the stream on the other side of the hill, she never would have wandered in this direction. And if she hadn't given herself a day off from her Dawson City nightclub, she never would have come to this remote spot northwest of town.

Fifty feet from the tail of the airplane, Betsy slowed to a walk to catch her breath, winded as much from nerves as from exertion. She couldn't help being afraid—both for the people in the plane and for herself. When her breathing quieted, Betsy strained to listen for sounds coming from the plane. Silence.

"Hello," she yelled. "Is anyone there? Hello?"

No one answered, but she was still hopeful. The passengers could be unconscious, she told herself. Or sleeping.

She circled around to the cabin of the single-engine craft, fear demanding she be cautious. She didn't know the make, though the design of the plane was familiar. There were plenty of four-seaters like it around Dawson City. The landing struts were snapped like toothpicks and the propeller was sheered off, the nose having apparently pitched into the ground. The plane seemed at rest now, settled and oddly peaceful in the sub-arctic wilderness.

She crept closer to the cockpit, not wanting to look, but knowing she had to.

Fabric. Faded red plaid. A little like her own jacket. Betsy's heart raced. Someone was inside.

She ducked under a wing of the plane and moved around to the front, part of her not believing that she was here doing this, and part of her determined to continue, driven by the understanding of what that bit of red plaid could mean.

She edged past the jagged nose, struggling through the churned-up brush until she reached a mound of earth high enough. Then she looked through the windshield....

And froze.

Goose bumps ran up her arms like a waterfall going backward. She was too late...much too late. The scream came a few seconds later—a long, piercing cry of horror.

It took Betsy a moment to recognize her own voice, then her legs backpedaled almost automatically. She crashed through the storm's debris and headed for the hill. Clearing the crest, she raced down the other side to the stream, scooped up her gold-panning gear on the fly and scrambled through rocks and brush and trees to the four-wheel-drive Bronco.

*Fleeing. That's what you're doing,* she told herself angrily. But a reasonable interior voice interceded, reminding her that she was heading for town to notify the Mounties. She'd tell them. First thing. But what if she couldn't remember the location? No, she would. She would never forget anything about the plane. Especially what she had seen slumped against its windshield, the skull with eye sockets as empty as an abandoned mine.

THE EVENING CELEBRATORS in the Fairbanks, Alaska, tavern throbbed to the primitive rhythms of a local rock band. Fueled by cut-rate drinks, the crowd wobbled and whooped as it marked the tenth anniversary of the Red Baron robbery.

In a corner booth, slightly removed from the noise of the room, Drew McKay chatted with a Canadian reporter and sipped a beer, amused by the antics of the rowdier party-goers, including the young redhead standing in front of him, who couldn't stop snapping her fingers. "Come on, Drew," she demanded. "Get out on the floor and *dance*."

He laughed. "Maybe after a while. It's not even dark yet. Right now I'm being interviewed, or at least I was." He nodded toward the reporter, Greg Harsted.

"Yeah?" The redhead gave Greg a once-over. He was the only man in the tavern wearing a sport coat and necktie. "Well, when you're done, *Mr.* McKay, come and find me. And that's an *order*." She saluted them and began weaving through the crowd to the dance floor, still snapping her fingers.

Drew shook his head. "One of my livelier acquaintances," he told Greg.

"So why aren't you out there bouncing with the rest of them?" the reporter asked, ready to scribble Drew's answer into his notebook.

Drew leaned back and shrugged. "Not my style, I guess. Maybe I'm getting old."

"Old?" Greg snorted, then emptied his glass and filled it again from the pitcher of beer Drew had bought for them. "Come on. I'm forty-four and I wish I were your age again." He ran a hand across salt-and-pepper hair that started well behind his forehead. "I'm losing my insulation, I've been divorced longer than I care to admit, and I'm scratching around in this crazy north country for a decent story that somebody will pay to read. But look at you. Fit, young bachelor... You can't be more than..." Greg let the sentence hang in the smoke-filled air, waiting for Drew to complete it.

"Thirty," Drew said, enjoying the parry with Greg. He'd watched the reporter work his way around the bar and tables, buttonholing various people and getting a feel for what he would call "local color." Greg had even taken a few photos of the more distinctive revelers.

"So, tell me more about yourself. I've researched the robbery itself to within a mosquito's eyelash," Greg said. "What I want now is human interest. You know, background on the partygoers, a cross section. I'm going to do profiles on a few of these people."

"Including me?" Drew asked. "About all I said was that some people will grab at any excuse for a party."

"Sure, but you're the only one who gave me that observation." Greg glanced at the crowd and looked back at Drew. "You're probably worth a quote or two."

"All right." Drew smiled. "Just spell my name right."

Greg cleared his throat. "You know, I really chose to talk with you because one of the people at the bar said you flew airplanes. That right?"

Drew nodded, vaguely wondering who had pointed him out, although it really made no difference to him whether his name ended up in some New York magazine. For a while, he'd keep talking and help Greg do his job. The guy seemed nice enough.

"Then I suppose you can really identify with this Red Baron stuff," Greg said with disarming casualness. "I don't mean the heist, of course, but the flying. Baron von Richthofen, the original Red Baron, was one hell of a pilot, a real ace. Shot down eighty planes in the First World War."

Drew shrugged. There was a big difference between his flying and the daredevil antics of the Baron. "No one knows for sure how the robbers left Fairbanks. They wore World War One aviator costumes: goggles, leather jackets and red scarves. So everyone assumes they escaped in a plane. The story's really snowballed along those lines. Guess everyone loves a mystery."

As Drew watched Greg make notes, he tried to think of something else to say that the reporter would consider quotable. "Naturally, I've had my scrapes as a bush pilot, but I'm actually a serious businessman. I have my own outfitting company. Best in Alaska. And I have a full day's work tomorrow." That ought to fix him, Drew thought.

"Then why are you here in this chaos?" Greg gestured toward the dance floor.

"Tradition. The robbers are a legend."

"*And* because you're a pilot," Greg went on, his tone encouraging, hopeful. "Two daring guys disappear into the bush with a sack of money, a couple million bucks. Admit it. This Red Baron stuff appeals to you."

"Sure, it's adventurous."

Greg jotted a few words. "What about the loot? No one's found it."

The money would be a natural hook for the story, Drew knew, so he strung Greg along. "I'm human. I could use a million or two. Buy another airplane, team of sled dogs, advertise NorthStar Expeditions in those slick New York magazines you work for. Might even hire you to do some publicity."

Greg stopped writing and laughed. It was obvious Drew was having fun with him. "You've gone too far now, McKay. I can't be bought like that. I've got ethics. But for two million..."

Now it was Drew's turn to smile, although he wasn't sure that Greg was kidding about wanting the money.

"Besides," the reporter said, "my article is for a New York *newspaper*. Let's get that right. And I wish you'd give me a straight answer. Look, I've got more than I need for your profile.'' He put his pen and narrow note-book in a pocket of his sport coat. "You can talk freely now. Off the record. What do you really think about the robbery?''

Drew cleared his throat. "Not a whole lot. Ten years ago today, on a sunny August morning, two men fired a few gunshots and robbed a Fairbanks armored car of two million dollars in cash. End of story.''

"Not quite,'' Greg corrected, wagging a finger at him. "They were never seen again. End of story.''

"Well, I know you've done your research, but the escape isn't really the end, either. The robbers haven't been *caught*. Where's your sense of justice? This is serious stuff, FBI and all that.''

"Ahh.'' Greg leaned across the table, raising his voice to be heard above the growing din of the party. "You're right. We're talking about a *federal* crime here. As far as the FBI's concerned, the heist was like a huge armed robbery from a bank. Federally insured money.'' He looked at his empty beer glass. "How about another pitcher? Help loosen you up while you give me more of your ideas on this Red Baron business.''

"Hey, you don't need *my* opinions,'' Drew said.

Greg waved a hand. "Forget the article. It's half-written already.'' Greg rolled the empty beer glass between his palms and gazed toward the band. "You know, it seems the only thing missing is the explanation of how these two guys pulled off such a perfect escape.'' He turned to Drew with a serious expression. "I sure would like to be there when they tell their story.''

Drew was amused by Greg's ambition. It was far stronger than his own. Still, he liked the reporter and enjoyed chatting with him. Suddenly, Drew had an idea.

He squinted at Greg and said, "You want another beer, right?"

"I wouldn't mind."

"Then why don't you buy yourself a six-pack and come along with me to my office? It's only a block away. And it's quiet. We could talk better there, if you still think I've got some rare insights into the robbery."

"Twisted my arm."

On the way out of the tavern into the long twilight Greg and Drew bumped into an older, bald-headed man.

"Good party?" the man asked.

"You'll love it," Drew replied, automatically, not breaking his stride.

Greg hurried to catch up with Drew. Frowning, Greg asked, "You know that guy?"

"Nah," Drew said, "you see a thousand like him at these blowouts. Takes all kinds, I guess."

Drew stuck his hands into his jeans pockets and led on. There was a chill in the air that he hadn't felt the previous night. The midnight sun was two months past, and summer was virtually over, the darkness now lasting less than nine hours.

Drew pulled a key from his pocket and unlocked his office door. When he flipped on the fluorescent lights a colorful array of clutter sprang into view. Large maps and photos of expeditions were tacked all over the walls, and a wide assortment of outdoor gear that customers could rent or buy ringed the room.

Greg took it all in. "You're the real thing. How's business?"

"It was slow for several years, but we're doing pretty well now."

"We?"

"My brother and I." Drew opened a door behind the counter and went in. "Come back to my office. It's more comfortable."

Drew switched on the brass desk lamp and motioned Greg to a small sofa in front of his desk. Drew eased himself into the old high-backed executive chair behind the desk. The walnut chair frame was scratched and pitted and the springs squeaked a little when he moved, but anything more up-to-date would have looked out of place. NorthStar Expeditions had worn linoleum on the floor and probably would have for the foreseeable future. Drew preferred to plow the profits back into the company to improve the service. The company image would have to look after itself.

He eased his boots onto the neat desktop and noticed Greg was already sprawled across the sofa, his sport coat bunched to make a pillow. The tab on a beer can popped.

"Want one?" the reporter asked.

"No. You go ahead."

Greg took a swig of beer. "Tell me about your brother. What's his name?"

"Pete."

"He's a pilot, too?"

"Sure. Dad taught us both to fly. Pete's probably better than I am. More cautious, I guess. And not just in flying. He's two years younger, which means he's had the chance to learn from my mistakes. I had to take over the business when I was twenty."

"Ten years ago," Greg said.

"That's right. The business was my father's but . . . Well, let's just say he's gone. Since I've been on my own, I've messed up enough to send five companies into bankruptcy." Drew grinned.

Greg laughed and drank more beer. "Maybe that's why these Red Baron guys took the money."

"Why?"

"Because *they* were going bankrupt."

"They had to be desperate, that's for sure. Or running from something. Fortunately, I've never been that bad off."

In the next half hour Drew talked about his business and Greg drained two cans of beer and started a third. Occasionally the reporter would bring up the robbery, but it was apparent that his thorough research on the subject had left little that Drew could add.

Drew looked at his watch. Although he was enjoying Greg's dramatic accounts of news events he'd covered, it was getting late. Drew was on the verge of sending Greg back to the celebration and going home when he heard the lock turn on the front door. "That's probably Pete," he said.

Drew's brother burst into the office, out of breath, with a grimness in his eyes, highlighted by his pallor. He didn't notice Greg.

"Thank God you're here," Pete said.

Drew popped out of his chair and went to him. "What's wrong?"

"You're not going to believe this. It's Dad. They've found his plane. Crashed."

"What?" Drew stared at Pete but could see only his father, stocky, graying, his face crinkled into a smile. Drew hadn't seen or heard from Sam McKay in ten years. His father had argued with his mother and disappeared the night before the Red Baron robbery. He'd been scheduled to fly three sportsmen into the bush the next morning, but the four-seat plane was already gone when the fishermen arrived. After a few days, Drew's mother, Nancy, had faced the inevitable and reported Sam missing. The Fairbanks police had been most interested in the time of his departure, hoping Sam would be the much-needed clue to the Red Baron robbery.

The days that followed were like a crazy string of bad dreams for Drew. His mother was sure that Sam had left them, and Drew was convinced his father would never have deserted his family. None of them would believe he'd had anything to do with the robbery. Nothing made sense. Sam's plane never turned up and neither did Sam. In the end, the police simply added Sam to their open file of missing persons and offered the usual, well-rehearsed assurances. That's when Drew started picking up the pieces of the family expedition business.

Now Drew looked blankly out the window into the darkness and then back at Pete. "Where is the plane? Does Mom know yet?"

"I just came from her house," Pete said. "She got this call from Canada. It was the Mounties, over in the Yukon. Someone stumbled across the wreckage in the Ogilvie Mountains north of Dawson City."

"Dawson City? Why on Earth..." Drew went back to the desk and dropped into his chair. He glanced at Greg, realizing he'd nearly forgotten him. Drew didn't want his father's story to be a matter of public record, but right now he had more to worry about than the invasion of his privacy. His mother would have to accept the obvious—that his father was dead. "Pete, did they...find Dad?"

"The Mounties didn't say."

"He must have been in the plane. Something went wrong. Dad tried to land and...he couldn't have survived." Drew pressed his elbows on the desk and wiped his palms down his face. He wasn't sure what he felt—sadness, relief, anger, confusion.

Greg, apparently picking up on the inappropriateness of his being there, jumped to his feet and grabbed his jacket. "Sorry, Drew. I'll leave you two alone."

Drew nodded and absently watched him leave.

Pete's voice cut into the emptiness. "Who's he?"

"Huh? Oh, just a guy I met at the Red Baron party."

They sat in silence a half minute, and Drew thought about how distant the celebration seemed now. And how ironic, considering the line of questioning the police had taken ten years before.

Finally, Pete said, "The Mounties want somebody from the family to go to Dawson City."

Drew shook his head. "That's it then. God, he's really dead, isn't he?" When Pete didn't answer, Drew got up and went to a wall map of Alaska and the Yukon. He ran a finger along what he assumed had been his father's flight path and said, "The Yukon. Damn it. I just don't understand." He pounded the map and leaned his forehead against the cool paper.

Pete moved to his side. "Are you going to Dawson City, or do you want me to?" he asked, his voice too calm and even.

Drew shoved his fingers through his hair. "I don't see how either of us can leave now. We've got NorthStar to run. You're involved in the business as much as I am. Maybe there's some alternative. Let's think about it. We can decide in the morning."

Pete left to go back to their mother's house and Drew locked up and walked to his small apartment. He'd lived there alone almost three years, but tonight it didn't feel much like home. The place seemed empty and suddenly artificial: lumber, paint, carpet and gypsum board nailed together in the middle of Alaska. The glue of permanence was missing, the feeling that things around him mattered.

Drew told himself tomorrow would be a fresh day, although he didn't believe it. He turned on the television and found that none of the programs held his attention. So he went to bed and stared at the ceiling. Sleep wouldn't come.

Minutes dragged by before he got up, shrugged on a robe and went to make a drink. But after he'd filled a glass with ice he forgot about the whiskey and instead went to a bookcase in the living room. He pulled out an Atlas and thumbed through the pages. North America. His right index finger went to the top of the continent. Top of the World. Fairbanks, Dawson City. Again, he traced an imaginary line. Two hundred fifty miles. The distance was reasonable for a good pilot.

He flipped off the lights and went back to the bedroom. But he didn't get into bed, just stood in the darkness by his nightstand with his fists jammed into the pockets of his robe. The question was haunting him again, he realized, but now there was a way to put it to rest.

He turned on his bedside lamp and phoned his brother. "Pete, sorry if I woke you, but I've decided. You stay here with NorthStar. *I'm* going to have a look at Dad's plane. I'll fly to Dawson City tomorrow afternoon."

Drew wasn't going just to see an airplane. He would have to tread carefully, he knew. The ghost of a doubt the police had raised ten years ago was alive and well again, and to put it to rest he had to find out what Sam McKay had been doing in the Yukon.

BETSY LIFTED the brilliant flounces of her cancan skirt and kicked up her left leg, swinging it, pendulum-style, from the knee. The piano music was loud and lively and the high-spirited crowd at Yukon Lights was clapping along. Tonight she was in the middle of a line of six female dancers and working hard not to be conspicuous. She'd never taken a dance lesson, but had found that the success of a cancan depended more on enthusiasm than technique.

Electrified gas lamps lined the walls of the turn-of-the-century saloon. Betsy loved the old place. She entertained tourists here: sang, danced, played honky-tonk piano, made drinks, whipped up good times. Now she tossed back her shoulder-length auburn hair and scanned the audience. A tall, black-haired man caught her eye as he angled with agility toward the stage.

She spun around and spotted him again. Blue jeans and tan windbreaker. There was something about the way he moved that intrigued her. He exhibited neither the hesitation of a typical tourist nor the overconfidence of a Dawson City local. When he reached the one empty table directly in front of the stage he sat down, eyed the dancers with appreciation and began to clap with everyone else.

Betsy shook her skirt and tried to ignore him. Tonight more than a hundred customers were watching her dance, and she was committed to entertaining them all. The crowd had gathered for Discovery Days. The town broke loose for three days every August to celebrate the Klondike gold strike of 1896. Although the formal festivities had wound down three days ago, revelers remained. She tried to concentrate on staying in step with the other dancers, but the man's handsome face caught her attention and she soon found herself smiling at him. She also found herself one kick behind.

Embarrassed, she quickly recovered and, focusing on the rosy-hued lights behind the massive wooden bar, finished the number in good form. Linking arms with the dancers on each side, she bowed, delighting momentarily in the whistles and shouts of appreciation. Dawson City was a rugged town; once peopled by dreamers, delirious with the fever carried by tales of gold, it was now filled with men and women tenacious in their desire to carve out a life there. Top of the World, they called the wild land around it. She loved it all. After the applause subsided, she took the side steps down from the stage, intending to circulate among the crowd as she often did.

When she walked by the black-haired stranger's table, he stood and said, "You're good, you know. Could I buy you a drink?"

She laughed and said, "No." His eyes glimmered in the hazy light. Lord, he was attractive. She reconsidered and said, "But I'll buy you one." She motioned for a waitress and sat down.

He scooted his chair close to hers and lowered himself beside her. "I asked first."

"I know." Betsy grinned. She liked the man's tanned skin, the lopsided slant of his smile.

The waitress appeared and took their orders. Betsy said, "Laura, put this gentleman's drink on the house."

"Sure, Boss."

The man's eyes widened and Betsy enjoyed his reaction. "Boss?" he asked, eyebrows raised.

"Betsy's modest," Laura said. "She doesn't often admit she owns the place."

He shrugged. "Well, in that case..."

The barmaid went away and he and Betsy laughed.

"You set me up," he said.

"It's part of the entertainment," she joked. "I'm Betsy Archer."

"Drew McKay."

He extended his hand and she shook it, surprised at the charge his touch sent up her arm. She gazed into his eyes. Blue-gray irises formed a counterpoint to his straight dark brows. She released his hand, suddenly aware that she had held it a shade too long.

He was smiling at her. "My first time in Dawson City since I was a boy," he said, "and I get to drink with the boss."

"Everybody's lucky sometime," she said.

He took the jest exactly the right way, Betsy thought. He hadn't seemed like a tourist, but he probably was. Too bad. He would walk out of her nightclub in a few minutes or an hour and disappear. Most of them did. But she couldn't complain. It wasn't easy to live alone in a town like Dawson City, but at age twenty-six she'd already made a place for herself. She was respected and secure. She had no desire to change a thing.

Their drinks came, and Drew said, "I was thinking. If you're the owner, why do you dance?"

"And wear a frilly dress and a feather boa on stage?"

He sampled his whiskey. "Yes."

"Simple," she said. "The cancan's fun. The tourists like the floor shows, all this gold rush stuff. Dawson City depends on tourists. But they're more than my bread and butter. Most of them travel a long way to get here, and I don't want them to go home disappointed. A little drink, a little food, a little dancing—everyone has a good time."

"I noticed your face when you were on the stage," Drew said. "I think you were doing it for yourself."

She was surprised by his perception and picked up her glass instead of answering.

"It's okay," he went on. "In fact, it's admirable. The other dancers were good, but you had that extra sparkle."

Betsy sipped her drink. "Really? I don't know about sparkle, but you're right. I do the cancan because it makes me feel good. Does that sound silly?"

"Not at all. Makes sense to me."

"Well, I've never been one to sit back and let other people have my fun for me." Betsy frowned. She couldn't believe she'd said that. She'd just shared an intimacy, although a small one, with a virtual stranger. What kind of crazy spell was he casting over her? "Our Klondike melodrama is going to start any minute," she hurried on, pointing at the stage. "The Yukon gold rush will be relived in its entirety, more or less. The actors do a great job. Want to see it?"

Drew kept his eyes on her. "Not really."

"Don't like gold?" Almost without thinking, Betsy's hand went to the gold chain circling her neck beneath the feather boa.

"I'd rather just keep talking," he said.

Betsy glanced at the bartender, busy with customers, and the waitresses, dressed in old-fashioned costumes, moving swiftly between tables. Everything seemed to be going smoothly. What harm would there be? She wanted to sit with Drew McKay and get to know him better. If someone needed her help, she could still be found. "It'll be noisy this close to the stage," she said. "Let's find a table in the back."

When they were seated again, Betsy said, "You don't seem like a tourist."

"I'm here on business. From Fairbanks." Drew's voice went flat. "But I got in too late to do anything about it."

"Well, I hope you found a hotel room for this evening." She knew how tough it could be to get one in Dawson City during the summer. Gold-panners from all over the country, eager to find a little "color" in the streams, reserved lodging well in advance. Discovery Days made bookings even tighter.

"As a matter of fact, I didn't," Drew said. "But I'm set for the Bonanza Hotel tomorrow night. Fortunately, they had a cancellation."

"Where will you sleep tonight?"

"I'll go back to the airport and bunk in my plane."

"You're a pilot?" Her heart began to pound. Plane crashes, skeletons in cockpits. Ridiculous, she told herself. She had to stop thinking continually about the wreckage she'd discovered. Lots of folks in the North had planes. Her *real* father had been a Yukon bush pilot, not that she'd thought much about him lately. When Betsy was two years old, he had died in a car crash, an ironic end for a skillful pilot who could land a floatplane on a tiny lake. Betsy had never seen him. When her mother became pregnant he had not offered to marry her, so she had fled to Vancouver, British Columbia, to escape him and ended up finding a husband in the process. Betsy had grown up with a wonderful stepfather, an adoring mother and two caring half brothers.

All that seemed far away now, forced to a dusty corner of her mind by recent history. But while Drew was saying, "I've been flying for years," the image of the crashed plane and its terrifying cargo loomed in her mind. Only two days had passed since she'd found it—too few to let the frightening memories fade.

Betsy shivered and Drew gave her a quizzical look. "You all right?"

"Sure," she lied. Last night had been hell. Every time she'd closed her eyes to sleep, the plane had materialized in her brain. It might have helped if she'd had someone to confide in. But her beloved grandfather, Conrad Parks, had been dead a year and she had no one else close—not here in Dawson City—except Evie Saunders. Evie, now fragile and ailing, had lived with Conrad for years. But Betsy didn't want to upset her with news of a skeleton in a plane crash.

Drew was staring and she rushed to say something. "I was just thinking about you sleeping out in the cold tonight. You really shouldn't. I heard it might frost."

"I'm used to roughing it," he said.

"In a plane?"

"And a sleeping bag. If you're in the expedition business, you get in the habit of carrying one. Never know when you'll need it." He told Betsy a little about his work, about taking fishermen and hunters into the bush around Fairbanks and the team of sled dogs he kept for winter treks.

Then the lights dimmed and the piano player pounded a few chords. The noise of the crowd became hushed as costumed characters ambled onstage, engaged in bantering dialogue. The Klondike melodrama was starting and Drew watched it a moment while he finished his drink.

Betsy shifted position in her chair and her boa slipped down over her strapless bodice. Drew glanced over at her and his eyes dropped to the thin chain around her neck—

and to the medallion. She noticed a muscle tighten along his jaw.

"That charm," he said, "where did you get it?"

"This?" She pulled the solid circle of gold out so he could see. Angular shapes covered the front of it. "It's an ancient Athabascan Indian design. Those people do beautiful gold work. It's even etched on the back." She flipped it over. "It was my grandfather's...." Her voice faded under the intensity of Drew's gaze. He was making her feel distinctly uncomfortable.

After what seemed like minutes, Drew spoke. "It's very unusual," he said in a restrained voice.

"I suppose so." She fingered the charm nervously. "You see similar jewelry in Yukon shops, but I think this one was custom-made. I've never spotted another quite like it."

"I'd like to look at it." Drew's voice was low and stern. "Take it off...please."

Betsy didn't understand what had caused this change in his manner, but she was on guard now.

"You must be kidding." She forced a smile.

He swallowed. "I want to see the medallion."

Uneasy, Betsy began to pull back. She didn't take orders from strangers. "Excuse me, Mr. McKay, I have work to do."

"Forget the work. This is important." Suddenly, he reached for the necklace and his hand scraped across her bare skin as he grasped the medallion.

Repelled by his aggression, Betsy jerked backward. Then the thin chain around her neck snapped and suddenly he was clutching her medallion, chain and all.

# Chapter Two

Drew's eyes opened wide with the realization of what he had done. Before he could speak, Betsy snatched the gold piece from his palm and hurried to her office twenty feet away. She closed the door behind her and leaned back against it for a few seconds, eyeing the medallion and its broken chain dangling from her hand. How dare Drew McKay make demands and break her necklace? How dare he even touch her? Everything had happened so fast. And for a while she'd thought she actually liked the guy. "I'm a fool," she muttered.

Then she crossed the tiny room and perched on the front of her desk. Her pulse had begun to slow, but she couldn't yet put the medallion down. Gradually she became aware of music. The muted familiar sounds of the piano and the actors' voices drifted in, and finally she felt safe and in control once more.

Then the door reopened. When it was shut again, McKay was hovering over her in the cramped space. "I want to apologize," he said. "I'm sorry. It's just that your medallion reminded me of one my father used to wear. But when I held it, I knew it was different."

Betsy stared at him. He *looked* sorry, she thought, but the damage was done. "Okay, I accept your apology," she told him, her voice showing her agitation over what he'd done and his closeness now. She needed space. When he didn't back away, she said, "You can leave."

He didn't budge. "I'd like to make this up to you. Maybe I could pay to have the chain fixed."

He glanced at the charm, still in Betsy's hand, and she felt threatened again. She put the gold piece on the desk behind her and slid away from him until she had room to stand up. On her feet, she didn't feel so intimidated. She was five feet six and Drew McKay was only four inches or so taller.

He stepped closer. And she moved backward. Then he pulled a battered wallet from a hip pocket and opened it. "Let me pay you." He looked into her eyes. "How much do you think it'll be?"

"I don't know," she said, not able to think clearly about the medallion now. "It doesn't matter, I'll take care of it. I just want to be alone." She turned away.

"But—"

There was a knock on the door.

"Come in," Betsy said.

The door opened and Betsy's six-foot-six, 260-pound bouncer lumbered into the office. The room was barely large enough for the three of them.

The bouncer looked at Drew, then Betsy. "You need any help, Betsy?"

"Thank you, yes," she said. "Mr. McKay was just leaving. Could you escort him to the street?"

"Sure thing," the bouncer said with a grin. For a moment, Betsy wondered if her muscle man took too much pleasure in his work. He opened the door and said, "Let's go, McKay."

"Now look," Drew said, eyes shooting between Betsy and the bouncer. "You're making a mistake. This isn't what you think. I'm not the kind of guy who—"

"Save it," the bouncer said as he thrust his chest out to Drew's chin.

Drew threw a pleading look at Betsy, but she dropped her eyes to the floor. She couldn't let sympathy endanger her. "Close the door on the way out," she said.

For several seconds after the door had shut, she stood still in the middle of her office, as if waiting to be sure that she was really alone. Then she sat down at her desk and tried to calm herself.

Betsy leaned back in her chair and closed her eyes, letting the sense of being in command that she always felt in her office wash over her. She relaxed as actors' voices drifted in again from the nightclub's stage. The melodrama was well rehearsed and predictable, and she could tell exactly how far along it was by hearing only a line. If only Drew McKay were that easy to figure out. She struggled to make sense of his outlandish behavior, but it was a futile endeavor. He was a stranger—an attractive one, she had to admit—and he was a customer. He *had* tried to make amends. Had she acted too harshly?

What a night, she thought. Suddenly, Betsy felt the energy drain from her body. Shoulders hunched, she studied the medallion on the desk in front of her. Its carved angles caught the light and shimmered like some distant constellation. The piece had belonged to her grandfather, Conrad. So had the nightclub. She'd come to Dawson City five years before to help him run Yukon Lights. He'd left her the club, her house in town and a cabin on forty acres in the woods, atop the Lost Lady gold mine.

Conrad's forty acres adjoined another parcel—land that had once belonged to Tom Fioretti, Conrad's old mining partner. They had worked the Lost Lady together until Fioretti had died in an accident there. He had left his land to some distant heirs but had sentimentally bequeathed the mineral rights on his property to Conrad.

But the gold charm was different. Conrad hadn't expressly willed it to Betsy. She'd simply found it among his things after he died. It was very odd, she thought, that it should have had such a disturbing effect on Drew McKay, even if his father had worn a similar medallion.

Betsy placed the pendant in the back of her desk drawer, then she shoved her chair away from the desk and snapped to her feet, disgusted with herself for being naive. McKay's motive for grabbing her medallion had probably been much simpler than it seemed. After all, the gold in the charm was worth hundreds of dollars.

Betsy stretched and straightened her shoulders, then went back out to the main room of Yukon Lights, confident that McKay had by now been shown the door. The evening had lost its luster, but she still had work to do.

"DON'T BOTHER to hang around, pal. When the boss says 'out,' she means it." The huge man gave Drew a shove, then wiped his hands on his jeans.

"Yeah, yeah." Embarrassed, Drew straightened his windbreaker and turned around. "I hear you." He began walking backward on the rough wooden sidewalk. The bouncer crossed his arms and chuckled, then disappeared inside the saloon.

*Damn!* Drew could not believe the scene he'd caused in Yukon Lights. What had happened to him in there? He should have known better than to come on so strongly about the woman's medallion. The boss, no less. Breaking the chain, then forcing the point. He wished she had accepted his offer to have it repaired. Or had at least allowed him to explain. She might have if muscle head hadn't interrupted.

Quickly, Drew headed down the boardwalk, away from the music and laughter that issued as a grim reminder from Yukon Lights. Betsy Archer's medallion looked so much like the one his dad had worn every day. Both were carved gold, both Athabascan and circular. Betsy's had shone like molten sun against her pale skin. Sam's was more worn and the designs, front and back, were slightly different. He wished he could have examined Betsy's medallion more closely.

Drew shoved his hands inside his jacket pockets. He knew his actions tonight were caused by his confusion about his father. Years ago, Sam would hold Drew on his knee and let him twist the charm with his boyish fingers. He'd loved his dad. What kid wouldn't love and respect the best pilot, the bravest and most skilled outfitter in the North? At least, that was how Drew had seen him.

Weathered planks thudded beneath Drew's boots as he walked. Ahead of him, a solitary streetlight cast the unpaved street and weathered storefronts into shadows. He'd been caught off guard tonight, that was all. The discovery of his dad's plane and the hasty trip to Dawson City had made him edgy. Drew picked up his pace. He'd made an ass of himself—in front of one of the most gorgeous women he'd ever laid eyes on.

As he stepped out of the shelter of buildings and into the street, cold air swirled from the Yukon River, sending a chill through him. He shivered and turned up his jacket collar. His heavy coat was still in the Piper Warrior, the plane he'd flown over from Fairbanks. Betsy Archer had been right. He *didn't* relish sleeping in his plane tonight. It was August, but tonight the wind had the brisk edge of winter.

Ahead, a neon light glared in the darkness—the Double River Inn. Drew had tried earlier to get a room there, before going to the Bonanza. Light shone from its windows, beckoning with a welcome warmth. Who knows, he thought, perhaps someone had canceled in the past two hours. He broke into a jog. It wouldn't hurt to check.

Drew pushed open the ancient wooden door. The Double River Inn had been recently refurbished, but like a lot of buildings in Dawson City, it was vintage nineteenth century. He crossed the carpeted lobby to the front desk. Although it was near midnight, several patrons were still sitting on sofas watching television.

The night clerk, a chubby blond woman, remembered him. She shook her head. "Still nothing. We're filled. Sorry."

Drew shrugged. "Me, too. It's getting a little fresh out there. This town needs a few more hotels, I think."

The clerk smiled. Drew gritted his teeth and resigned himself to a night in his plane. He was moving toward the door when he heard his name.

"Drew McKay...well, I'll be."

Drew stopped and twisted at the sound of a vaguely familiar voice. Greg Harsted was crossing the lobby toward him, from the direction of the pay phone. He carried an attaché case, and a camera hung from a strap on his shoulder. "Greg, what are you doing here?" Drew asked in surprise.

"I could ask you the same thing." The reporter stopped and lowered his case to the floor. "I had a feeling you'd come to Dawson City, but I didn't expect to see you in the same hotel as me.''

"I'm not. I don't have a room here. Not that I haven't tried to get one.'' Drew glanced over his shoulder at the clerk. The woman had been staring at them, but quickly dropped her gaze and busied herself checking a ledger. "Over here.'' He moved toward the center of the lobby and Greg followed.

"You know why *I'm* here.'' Drew swiveled to face the taller man. "But you didn't answer my question. What about you? I thought you were knee-deep in Red Baron robbery stuff in Fairbanks. Dawson City isn't exactly next door.''

"When I'm on a hot story, I never know where I'm going to end up. Of course, I've developed a few sources here and there to keep me in touch.'' Greg grinned, as if acknowledging that his last statement had been intended to impress.

"You must have got here early,'' Drew said. Greg brought the specter of doubt that the police's suspicions about Drew's father ten years ago had erupted into view again, and a sensation of being smothered by that doubt closed in around Drew.

"I did. Chartered a plane this morning. Even then, I almost didn't get a room. Too many tourists in town. And yes, I'm still knee-deep in the Red Baron case. It seems the story is taking a new twist. The Mounties may have found a key to the case. Unfortunately, I'm not the only reporter here. They're coming in droves.'' Greg spread his arms wide. "We might be sitting on the story of the decade.''

"What's the key you mentioned?'' Drew fought the stifling sensation only to find that fear was there to replace it.

For a second, Greg looked as if he were really going to tell him. Then his expression turned blank. "Sorry. Can't say yet." Greg clapped one hand on Drew's shoulder and gave it a quick squeeze.

Drew frowned. He knew Greg had a professional reason for keeping quiet. But the friendly touch on his shoulder made him think Greg also had a personal reason.

"Everything's speculation right now," Greg said, "but the Mounties plan to call a press conference in the morning. Exciting, isn't it?"

"Guess so." Drew was too frightened to share Greg's enthusiasm.

Greg glanced at the clock behind the front desk. "Look at the time. It's almost midnight and I've got to get going early tomorrow." He picked up his case, then paused. "Good luck with your own business, Drew. Tough—your dad's plane being found like that. Try not to let it get to you."

"I'm all right," Drew said curtly. Then he smiled. "Really." He couldn't let Greg know how disturbed he was.

"Okay, see you around," Greg said.

"Yeah, right." Drew watched the reporter disappear up the stairs. Then Drew bolted outside. For several seconds, he had no idea where he was going. But the chill wind quickly reminded him why he'd gone into the hotel and what kind of night he could look forward to.

The hotel van was parked across the street. Drew signaled the driver and persuaded the man to give him a lift. Soon they were headed east to the airport. Drew's four-seater Piper was sitting at the far end of the paved strip. The familiar name, NorthStar, was lettered on the fuselage. Suddenly, he couldn't believe how comforting the plane looked. The cockpit would be cramped and cold tonight, but at least the plane was his—solid and safe. His mind felt numb. He wanted privacy now. And the chance to sort out his thoughts.

Drew unlocked the cockpit and crawled in. He put on the parka he always carried and took his sleeping bag from the rear. When he'd wrapped the bag around him, he felt more comfortable. Then he leaned back in the seat and focused on the moonlit hills. Somewhere out there in the wilderness was his dad's plane. He wondered who had found the wreckage. He should probably thank them. He pressed his eyes shut and tried to imagine what his father's last moments had been like. He could feel Sam's anguish when he realized the plane was going to crash. Sadly, he could also begin to imagine what his dad might have been doing in the Yukon.

Drew shifted, trying to stretch his legs. He also wondered about Greg's reasons for being in Dawson City. Sure, the reporter was pursuing a hot story, and he was a Canadian—he had a right to go where he wanted in his own country. But Greg had been more circumspect than he needed to be to merely protect his story.

"Ridiculous," Drew muttered. Now he was letting his imagination run wild. Harsted couldn't hurt him. He twisted sideways and wadded his windbreaker under his head. Maybe Sam's ghost would materialize in the seat beside him and explain away his questions. Sam McKay had been a kind man. He'd cleared up countless mysteries when Drew was a child. Drew closed his eyes again and this time didn't see Sam. This vision had velvety skin and clouds of wavy auburn hair.

"Betsy...Archer." Drew sampled the sounds, welcoming their pleasant intrusion. His brain needed a break. What a woman, he thought. Slowly, he sank into the sleeping bag. She was vibrant and sexy, and she had danced with flair and energy. And those eyes: huge and green, in a shade he'd never seen before. His mouth curved into a smile. He'd like her slim legs, too, and that lacy red garter.

Then Drew remembered the medallion and its broken chain. And the bouncer. "Damn it all!" He hunkered down in the narrow seat and yanked the sleeping bag over his shoulders. Thinking about Betsy Archer was almost as frustrating as thinking about his father.

THE ALARM ON THE NIGHTSTAND blasted through Betsy's sleep. She pushed blindly from beneath the comforter and turned it off. She'd worked too late, and though the clock said eight-thirty, her body felt as if it were still the middle of the night.

It hadn't helped that images of Drew McKay had invaded her dreams. She'd momentarily forgotten her disgust. Her mind had kept replaying only her unexpected pleasure when they'd touched, and the perplexed look on his face as the bouncer had forced him out. Then she'd pictured him sleeping in his plane, struggling to keep warm. Now she wondered if she'd see him again.

Betsy got to her feet and rummaged through the closet for a turtleneck sweater and jeans. The chain holding her medallion curled on the dresser like a broken golden thread. She had to go to Yukon Lights this morning to give Laura Bertino her paycheck. After that she would walk down to Front Street and have the chain repaired.

As usual, her small house was chilly. Hastily, she dressed, then scuffed down the short hallway to the kitchen. Brilliant sunlight shafting through the window made her blink. Another nice day. Brisk. Good for tourists. Good for Mounties searching mountainsides. That was what they'd probably been doing the past two days. She twisted on the radio and poured a glass of orange juice. A country tune filled the room. The AM station was CBC North in Whitehorse, the territorial capital almost three hundred miles south.

Betsy leaned against the counter and sipped the orange juice. The tune ended and the newscaster's hyped-up voice broke in. She listened for several seconds. A fire was raging in downtown Whitehorse, and a fishing boat had sunk in the Gulf of Alaska. When the announcer said a plane had crashed near Dawson City, Betsy nearly choked on her juice.

"A four-seater Cessna was discovered two days ago in the Ogilvie Mountains north of Dawson City," the man said. "Sources indicate a Dawson City woman may have found it."

Betsy coughed. He was talking about her.

The announcer went on. "Details are sketchy, and the Royal Canadian Mounted Police have maintained official silence on the matter so far, but there is speculation that the plane may be linked to the legendary Red Baron robbery, which took place ten years ago in Fairbanks, Alaska."

Betsy shuddered. The announcer related a short, sensational version of the Red Baron story, but she barely heard him. She already knew the tale anyway. The robbers were famous. Even though Fairbanks was a couple of hundred miles from Dawson City, she'd had a few customers in her place who'd used the daring, unsolved crime as an excuse to celebrate.

"The robbers escaped with two million dollars," the announcer said. "No trace of the two missing men or the money has yet been found, until possibly now." The announcer read another news item. Then the music started again.

Betsy's fingers shook as she placed the juice glass in the sink. The radio announcer hadn't mentioned the body. The dead man in the cockpit must have been a robber. But where was the other man? His remains were probably close to the plane. She was glad she'd been too scared to stay and look around.

Betsy turned off the radio. Most of the report had been speculation, but she had a dark feeling it was all true. And why had she had to hear about it on the radio? She would have to stop by the RCMP station on her morning errands and get updated. Constable Selkirk had said he'd keep her informed.

Ten minutes later, Betsy jogged across the dirt street in front of Yukon Lights, the broken chain coiled in her jeans pocket. Familiar neon lights scrolled above the weathered wooden entrance. In the summer, she opened the club at eleven for lunch and, although it was only a little after nine, several employees would already be working.

The front door was ajar and Betsy nudged it open and slipped inside. For several seconds, cool darkness enveloped her. The club had always been her refuge, filled with happy times. Thanks to Conrad. She paused to let her eyes adjust. The sounds of clattering dishes and of voices wafted from the kitchen.

"Hi, Boss," Laura Bertino called from behind the bar.

Betsy went over to her. "Hi, Laura. Thanks for working overtime last night."

"No problem." Laura smiled. "I like extra hours. You know me. My paycheck's usually spent before I get it." The young woman slid a rack of glasses under the counter.

"Speaking of paychecks, I'll go make yours out. You still want it early, right?"

"Sure. If you can do it. I'm driving down to White-horse tomorrow morning to meet my sister." Laura straightened and wiped her hands on her apron. "By the way, you've got company in your office."

"Who?" Betsy wasn't expecting anyone. For a second her mind flashed on Drew McKay. No. He probably wouldn't come back, but a tingle of excitement began to build when she considered the possibility. Perhaps she should apologize for having him thrown out.

Laura lifted her shoulders. "He said he was a friend."

*A friend.* Was that what McKay thought? Some people used the word loosely. Still, it was a beginning, and Betsy felt a tightness in her throat as she wove between tables to the back of the building. But was it really McKay who was waiting for her? Surely Laura would have remembered him. She'd brought their drinks the night before.

Betsy slowed her pace. A sliver of light showed along the edge of her partially open office door. She stopped when she saw a man's shoulder and head. She curbed her disappointment. It wasn't McKay. The man's back was to her. His head was nearly bald, banded by thinning gray hair. He seemed to be picking through papers on her desk. Snooping.

Angry, Betsy threw open the door. "Can I help you?"

The tall man in a gray plaid business suit dropped the papers and swiveled around. "You surprised me."

"So I see." Betsy's glance shot from his empty hands, behind him to the items he'd been looking at, then back to his face.

"Forgive me," he said. "The street door was open. One of the employees told me it was all right to come in. I'm waiting for the owner." The man smiled and his cheeks wrinkled. "We're old friends."

"Really?" Mid-fifties, Betsy decided. Prematurely worn out, along with his suit. It was rumpled and ill-fitting, like something you'd get at a charity store. And why was the man wearing a suit? Dawson City wasn't a dress-up kind of town. Betsy moved behind her desk and picked up the papers and envelopes he had so hastily dropped, aware that he had turned to watch her. "You see, I'm the owner. This is my office. And I've never seen you before."

"You?" The man stepped back. "What happened to Conrad Parks?"

Betsy tossed the papers face down into a basket on the corner of the desk and crossed her arms. Something about the man seemed familiar. And she was sure he'd been looking for more than her grandfather. "May I ask who you are?"

"Of course," he said. "My name's Jacob Talbot. I've known Conrad a long time. I own a parcel of land in the hills northwest of here. Near the Lost Lady Mine. Bought it from Tom Fioretti's family about nine years ago."

Now Betsy remembered when she'd seen this man before. Talbot had met with Conrad on several occasions, although Conrad had said little about him. As far as she knew, their last meeting had been more than a year ago.

Talbot had bought out the Fiorettis, so now she held the mineral rights to his portion of the mine. Conrad had been adamant about retaining them—to keep the mine, and his dream, whole. Since the gold rush, it had become common practice to separate ownership of the land's surface from what might be underground. Even though the easily accessible gold had been mined out long ago, the hope for a big strike died hard.

As Betsy recalled, the Fiorettis had not seemed to mind the arrangement, but Talbot had tried to negotiate with Conrad on his last visit. Perhaps he was here to try again. She had no desire for a confrontation, so she chose her words carefully. "If you haven't been in Dawson City lately, then you wouldn't know that Conrad Parks...passed away a year ago."

"Conrad? Gone?" Talbot seemed stricken by the news. His shoulders sagged, and the ruddiness of his cheeks faded. "It's been at least a year since I was here. I didn't realize. I'm sorry. What happened?"

Betsy paused. The man did look stunned. She softened her tone. "He had a heart attack. I'm his granddaughter."

"You ...you're Betsy. I should have known. You look a bit like Conrad. The same green eyes." Talbot squinted. "And I'd imagine that Conrad's hair was reddish once, like yours."

Betsy nodded, warming to the man.

As he folded his hands, Betsy noticed that they were shaking. The news of Conrad's death had obviously disturbed him.

"I hope you don't mind if I sit down." Talbot lowered himself into a chair. "Conrad's passing is quite a shock, believe me." He wiped one palm across his shiny forehead. "He and I have shared a lot."

"I had no idea." Betsy leaned against a shopworn credenza. Talbot studied her with a disturbing spacy gaze, his pale blue eyes red-rimmed. "Mr. Talbot, you came here to speak with my grandfather. Maybe I can help you instead." Betsy forced another nagging question to the back of her mind: *Why were you snooping through my papers?*

"Maybe you can." Talbot bent forward, pressing his elbows into his thighs. "I'm disappointed and upset, of course, about Conrad. I came to Dawson on business and planned to visit my old friend. I'll be here several days. I have a lot to do, but I should have a few free moments. Maybe you and I can get together again. You know, talk about old times? Our common . . . concerns. Conrad and I didn't keep in touch regularly, but we were close. You wouldn't believe the stories I could tell about him. Probably sounds crazy, but I think it would be nice to know my old buddy's granddaughter."

His hesitation over "common concerns" led Betsy back to her earlier suspicion. He does want the mineral rights, she thought. "I don't know, Mr. Talbot," she hedged. The man seemed sincere and it would be nice to talk to him about Conrad. . . . *Maybe you've just spent too much time in big cities, Betsy,* she thought, remembering her assumptions about Drew McKay's interest in her medallion. *You're too suspicious for your own good.*

Talbot spread his hands. "Please call me Jacob. And don't say no about getting together. We're bound to meet again anyway."

Betsy stood. It would be best to be direct, she decided. Once the air was cleared, she would have a better idea about the man's true intentions. "Look, Mr. Talbot, I think I know why you're here and I can save you a lot of trouble. You and my grandfather discussed the mineral rights at Lost Lady. It's unfortunate that the mine runs under both our properties, but those rights on your land were Tom Fioretti's legacy to Conrad, and now Conrad's to me. Conrad never wanted to sell them, and I won't sell them, either."

Talbot stiffened. "I appreciate your honesty, so I'll be straight with you. Of course, I'd like the mineral rights to my own land. Who wouldn't? But I gave up trying to persuade your grandfather a long time ago. I'm not as hard-nosed as you seem to think. I understood his sentiment. And I won't press you, all right?"

"Okay," Betsy said quietly. Well, at least that matter was cleared up. She shoved her hands into her pockets. The broken chain. She'd almost forgotten about getting it repaired—and about going to the Mounties. She still had a lot to do before Yukon Lights opened for lunch. Without thinking, she fidgeted.

Talbot noticed and jerked to his feet. "Forgive me. I've taken too much of your time already. We'll see each other again before I leave?"

Betsy started to reply, but Talbot interrupted. "No arguments." He went toward the door. "I'll call. Maybe we can have dinner. You know, I'm glad you're running the show here now—Yukon Lights and all. Conrad would have wanted us to get acquainted. I'm sure of it."

Before Betsy could react to Talbot's illogical conclusion, he vanished into the darkness of the club, his footsteps echoing on the wooden floor. Her instincts were usually right, but perhaps she'd been wrong in distrusting this man. The question remained: what *had* he been looking for in her office? But he seemed harmless enough, and it could have been a distracted act, the sort of thing people who read everything in sight, including cereal boxes, have been known to do.

Betsy stared at the gaping doorway. Although she'd agreed to nothing, she believed Talbot when he said they would meet again. Maybe she would ask Evie about him. Or would that, too, be upsetting to her? Evie had loved Betsy's grandfather unconditionally and understood more about Conrad than he would ever have admitted. If Conrad had spoken to her about Talbot, maybe Evie would be able to put Betsy's suspicion to rest.

Betsy sat down and unlocked her top desk drawer. She would talk to Evie later. She pulled out her business ledger and hastily wrote out Laura's paycheck. A few minutes later, Betsy had delivered the check and was walking down Queen Street toward the intersection at Front, heading for the jewelry shop to get her chain fixed.

She quickened her steps. Luckily for anyone on foot, Dawson City wasn't a large town—a little more than one thousand permanent residents, although estimates of the population at the height of the gold rush in 1898 ranged up to thirty thousand. Five minutes after leaving Yukon Lights, Betsy had reached Front Street, at the intersection near the police station. The building was new and big-city efficient but the old horse stables had been preserved, mainly for the benefit of tourists. A large group of men and women, some with notebooks and cameras, were gathered in front of the station.

Curiosity led Betsy to stop across the street from the RCMP station. She saw a constable open the door and say something to the group. Questions were asked. The officer shook his head and went back inside. Betsy couldn't hear what had been said but it was clear the people were reporters. She crossed the dusty street, wondering what the commotion was about. Must be the Red Baron robbers, she thought.

Then Betsy heard a woman tell her colleague that a local woman had found the wreckage. Betsy cringed. It seemed everyone was talking about her. *Enough was enough.* She thrust open the door and went inside the station. Several people were waiting, but she paid little attention to them as she rushed across the room to the counter. Behind it, an officer, dressed in blue and tan, sat drinking coffee.

Betsy leaned across the countertop and caught his attention. "Constable, what's going on with the plane? I heard the radio report and saw those people outside—"

"Miss Archer," Constable Selkirk cut in, with a touch of reprimand in his voice. He hurried to the counter, eyes flicking across the waiting area.

The constable was tall and thin and when he breathed in, his cheeks went hollow. Betsy placed his age at thirty-five. "We were going to call you later this morning," Selkirk said. "This way, please." He went to the end of the counter and gestured to swinging doors.

As Betsy headed to the back with him, she glanced at the waiting area for the first time. Her heart dropped to her stomach when she saw the man sitting only a few yards away, his arms folded casually across his chest. The haunting eyes staring at her belonged to Drew McKay.

# Chapter Three

"Good morning." Drew's gaze was unflinching as it caught and held hers. He stretched out one lean leg.

"Morning." Betsy quickly recovered. She noticed the sexy way faded denim tightened around solid thigh muscle. *Nice*. Then she looked at Drew's handsome face, clouded now with exhaustion. Dark stubble covered his jaw, and his jacket was wrinkled.

"What are you doing here?"

Drew shrugged. "Business."

"I see." Betsy wished she hadn't asked. She knew that Drew had planned to sleep in his plane the night before. But that didn't explain how ragged he appeared this morning. He looked as if he'd been carousing—probably drinking and gambling at Diamond Tooth Gertie's. Maybe he'd been kicked out of the casino, too. That would explain why he was sitting in the RCMP office at ten in the morning: he'd been picked up for disorderly conduct.

"Miss Archer?" Constable Selkirk's voice interrupted her thoughts.

Betsy felt her face grow hot. The Mountie was waiting, a large manila folder under his arm. He must have surmised what was distracting her.

Betsy swiveled and followed Selkirk down a hall to an office with barely enough room for the desk and two chairs it contained. He led her inside and closed the door. She wasn't sure what to expect from Selkirk. He'd been in Dawson City just a few months, and she'd said little more than "hello" to him on his foot patrols around town.

"Have a seat." He went behind the desk and nodded toward a chair. "I'm sorry you had to hear the radio report. But it's just speculation at this point. Nothing to get excited about. We intended to speak with you about it, but we know you have to keep late hours at your club, so we didn't bother you early."

"I appreciate your consideration. But the report's true, isn't it?" She sank onto the chair. "Why else would all those reporters be out front?"

"Rumors, that's all."

Betsy was silent.

Selkirk sat down and looked at her grimly. "All right, Miss Archer. You'll find out soon enough. We do have a tie-in to the Red Baron robbery. Sergeant Randall will be making an official statement soon."

Betsy shook her head. "Incredible. That robbery happened in Fairbanks years ago."

"Yes, ten years to be exact." Selkirk sighed and flipped open the folder. "An unsolved crime the public has taken delight in. The robbers have become heroes to some, but they're criminals all the same. We would never have linked the crash with that heist if it hadn't been for what we found in the wreckage."

"You mean besides the body?" Betsy's palms grew moist.

Selkirk nodded. "We also found stolen bills and vintage aviator glasses in the cockpit. As you probably know, the Red Baron robbers wore costumes. It seems now that they tried to make their getaway in our direction.''

''But there was only one body, Constable. What happened to the other robber?''

''We're working on that now, Miss Archer, among other things. I didn't catch the news report, but this Red Baron robbery seems even bigger than we imagined. The media are having a heyday.'' Selkirk looked distracted. ''Somehow word got out and we had to acknowledge that the plane had been found. It was only last night that we informed the family of the plane's owner about *recent* developments—the goggles and cash.''

A woman knocked on the door, then opened it. ''Excuse me, Constable, we need you for a few minutes.''

Selkirk smiled. ''Sorry, Miss Archer. I have a bit more I want to say to you, since you've come by. Hope you can wait. I'll try not to be long.''

Betsy relaxed against the vinyl chair. As soon as the door shut, her thoughts shot back to Drew McKay, and she again fingered the broken strand of gold inside her pocket. She was still curious about why Drew was at the station this morning. Away from his disconcerting stare, her theory that he'd been picked up for disorderly conduct seemed ridiculous. There had to be something else. ''Business,'' he'd said. He'd said the same thing the night before. Of course, if his ''business'' was important, she supposed she'd hear about it soon enough. Secrets had a way of getting around small towns. Her mind wandered and she stared at a wall map of the Yukon until the Klondike River began to blur.

Footsteps approached along the hallway, then passed by her cubicle. Another door nearby opened and shut.

"Have a chair, Mckay." The policeman's voice was audible through the thin wall.

Betsy straightened. Drew McKay was in the next room.

"I got in as quickly as I could, Sergeant Randall," Drew said. "It would have been yesterday afternoon, but I had obligations in Fairbanks and I couldn't leave as early as I'd hoped. When I finally did arrive, you'd already gone home."

"I see."

There was a moment of silence and Betsy strained to hear. She drove whatever qualms she had about eavesdropping from her mind and hoped Selkirk wouldn't return until she'd had a chance to listen a bit longer.

Randall cleared his throat, then went on. "We appreciate your coming all this way. It must be quite a shock. You have our sympathies."

"Thanks." Drew's voice sounded strained. "I saw the news media out front. What's going on?"

"We'll get to that. As you know, a local found the plane...."

"Can you tell me who?" Drew interrupted.

"A woman. Beyond that, I'm not at liberty to say."

Betsy stiffened. Drew was involved, somehow, in this murky Red Baron stuff.

"Okay," Drew said. "Was anyone . . . in the plane?"

Silence again. Betsy wrapped her arms tightly around herself and stifled a shiver. She could see the horrible skull so clearly. How could Drew McKay possibly be mixed up in this? Maybe she should stop eavesdropping now. She wasn't sure she wanted to hear more.

The sergeant went on. "Yes, there was a body. It's our policy to notify family first, and we did speak with your mother last night. We tried to locate you, but couldn't find you in any of the hotels. There was evidence the victim was wearing a parachute.''

Betsy's thoughts raced. *Family.* What did Drew's family have to do with this? When Drew spoke again, she could hear the fatigue in his voice. ''The victim...you mean the 'body','' he said. ''It's all so impersonal. You know what I mean, Sergeant?''

''I understand, but we have no positive ID yet.''

''Why the reporters? Somehow, I find it hard to believe that a parachute is newsworthy. Why are the news media so interested?''

''Well, Mr. McKay, I'm afraid they found out about the aviator goggles and stolen money.''

''What are you talking about?''

''We're still sorting through this mess,'' Randall calmly answered. ''Probably will be for some time. I'm really sorry, but new evidence suggests the plane was used in the Red Baron robbery getaway.''

''Impossible,'' Drew snapped. ''That was in Fairbanks.''

''Maybe I'm going too fast, McKay. Let's talk about the plane itself. The Department of Transport has already picked up the engine and taken it to Edmonton for analysis. Of course, the registration in the cockpit was still intact and that's why we called your mother's house in the first place. We felt it best to have someone from the family look at the wreckage.''

''What about the numbers on the outside?'' Drew asked.

''They're faded, but readable,'' Randall said. ''We were able to trace them. Got the answer back late yesterday, probably while you were on your way over. McKay, I regret to inform you that the plane did belong to your...father.''

Betsy felt a chill pierce through her. What if the remains she had found were those of Drew's *father*! Somehow, the possibility made the horror of the discovery more real for her than it had been at the time. And it added to her confusion over Drew. With all of this on his mind, it was no wonder that he had reacted so strongly to seeing her medallion. She'd already spent half the previous night remembering his boyish smile and teasing eyes and wondering if he could understand why she'd had him thrown out. Now she could imagine what Drew would say if he knew she was the one to bring his father's plane and possibly his reputation into the open for public scrutiny. If he had forgiven her for her actions at Yukon Lights, he would never be able to forgive her for this.

Betsy rubbed her fingers along her brow and wished to God she'd never found the plane or its cargo, and that she'd never met Drew McKay.

DREW FORCED HIS shoulders back in the chair. He didn't want to believe what Sergeant Randall was saying. "What proof do you have, Sergeant? I want the whole story and I don't want to hear it on the street or on the news."

Randall's brow furrowed. He was about forty-five with a craggy face and close-cropped graying hair, but there was something much older in his eyes that spoke of many years on the force and many questions like Drew's. "All right, McKay, I'll give it to you straight. We found a number of items in the airplane that link your father to the armored car robbery in Fairbanks. I guess you Alaskans call it the Red Baron robbery."

"That's what everyone calls it." Drew was seething. For years, he had managed to push the suspicions of the

FBI and the Fairbanks police to the back of his mind. His father was a missing person, not a criminal. He'd gone to the annual celebrations, which painted the Red Baron robbers as heroes, but now the whole idea made him sick.

"Besides the old goggles, we also found a khaki World War One pilot's jacket," the Mountie said. "Neither was on the body, but since there was only one person on the plane...well, for now, we still have to make certain assumptions."

"And the money?"

"A thousand dollars U.S. A packet of twenties. All of them at least ten years old. The serial numbers match. The money was from the armored car, all right. Sorry, McKay, but none of us can change history."

Drew couldn't argue about the money, but he did see a flaw in the Mountie's logic. "Okay, you found a thousand dollars, but where's the rest of the loot? Two million in cash. And there were *two* robbers. Why aren't you out looking for the other guy?" Drew thought about what he'd just said. Did it mean he had accepted his father's guilt?

"Where would we look, McKay?"

"How should I know? You guys are the experts. I thought the Mounties always got their man."

"So the saying goes. But we have only a few policemen for a very large area. The Yukon Territory isn't as big as Alaska, of course, but it's still a sizable chunk of real estate. We've got more square miles than California—without the freeways. The road to Whitehorse was paved only a few years ago, and, as you've seen, most of the streets of Dawson City are still dirt on top of permafrost. Even if we knew who 'our man' was—and at this point we don't have the least idea—we'd have to track him across forests, mountains, rivers and Arctic ice. Nothing is easy here. You're from Fairbanks. I'm sure you understand.''

Drew knew only too well. His livelihood depended on his skill in transporting people where they couldn't go by ordinary means. ''You can't just quit now. Don't you have any clues?''

''You're a thorough man, McKay. Might make a good policeman yourself. Unfortunately, your question, as valid as it is, leads us nowhere. What we have is the plane and what was in it. Nothing more. Not at the moment anyhow.''

''There has to be something,'' Drew said.

''Probably,'' Randall acknowledged. ''But we don't know where to begin. We also have to consider the possibility that the rest of the money never made it to the Dawson City area. It could have stayed in Fairbanks. And by now, after ten years, it could be anywhere in the world. Of course, the FBI tells me that not one dollar of it has ever turned up. So, if one of the robbers *is* still at large, he's obviously afraid to spend it.''

Drew thought for a moment. ''I don't see why the money hasn't been spent. Isn't there a statute of limitations?''

Randall nodded. ''Five years on the robbery, the U.S. attorney says. But it isn't that simple.''

''What do you mean?''

''As I understand it, this Red Baron pair is home free in terms of the robbery itself, but if one of them is in possession of the cash, he's still breaking the law. And if anyone else is holding the money for them—a friend or relative, say—then that person probably could be prosecuted, too.''

Drew let the mention of the relative pass. He knew Randall was testing him, but he couldn't let himself be goaded into anything. There was too much he didn't know, although he was beginning to make sense of the legal distinction. "Then you're saying that robbery and possession of the money are separate crimes."

"Exactly," Randall said. "The limitation on possession is also five years, but that technicality probably won't come into play. You see, the five-year clock starts when the robbers last had the money, but we have to assume that at least one of them is still hanging on to it."

"So the clock hasn't even started," Drew concluded. He felt a charge of excitement. Until now, he'd never thought of searching for the Red Baron robbers. Drew knew scores of policemen had failed, but he had a better reason to succeed than anyone else. The robbers had used his father's plane and... Drew didn't want to think about the possibilities.

"Do you think the robbers know they're still in jeopardy?" Drew asked.

Sergeant Randall stroked his chin. "Hard to say. They were apparently clever enough to make a clean escape, but not smart enough not to take the money in the first place. Everybody has blind spots, but criminals seem to exaggerate theirs. A criminal often believes so much in his own scheme that he doesn't notice its weakness."

"So if a Red Baron robber is ever found with the loot," Drew said, "there's still a case against him."

"True. But I'd like to caution you not to get your hopes up. It's been a long time."

*A long time.* A fresh wave of sadness swept over Drew. He'd never dreamed he would be learning about Sam like this. But at this point, he was more confused about his father's fate than enlightened. "What about the . . . body, Sergeant? I made a special trip over here."

Randall sighed. "The remains have been removed but, as I said, we don't have positive identification yet."

*Remains.* Drew flattened his palms against his thighs. He resisted the sickening implication of Randall's word but knew he had to accept reality. What could he expect after ten years? "When will you know?" Drew asked. "Maybe there's some way I could help."

"If the crash had been last week, perhaps . . . but not now. We've sent X rays to Fairbanks. Your mother was kind enough to provide the name of your father's dentist. We should be getting confirmation any time."

So the Mounties were sure, Drew thought. His father was guilty and there wouldn't even be a trial. "I'd like to look at the plane."

The Mountie nodded. "Fair enough. I'll need to clear up a few things here first. Can you come back in, say, twenty or thirty minutes?"

"I don't have anything else to do."

"All right, I'll drive you out. By the way, I take it your brother didn't come along."

"No," Drew said. "Somebody had to mind the store."

"Then he's in Fairbanks?"

"Of course," Drew said. He didn't like Randall's attitude, pinning down Pete's location.

"Do you have a room yet?" Randall asked.

"I'm checking into the Bonanza Hotel a little later."

"Good." Randall stood and Drew got up, too. "If it's not a major inconvenience," the policeman said, "I hope you'll spend a couple of days with us—just until we get a few matters figured out. Enjoy the town while you're here. Dawson City has more going on than you might expect. You can pan for gold or even do a little gambling at Diamond Tooth Gertie's.''

Drew scratched the stubble on his face. Damn it, if he wanted to leave town, he would. It seemed as though he and Pete were under suspicion as accomplices. He knew better, but felt so gloomy and mixed up about his father that it didn't matter to him what was convenient for the police. Still, he might look around as long as he was here. After all, there was Betsy. ''What about this other place I saw?'' he asked. ''Yukon Lights?''

Randall glanced at him oddly for an instant, then smiled as he opened the door to let Drew out of the office. ''Ah, yes. One of Dawson City's finer establishments. Excellent food. And be sure to take in one of the cancan floor shows. The ladies are easy on the eyes.''

Yeah, Drew agreed silently. Especially the lady who owns the place.

Drew went outside, carefully swinging wide of the reporters. They hovered like vultures, waiting to feast on his father's ambiguous misfortune. He looked up and down the block and felt lost. He was familiar with landscapes like Dawson City's, towns perched precariously on the North's rugged terrain, and he might even have been able to appreciate nature's gifts under different circumstances. But he didn't want to be here; he wanted to be back in Alaska doing the work he enjoyed.

Besides, he wasn't here to appraise the town. He had a mission he couldn't ignore. As he walked along, he started thinking again about his father and the wrecked plane. Everything would be just as it had been before if this local woman hadn't stumbled across the wreckage. Who was she? Obviously, she didn't want to get involved.

He sauntered along the boardwalk a few more yards. Then it hit him. Why had Betsy Archer burst into the Mounties' office, asking about the plane and the reporters? And why had she been closeted with that officer? Could she be the one who had found the plane? He had to talk to her soon. He tried to remember whether he had seen her leave the station but couldn't. He'd been so caught up in his own affairs that he'd failed to notice much when he left. Now he had to meet Randall in fifteen minutes.

Great, Drew thought ruefully. Wonderful timing. He'd finally figured out that Betsy Archer had found the plane and he didn't have time to see her.

A DOOR SLAMMED in the next room and footsteps scuffed, then faded. Betsy was jolted back to reality. She was still waiting for the constable to return, but after overhearing the conversation next door she felt a lot wiser—and sadder.

She wished she could have seen the two men in conversation next door. Drew had sounded disturbed, just as he had last night when he'd seen her medallion. The RCMP wanted him to stay in town. Was he under some kind of house arrest? Maybe the police suspected *he* was involved in the robbery, or that he was looking for the two million dollars himself.

Selkirk opened the door. "Sorry for the delay, Miss Archer. When I transferred to Dawson City in June, I had no idea I'd be so busy here."

He sat down and Betsy said, "You can blame me. If I hadn't found that plane we'd all be better off."

The Mountie studied her. "It hasn't been easy on you, has it? I know it won't make you feel better to hear that the RCMP appreciates your help. What you saw has to be upsetting. But when this is all over, I think you'll be glad you reported what you did."

"I don't know. After this morning and..." Betsy stopped herself from mentioning what she'd overheard next door.

"And what?" Selkirk arched a brow.

"I just don't want to be involved."

"We don't intend to release your name. There's no need for anyone but the RCMP to know your role, although it wouldn't hurt for you to be extra careful for a while. We're undoubtedly going to see treasure hunters descend on Dawson City."

"But you haven't told the media where the plane is, and you've already taken the money off it."

"A thousand dollars," Selkirk answered. "The rest of the two million could be anywhere—somebody's backyard, the goldfields, a hollow tree, maybe even a bank. Wherever it is, I expect a few greedy souls to move in for a killing."

Betsy grimaced at the word, and Selkirk noticed. "Sorry. But I think you know what I mean."

"I guess so," Betsy said. "Just remember some of those visitors might be my livelihood."

"Agreed." The Mountie paused. "I don't mean to scare you, but these fortune hunters really could be dangerous. So call us if there's any trouble. That's about all I can tell you."

Betsy immediately thought of Drew and wondered if she'd already encountered a fortune hunter—or worse. Confusion filled her. Mere moments ago she'd felt sorry for him, and now she couldn't help but think about the possibility that he was somehow involved with the robbery.

Betsy stood and headed for the door. Then she stopped and turned. "Don't worry, Constable. I keep your number by my phone."

Selkirk nodded. Betsy returned him a confident smile that lasted until she reached the sterile hall outside his office. She wasn't confident at all. She was beginning to be frightened. At this point Drew McKay knew more about her than she did about him—such as where to find her. As far as Betsy was concerned, he might be the most dangerous man in Dawson City.

As she left the police station, she scanned the crowd for Drew, but he was already gone. She was thankful. But she still had to push through the clump of reporters waiting on the street. She'd never seen so much activity at the RCMP station. Sergeant Randall quickly followed her out and met the people. The small crowd surged around him.

She stood aside. Two men started filming Randall with small video cameras, and a woman with a Nikon snapped his picture. At the same time, five people began simultaneously asking questions—about the Red Baron robbery and the plane.

Betsy inched backward. She'd been naive not to consider the threat of the news media as well as that of treasure hunters. Unlike her native Vancouver, Dawson City was virtually outside the rings of the media circus. It had its little newspaper, and television and radio were available, but the scale and impact of journalism there were smaller and less intense.

When a couple of the reporters glanced her way, Betsy quickly moved on. Talking with the press was the last thing she wanted to do.

Betsy edged behind the crowd and toward Front Street. Then, away from the clamor outside the RCMP station, she took comfort in the ordinariness of commercial life in the storefronts as she made her way to the jewelry store to see about having her chain repaired.

An old-fashioned bell over the door announced her, and she was relieved to see that there was no one but Frank Saunders, Evie's brother, in the shop. Frank was sitting behind the counter on a high stool, next to the old assay scales that were the focal point of the period decor of the shop, peering intently at something through the small black-edged jeweler's loupe wedged firmly in his eye.

*The bell isn't much use to him,* Betsy thought, as she stood unnoticed for what seemed like minutes. Finally, she cleared her throat and Frank looked up, loupe still in place. Recognizing her, he broke into a broad welcoming grin, pausing only to catch the eyepiece as it tumbled out of place.

"Betsy! Great to see you. Everything okay?"

"Hi, Frank. Hope I'm not interrupting—" Betsy gestured to the orderly array of jeweler's tools spread out on the counter in front of him "—but I've got a small repair job for you that I was hoping you could do while I wait." She reached into her pocket, pulled out the pendant and held it out to him.

"No problem," Frank said, taking the broken chain from her. "I can make time for *this*. I know you wouldn't want to be separated from it for long." Affection showed in his sparkling gray eyes. "Won't be a minute. Make yourself at home."

While Frank fiddled with tweezers and magnifying glass, Betsy walked around the shop, looking at the display cases. Frank was a skilled goldsmith, and though most of his work was designed to appeal to the steady stream of tourists that flowed through Dawson City, even the pickax and gold-pan charms showed his love of the subject in their careful detail. The warm sheen of the precious metal objects brought memories back to her of happy times when she would sit with Conrad and Evie while Frank recounted tales of the lore and lure of gold. It was there that she had come to understand the dedication and fervor of that brotherhood of dreamers who devoted their lives to chipping away at surfaces to get at the richness beneath.

With these memories came the realization that Drew, too, must be haunted by distant happy times and, not least of all, by an uncertain future. Was she being too suspicious, too hasty in her evaluation of the situation to look beyond the surface to glimpse what was beneath it? *Conrad would be disappointed in you,* she thought, and as the tears welled up she fought them back with an unspoken vow that she would speak to Drew, would keep an open mind. She also decided that she would indulge Talbot in a few hours' reminiscence if he should ask again. As composure settled over her she turned back to face Frank.

"Almost done, Betsy…there." Frank beckoned to her to turn her back and he fastened the clasp behind her neck. "I put in a new link for you. That way there won't be a weakness anywhere in the chain. Good as new."

*Weakness.* Doubt rushed in again, eroding Betsy's resolve. Was her desire to believe in Drew McKay despite the circumstances just a sign of weakness? Confusion threatened to overwhelm her again.

"Thank you, Frank. How much do—"

Frank dismissed the question with a gesture. She thanked him again and said goodbye.

The shop bell sounded and she was back on Front Street. Despite the period storefronts, it was a modern world full of modern dilemmas that Betsy walked through as she made her way back to Yukon Lights.

WHEN SHE REACHED the saloon, Betsy went directly into her office. She needed its security. But once there, she could think only of Drew's appealing smile, his teasing warmth, his devastating blue eyes—and the disconcerting knowledge that he might be involved with the Red Baron robbery. For the first time since she'd come to Dawson City to stay, she felt confused, cornered and vulnerable.

Then Betsy heard it. Noises from the back of Yukon Lights—an intermittent pounding. It couldn't be a customer. It was still too early to open for lunch. She went to her office door and scanned the main room of the nightclub. Nothing unusual. The place had only two small windows on the street side and even on a bright summer day was fairly dark.

She was about to blame her state of mind for the imagined sounds when she heard another one. Soft, grating. She decided to check. The short hallway to the back was like a tunnel. At the other end a man was twisting the knob of the delivery door and peering through its window.

Betsy set her jaw. She was in no mood for more problems. Now it looked as if she would have to deal with a burglar. For a moment, she hung back in semidarkness, where the man couldn't see her. She probably shouldn't confront him, but she was angry.

She charged down the hallway, unlocked the door and flung it open. But before she could tell the guy to get lost, he said, "Hi, I'm Greg Harsted—a reporter. I'd like to ask a few questions about this Red Baron plane."

Betsy glared at him. In full daylight, she recognized Harsted as one of the media people she'd seen questioning Sergeant Randall at the RCMP station. How had he found her? The Mounties were supposed to be keeping her name out of it. Surely there hadn't been a leak.

"I'm not the one you want," she said calmly.

"Oh, I think you are." Harsted leaned against the doorjamb, forcing Betsy to retreat slightly. He crossed his arms and said, "It's common knowledge that a Dawson City woman found the plane, and when I saw you leave the police station a few minutes ago, I had a hunch. So I asked a few questions and I was directed here. I knocked at the front door, but when no one answered, I came around to the alley. Sorry if I startled you."

Betsy found his apology inadequate. She didn't like having her privacy invaded. Slouching against the molding, the reporter was pretending to be casual, but he clearly expected her to tell him whatever he wanted. She supposed a good reporter had to be skilled in getting other people to talk, but she didn't have to be an easy subject.

"If you're waiting for lunch," she said with determination, "we'll be opening in twenty minutes. You'll find the *front* door open then." Fortunately, she'd locked the street door when she'd returned.

"I'm not here to eat," Harsted said. "I'd like to interview you. You're nervous now, but you'll get over it. When the other reporters eventually beat a path to your door, you'll be glad you talked to me first. I'm nice and I won't stick a microphone in your face."

"Look, there are a lot of tourists in town, and I've got a business to run," Betsy said. "I don't have time to chat."

Harsted pulled away from the building. "Okay," he said, "I've caught you at a bad time. I can come back after lunch, when it's slower. Will you talk to me then?"

"No."

"Loosen up, Miss Archer," he said. "You're about to become famous. Or maybe 'more famous' would best describe it. I cornered a local and described you. Which wasn't hard to do with your looks. You're apparently well-known in this town."

She didn't fall for his flattery. "I'd like to limit my fame to Dawson City. If I wanted to be a celebrity, I'd go to Hollywood. I don't need to have my name in every newspaper in North America."

Harsted lifted his chin, a knowing smile on his face.

Betsy moved back a pace into the building. Damn! She'd as much as admitted she was the one who had found the plane. It didn't matter. She wasn't going to let him interview her.

Betsy was reaching to close the door when Harsted asked, "Has Drew McKay found you?"

"McKay?" She stopped. Harsted had caught her off guard. "You know him?"

"Sure, met him in Fairbanks a couple days ago." He paused. "And I saw him leave the RCMP station shortly before you did."

"Does it matter?"

"I'm just warning you, that's all. You should be worrying about people like him, not me."

Betsy bit back a retort. She knew Harsted was trying to force her off balance, but already realized there might be some truth in the reporter's words. "I don't know what you mean."

"You'll learn," Harsted said smugly. "McKay's short of cash and he told me himself he'd like to find two million dollars. And that was *before* his dad's plane was linked to the Red Baron robbers. Don't you think he wants that money even more now?''

Betsy didn't know what to think. ''The police wouldn't let him keep the money even if he found it,'' she protested. ''It's stolen.''

''You think criminals bother to consult the police? I doubt if anything would stand in the way of a guy like McKay. Talk to me first and I'll see that you get to speak your mind. You know, tell the raw truth: *How I Found the Red Baron Plane,* by Betsy Archer.'' He held up his hands, as if to suggest a gigantic headline. ''If everybody's convinced you don't know where the money is, they'll probably leave you alone.''

Suddenly, a man's voice sounded from inside the nightclub. ''Betsy? You back here?'' The voice grew louder as it echoed along the hallway.

*Thank goodness.* The cook's timing was a bit off; she would have preferred him to cut off Harsted a minute or two sooner. But his interruption was welcome.

''Oh, there you are.'' The middle-aged man stopped when he saw Harsted. ''Sorry to bother you, Betsy, but we may have a problem with a couple of the menu items. We're running short of corned beef.''

She turned to the cook, glad for an excuse, although at the moment her mind couldn't have been further from the concerns of the kitchen. ''No problem,'' she told him. ''Let me show you.'' Again, she started to close the door.

Harsted retreated to the middle of the alley. ''I'll be back. Or you can look me up at the Double River Inn. I hope you change your mind soon, Miss Archer, even though I'm prepared to wait. You may not realize it, but this is an important story. And *I'm* going to get it.'' He put on sunglasses and swung away.

''Don't hold your breath,'' Betsy muttered. She watched him disappear around the corner of a building, then shut the door and locked it. Well, at least Conrad would have approved of that, she thought.

A HASTILY CONSUMED SANDWICH churning in his stomach, Drew rode in the passenger seat as Sergeant Randall's four-wheel-drive Chevy Blazer bounced over the rock-studded ground. Neither Drew nor Randall talked, and only the groans of the vehicle's suspension system broke the silence. They'd left the good road long ago. Now they were driving down nothing more than a trail. Although he was confident Randall would get him to his father's plane, Drew was lost.

Fifteen minutes later, the Mountie stopped the Blazer and said, ''We walk from here.''

Drew got out and surveyed the brush and winter-stunted birch and spruce. ''Is it far? I didn't bring hiking boots.''

Sergeant Randall glanced at Drew's running shoes. ''Those'll be fine. It's only about ten minutes in. Watch out for broken branches, though. We had a bad storm with high winds several nights back. The plane probably wouldn't have been found if the wind hadn't chopped off trees around the wreckage.''

Drew was silent. He thought he knew what to expect, from the crash site and from himself, but as he followed Randall across a stream and up a hill, he realized he was afraid. It was one thing to identify an airplane; it was another to look at the place where someone had died, perhaps your father.

At the top of the hill, Drew got his first glimpse of the plane. Blue and white were the colors, of course, and as Drew and Randall got closer, the numbers on the Cessna dispelled all doubt.

Drew and Randall didn't speak until they were twenty or thirty feet from the aircraft.

Drew said, "It's the one, all right. Cessna 182. I've flown it myself." He walked around the Cessna for a few minutes, trying to absorb some feeling from it, some vibration about the Red Baron robbery and why the pilot had lost the advantage. But he got no hint at all from the twisted hunk of scrap. Wherever the answers were, he decided, they weren't in the wreckage.

He was tentatively playing with the idea that Sam McKay had been that pilot when Sergeant Randall calmly said, "A problem has come up."

A problem? Drew thought Randall must be joking. How could matters get more complicated? "What is it?"

"It's those dental records I told you about. I received a report from Forensics just after you left the station this morning. Your father's records don't match."

"What?" Drew wasn't sure he was understanding what he'd heard.

"I'm as confused as you," Randall said. "All I can say is that the body in the wreckage was not your father."

Conflicting emotions tugged at Drew. A minute ago he had decided to work at accepting that his father might be dead, but now even that sad certainty was being denied him. Or was it?

"You mean my father is still alive?"

"I don't know," Randall said.

"You don't know?" Drew felt his adrenaline rise. "Who the hell was the guy in the plane?"

"I'm trying to find out. The dental charts are being sent all over Fairbanks." The Mountie stared at the battered fuselage, then turned back to Drew. "There's something else. I didn't want to tell you before, not until we knew whether or not it was your father."

Drew steeled himself for another shock.

"The man in the plane," Randall said, "died from a blow to the back of his skull."

## Chapter Four

"Oh, my God." Drew's legs crumpled under him and he sagged onto a rock. He didn't want to hear more, or to stay in this place.

The ride back to town was as silent as the one to the wreckage. Drew had gone out there thinking that Sam McKay *might* be dead, but he was returning with the sure knowledge that Sam McKay, dead or alive, was the chief suspect in the murder of the unknown passenger. Earlier, Drew had been forced to consider that his father might have robbed an armored car. Now he was compelled to think that his father might have killed a man. Whatever the evidence, Drew couldn't accept either possibility. There had to be an explanation. But the man who could supply it had been missing for ten years.

When Drew got back to Dawson City, he checked into his room at the Bonanza Hotel. He was weary—a night in his airplane hadn't provided much sleep—so he kicked off his shoes and lay down on the bed. His need to talk to Betsy seemed greater now, but he decided to rest first. He closed his eyes. Minutes stretched hazily, and when Drew finally rubbed his face and got up, he realized he'd been asleep. Disoriented, he looked at his watch. He'd slept more than an hour. Though the northern sky was still bright, the day had slipped into evening. He wiped one palm across his forehead, feeling groggy. Worries about his father came flooding back. The nap had let his body rest but had done little to ease his mind.

Drew went to his second-story window. Below, tourists crammed the sidewalks, and he felt a need to join them; to take some kind of action. He had no idea how to find his father, and that inescapable helplessness sat heavy on him.

He concentrated on the crowd again and felt a sting of loneliness. It was a special comfort he longed for. Softness, compassion. A woman's touch. And he knew whose. An image of Betsy rematerialized in his brain and he sensed a sudden warmth. He hadn't just imagined that there was an attraction between them. Now he had several reasons for wanting to see her. But he would have to proceed cautiously. He couldn't risk a repeat of the previous night's embarrassing performance. He began to strip for a shower.

TWENTY MINUTES LATER, Drew was on his way to Yukon Lights. As he neared the nightclub he heard piano music. The overflow crowd filled the narrow boardwalk. He swung between groups of laughing customers and accidentally bumped into an older man leaning against the building.

"Excuse me." Drew stepped around him and hesitated. "Looks busy tonight."

The man seemed amused. "Tonight? Yukon Lights is busy just about every night from what I hear. If you think this is jammed, try to fight your way inside."

"Maybe I will." Drew grinned and straightened his jacket. The man beside him was nearly bald, mid-fifties, his ill-fitting suit draped around a body well past its prime. "I've always enjoyed a challenge."

The older man's answer was a short, high-pitched giggle. Drew felt uncomfortable. He paused a second, then headed inside the club. Cigarette smoke stung Drew's eyes and he frowned. Where had he seen that man before? For a moment, he considered going back for a second look, but Betsy's voice, soft and slightly husky, echoed through a microphone and lured him farther into the haziness of the club.

"Hope this next number gives you a little Klondike fever," Betsy said, gripping the microphone as she gazed from her side-stage piano into semidarkness. "The original sheet music for this song was found during the remodeling of the old Nugget Theatre down the street. It's ripe with history and should really take you back."

A beer bottle clanked somewhere in front of her. The club was nearly silent. She looked at the well-lighted piano keys, let her fingers hover a second, then broke into the raucous melody. Her kind of music. She bounced on the stool, loving the vintage honky-tonk tune. It was still early, or at least the sun hadn't set, but Yukon Lights was already nearly filled. Most of the people there were finishing dinner. The evening crowd wouldn't start drifting in for another thirty minutes.

It was the night off for the melodrama. Later the other piano player—the lounge pianist, she liked to call him— would spin out requests and dance music on the baby grand down by the bar. She needed someone besides herself to play piano at Yukon Lights. She didn't have time every night, and her hired hand's repertoire and technique frankly outshone hers, except in honky-tonk. He had joked to her that her old upright was fifty years out of tune. Conrad had bought the piano used, so maybe the lounge pianist was right, but for now the audience was hers. She was grateful for that. At least, for a little while, she might forget her worries.

But when Drew came in, Betsy noticed immediately. Although she'd been half expecting him, she still faltered a beat. Handsome, once again seemingly in control, he sat down at one of the few vacant tables. She closed her eyes, searching her brain for the notes she'd memorized. What if he talked to her again? She'd never be able to keep it a secret that she'd found his father's plane. For the first time since she'd come here, she longed for the anonymity of big-city life.

Between tunes, Betsy took a chance and casually glanced at Drew's table. He sat in the dusky light, only twenty feet behind her on a diagonal to the left. Thank goodness he was occupied scanning a dinner menu. He looked much better than he had at the RCMP station. He was clean-shaven now, his black hair combed, curling in wisps around his ears. Broad shoulders neatly filled a blue plaid shirt. Only the slightly weathered cast of his tanned face betrayed an outdoors occupation. A waitress stood over Drew as he ordered. He's going to be here awhile, Betsy thought. Then Drew glanced up at her and grinned.

Involuntarily, she returned the smile. It was all she could do to play another song. She peered at the keys, then began to beat them with clammy fingers. She couldn't look at him again—not until she felt more in control. She had planned to do another four or five tunes before taking a break, but now she'd be lucky to struggle through this one. She would skip the rest of her honky-tonk program. Only the staff and a few regulars would notice.

Finally, Betsy finished the tune. People clapped. She stood and bowed. But she was disappointed in herself. The notes had been right, but her usual spark was missing. She went behind the bar and poured herself a glass of red wine. Although she was facing the wall, instinct told her Drew had followed her. As she turned, he came up to the bar and put his elbows down on the dark polished wood between them.

"I forgot to order a drink with my dinner," he said.

She put down her wine. "I suppose I can help you."

"I was counting on that."

"What do you want?" Immediately she regretted asking. The question was loaded and she was sure her voice had betrayed her. A knot rose in her throat.

He threaded his fingers together. "I want to say I'm sorry. I behaved like an idiot last night."

"Yes, you did." Amber lamplight from behind the bar accented the attractive angles of his cheekbones and jaw. She was suddenly aware of the medallion beneath her blouse. She took a step back when a tremor of excitement rippled through her. "But I accept your apology. What are you having for dinner?"

"A steak."

"Then how about a glass of burgundy?" She held up her own wine, trying to ignore the harnessed sensuality in Drew's eyes. She was, at once, compelled and frightened by it. "The house special. *Vin rouge de maison.* It's quite good."

"I'll try it," he said.

"Fine." She looked around. *Damn!* The rest of the staff seemed busy. "I'll . . . bring it to your table."

Betsy poured the burgundy and carried both their glasses to the dining area. Drew lagged behind a moment, enabling him to reach the table at the same time she did.

"Would you join me?" He eyed her glass and pulled out a chair. "I could use a little company. I promise I won't go off the deep end again about your medallion."

Betsy started to protest, fighting against the attraction she felt to him. "I really don't think . . ."

"Please, Betsy." His fingers gripped the back of the chair. "I want to talk with you."

Betsy's temples throbbed as the litany of confusion echoed in her mind. Maybe Drew knew she'd found the plane. After all, the reporter had figured it out. Maybe he wanted her to help him look for the money. Maybe he was lonely and needed a compassionate ear. Maybe . . .

"Betsy?"

She looked at him. His shoulders had become rigid, his unreadable eyes as cool as steel. But his voice was low and gentle, and the easy way he'd said her name relaxed her, made her warm. She thought about the vow she'd made at Frank's. Perhaps Drew deserved a chance. "All right, but I can stay only a few minutes." She dropped into the chair.

Drew sat opposite her and lifted his goblet. "Let's toast."

"To what?"

"To a quiet evening at Yukon Lights."

"I'll go along with that." Betsy touched her glass to his, then sipped. "What did you want to talk about?"

Drew tilted his glass and focused on the shimmering liquid. "You're the one who found my dad's plane." His words were a statement, cold and even.

Betsy gulped and put down her wine. A swallow of burgundy caught momentarily between her mouth and stomach. She'd feared this moment, had been expecting it. Still, her brain scrambled for the right words.

Before she could respond, Drew said, "I'd been wondering who the woman was—all day yesterday, and last night after your bouncer kicked me out. At first, I was surprised to see you at the police station. Then I knew..." His voice trailed off.

"I'm sorry," Betsy whispered. Her condolence sounded insubstantial, but it was the best she could muster.

Drew didn't respond, just stared at her as if he could read her mind. She didn't want to lie. Impulsively, she stretched her arm across the narrow table to touch him. The fine dark hairs on the back of his hand were feathery, his skin taut. The brief contact titillated her. He lifted a brow and glanced down at her fingers. Confused, she slid them away.

"Thanks." His mouth slanted into a smile. "For the sympathy..."

Betsy looked down at the wineglass in front of her and then gave in and allowed her glance to meet his. "I had no idea it was your father's plane. I stumbled across it. Then I reported it to the Mounties. The police weren't supposed to mention me."

"They didn't—not by name. All they said was that a local woman had found the plane."

"I'm not the only woman in Dawson City." Betsy toyed nervously with her glass.

Stretching back in his chair, Drew sighed. "No, you're not the only woman in Dawson City, but you're the only one who counts. You tore into the Mounties' office this morning, remember? I didn't think that after a late night here you'd want to get up early to see those guys. Not unless one of them is your boyfriend."

"I don't have a boyfriend."

"Well, that's good anyway. For me."

Betsy's face flushed.

Drew slid forward and braced his arms on the table. "Forget the airplane for now, Betsy. Sure, the whole thing has been a shock for me. But it's also a relief. For years we heard nothing...." He bit down on his lip, then hurried on. "Look, I came in tonight to get cheered up. I liked your piano playing a lot, but I'd hoped you might be dancing that cancan again."

"I haven't decided." Betsy gave her nearly untouched wineglass a twist. She didn't need alcohol. Sitting so close to Drew McKay was already making her head light.

"Got something better going?"

"Maybe." Betsy tilted her chin almost defiantly. His eyes were locked on hers. *Slow down,* she told herself. "I'm waiting to see how things turn out."

"You and me both." He frowned. "I *am* sorry about breaking your chain. But as I said, my father wore one like it. Knowing what you know now about the crash..." A tiny muscle jerked at his temple.

"I understand," Betsy said. "You were upset. That's natural. I don't blame you for being so interested in my medallion. I like it myself." Beneath the cotton of her blouse, the medallion burned against her flesh.

"You don't find much of that stuff in Fairbanks. Dad got his from an Athabascan who worked for us once. One of the best guides we ever had. I feel terrible about what I did to your chain...and about how I acted. I wish you'd, at least, let me pay for repairs."

"Drew, don't worry about that. It's already fixed and there was no charge." Betsy shook her head. "The medallion's not that important. I don't wear it much anyway." More lies, she thought. But something vulnerable in Drew's expression made her want to ease his burden.

His features softened. "My name sounds good when you say it."

Betsy smiled weakly. She'd accidentally used his first name. A dangerous precedent. "What happens now?" she hurried on. "About the plane—and your father?"

Drew shrugged. Suddenly, he looked tired and worried again. "That's a good question. You might be seeing more of me. The Mounties have asked me to hang around awhile."

"Why?" Betsy noted the nervous crack in his voice. "Something else is on your mind."

"Is it that obvious?"

"Maybe I can help."

"You already have. More than you know."

Betsy took a deep breath and went on. "Look, I already feel involved. Sometimes it's better to talk."

Drew studied her, emotion crisscrossing his face. Finally he spoke. "I tried to put all this out of my head, at least for tonight. I wasn't going to tell you, but you'll find out soon enough anyway. Those reporters are going crazy. Probably better to know the truth from me."

"What truth?" Betsy's mouth dried. He edged closer, so near she caught the male scent of him, woodsy and clean.

"When you found the plane, you saw the ... body, didn't you?" Drew suddenly reached out and folded one of her hands in his. His thumb moved, aimlessly, across her knuckles. "They told you it was my father, didn't they?"

This time Betsy didn't mind his touch, although it made concentrating difficult. Her mind zoomed back to what she'd overheard Sergeant Randall tell Drew. "Not directly," she answered. That was the truth. They *hadn't* told her.

"Well, here's even better news. And more unbelievable." Drew's fingers tightened. "Now the Mounties have learned that the man in the cockpit wasn't my dad. Betsy, he might still be alive."

She blinked in shock. If she hadn't found Drew's father, than whom had she found? It was obvious Drew was judging her reaction. She had to say something. "Why, that's . . . wonderful," she stammered.

"Yes." His mouth flattened. "But that possibility gives them even more reason to think my dad's one of the infamous Red Baron robbers. And that he's escaped with the loot."

"They told you that?"

"Not in so many words, but the Mounties found evidence in the plane."

Betsy pulled her hand away. "Surely, you would have heard from your father if he were still alive." She waited for an answer, but didn't get one. "Anyway, why do the Mounties want you to stay in town?" She felt a sudden chill, even though the air in Yukon Lights was warm.

"I don't know—unless they think I might know where my dad is. But that's crazy. If I knew, I wouldn't be here, would I?" Drew laughed bitterly. "I'm sorry you had to get mixed up in this, Betsy. I should be grateful to you for finding the plane. Seeing what you did had to be frightening. I only wish the nightmare was over."

Betsy moistened her lips. As Drew spoke, the nightclub slowly closed in on her. "I don't understand," she murmured.

"Let me explain." He formed the words carefully. "You found a body in the plane. It wasn't my dad. But the plane crash didn't kill that man in the cockpit." He pressed forward. "That unknown man received a blow to the back of the head. Add another accusation to my father's apparent list of crimes. The Mounties also think he's a cold-blooded murderer."

Betsy felt as if someone had punched her in the stomach. She sagged, and the sickening moments when she'd discovered the wreckage zoomed back. She'd spotted red plaid flannel, seen the skeleton slumped over the wheel. There must have been a crack in the skull, but she hadn't noticed it. *Thank God.*

"Don't worry about any of this, Betsy," Drew said. "This whole mess is my problem. I was an idiot to even tell you. But there's something about you ... I don't know. I can't explain it, except that I feel close to you. I have the wacky feeling that you understand."

Betsy didn't answer. She couldn't let him know that she felt the same about him. And that she'd been suspecting him of God knows what. She was wondering how to change the subject when a voice came from behind her. "Hey, Betsy, you really know how to pack 'em in."

She jumped as she felt fingers on her shoulder. Twisting around, she faced Jacob Talbot. "Oh, hello."

He dropped his hand. "Sorry to startle you. Seems I'm good at that. I just wanted to say hi ... again." He lifted a nearly empty beer mug in his other hand.

"Mr. Talbot." Betsy hadn't expected him to come to Yukon Lights. Most of her evening customers were young and boisterous. "Hope you're having a good time."

"I am." Talbot surveyed the bustling room. "I always like a little excitement. Takes my mind off the pressures of the day."

Then he laughed, somewhat oddly, Betsy thought. She glanced back at Drew. He was studying Talbot, an absent, perplexed look on his face.

Talbot seemed to notice. He gave Betsy's shoulder another almost fatherly squeeze. "The bartender's drawing another beer over there. And it seems to have my name on it. I still hope we can get together before I leave town, Betsy. I'll keep in touch. Well, have a good one." His nod included Drew. "You, too." Then he headed to the bar.

"You know him?" Drew asked.

"Not really." Betsy watched Talbot sidle up to the wooden counter. "He used to know my grandfather, Conrad Parks. Grandpa owned this club. Also some mining land in the hills." She looked back at Drew. "The land's mine now and Talbot has a parcel next to it."

"I've seen him before," Drew said, shifting his gaze back to Talbot.

"Maybe you ran into him here in Dawson. He's been around at least since yesterday."

Drew frowned. "I did see him out in front when I was coming in here. But he already seemed familiar then."

Betsy couldn't help Drew. She didn't know much about Talbot, either. Only that he still made her nervous, even surrounded, as she was, by a houseful of revelers. She peered through the smoky air at the entrance. Virtually every seat was occupied, but people continued to push inside. Another man she recognized stood by the bar: Greg Harsted.

"Damn it," she muttered. "Not him, too."

Drew leaned closer. "What did you say?"

"Oh, nothing really." She tipped her head toward the door. "I just noticed someone else I'd rather not see. A reporter. He cornered me earlier today, but I was in no mood to be interviewed."

Drew followed her gaze. "You mean Greg Harsted?"

Betsy remembered that Harsted said he'd met Drew in Alaska. "Has he pinned you down, too?"

"You might say that." Drew's voice had an edge now. "He's pretty smooth. Free-lances for a New York newspaper. Told me he was Canadian, but borders don't seem to stop him. He interviewed me in Fairbanks. That was two days ago, during a Red Baron anniversary party. Weird, huh?"

"Yeah." Betsy dropped her glance. She didn't want Harsted to spot her.

Drew bent down, too. "Be careful with Harsted," he warned. "I have a feeling he'll do anything to get a good story."

"He turned up here after I got back this morning. He knew I found the plane."

"I wonder how much more he knows."

That was a good question. Betsy watched, absently, as the lounge pianist settled himself at the baby grand and began a lilting tune.

"Harsted's coming our way," Drew whispered.

"Then dance with me."

"What?" Drew looked pleasantly surprised.

"Come on." Betsy reached for his hand, then rose, tugging Drew to his feet. "I don't want publicity any more than you do. Harsted won't bother us if we're on the dance floor."

"Good thinking." Drew placed his arm, protectively, around her shoulders. He stopped a waitress hurrying by. "Tell the cook to hold my steak."

Betsy and Drew headed to the center of the room, where they joined several other couples. Then Drew gathered Betsy into his arms.

After they'd settled into a rhythm, Drew said, "I like your methods for dodging reporters. I couldn't have planned this better myself."

"Thanks. You're a good dancer, you know that?" Betsy had only imagined being so close to Drew. In her fantasy, she was calm, not deafened by her hammering pulse.

"I've never taken lessons." Drew moved his palm across her back, swaying to the music. "But no one's complained."

"I can see why." His eyes caught hers, darkened and held. She was intoxicated. But not with wine. Her movements became natural and when she leaned against him, his arm tightened against her back. She threaded her fingers behind his neck and said, "I think it worked. Harsted's going the other way."

"Good," Drew murmured against her cheek. "You nearly made me forget him."

The piano music lifted and they circled together. Harsted had stopped several feet from their table and turned back. They had evaded him for now, Betsy thought. Harsted headed for the bar, hesitating several yards from Talbot. The older man seemed occupied with a vivacious brunette woman at least thirty years his junior.

"Uh, Betsy? I don't mean to bother you." A waitress in her early twenties appeared beside them. "But we need your help in the kitchen." The younger woman glanced at Drew, looking slightly embarrassed. "Just for a second. I'm really sorry."

Drew released Betsy and stepped back. "You're the boss, Betsy. But if it's longer than a second, I'll come and find you."

Betsy caught the teasing sparkle in his eyes and laughed. By the time she reached the swinging double doors leading to the kitchen, Drew had returned to his table. And Harsted was again crossing the floor in Drew's direction.

Betsy stepped behind a potted plant. She couldn't believe her eyes. The two men stood and greeted each other like old friends, she thought. Drew and the reporter shook hands, clapped shoulders, then sat down at the table. Then Harsted pulled a notebook and pen from inside his jacket. He had caught up with Drew and, as far as Betsy could tell, Drew was falling for his line.

Betsy wiped her palms on the folds of her skirt. She was needed in the kitchen and couldn't watch the two men any longer. Each man had warned her about the other one. But she felt Drew had deceived her. It was all so confusing. She couldn't deny enjoying the feel of his strong arms about her. Although she'd dated in Dawson City, it was a long time since a man had interested her the way he had. But what if he and Harsted were working together?

*Nobody's what they seem.* In disgust, Betsy headed for the kitchen, pausing again at the doors for one last look. Drew and Harsted were ordering drinks. And on the other side of the floor another man was sitting next to the brunette. Jacob Talbot was gone.

BETSY WADDED THE WET RAG and gave the refrigerator door a final rubdown. It was one o'clock in the morning. Since abandoning Drew, she'd managed to spend most of her time in the kitchen helping out for an assistant who'd gone home sick, and now the diminishing din beyond the swinging doors told her that some of her customers were calling it a night. With any luck, Drew would be one of them. She'd torn lettuce for salads, grated potatoes for hash browns, even scrubbed the grill. And her distrust of Drew, justified or not, had continued to build.

Thirty minutes later, she put on her jacket and wearily stepped into the alley. The late cook, as usual, would lock up. A cool breeze from the Yukon River rustled leaves on nearby trees. Overhead, stars flecked the velvet sky. She tipped her jacket collar against her neck and headed for the street.

"Betsy, there you are. Let me walk you home." A tall form materialized out of the darkness.

Betsy jumped. "Who's there?"

"It's me." Drew stepped into the silvery fan of a streetlight. "I've been waiting for you a long time. I had a hunch you'd probably leave through the alley."

Betsy's heart was pounding. "Damn it. Why can't you leave me alone?" she shouted. "You scared me out of my wits." She was angry with Drew for startling her. And mad at herself for underestimating him.

"Sorry, I didn't mean to." Drew spread his arms wide. "I just don't think women should be out on the streets this time of night. There're a lot of kooks around."

"That's for sure." Betsy fumed. "The gallantry isn't necessary. I leave my club when I want to. I've survived just fine in this town for five years, and I can take care of myself."

Drew's jaw fell. "Hey, I said I was sorry."

"Then you've said enough." She swiveled on her heel and strode away, not daring to look back to check his reaction. At the corner she finally turned around, but

Drew had disappeared. *Fine. Maybe I'll get some rest this evening,* she thought. *Not much chance of that,* a voice in her head retorted.

But by the time Betsy had walked the five blocks to her home, she was even more exhausted. The past eighteen hours had been devastating, and she longed for the warm comfort of her bed. She could barely manage to release the gate in the picket fence surrounding her tiny yard. As she fumbled with the latch, she noticed an unusual slim line of blackness edging the side door of the garage.

Betsy hurried in the dark to the weathered wooden structure beside and behind her house. Gravel crunched eerily beneath her feet. The main doors were rickety and the old lock was broken, but they were secure, bolted from the inside. The fear turned Betsy's legs to rubber. The ebony strip was a shadow from within the garage. The side door was ajar. Someone, sometime that evening, had been inside.

Setting her shoulders against her rising panic, she pushed the garage door open and stuck her head inside. The room was silent. Light from a vapor lamp on the street cast diluted streams through the one large window. Fruit jars, filled with Evie's handiwork, still lined one wall. Conrad's battered '68 Chevy pickup loomed in front of her.

Then she looked at the dirt floor and gasped. Papers and magazines had been strewn everywhere, boxes of old clothes and business records maliciously torn apart. She jerked backward and ran inside. If the burglar was still in the garage, she didn't want to find him. Hurriedly, she bolted the front door and stood panting in semidarkness. When she caught her breath, she went to the phone and called the Mounties. But as she did, her fingers trembled. She felt violated. And painfully alone.

# Chapter Five

Drew's eyes popped open and he was on the edge of terror. He had no idea where he was. Or why. The ceiling stared back at him for a few long seconds, then recognition gradually surfaced: bed, room, hotel.

He rolled over and checked his watch on the nightstand. He'd slept only an hour, but he was wide awake now. Noises from partygoers filtered up from the street. Dawson City was even more awake than he was.

Drew pulled back the covers and sat on the edge of the bed in his underwear. A chill enveloped his bare legs instantly. The room was cool because he'd cracked open the window. He stood to close it, then sank back on the bed. Fresh air might clear his head, let him think. Especially about Betsy.

Holding her in his arms when they'd danced had been impossibly good. He'd felt the electricity. But that was only part of the spell. There had been something extra, something deeper that made her nearness so satisfying. Their rapport had been amazing, he thought. As natural as breathing. For a while, they'd talked as if they'd known each other for years. That had probably been a big mistake: he'd told her too much about his father—and about himself. That was why she pulled a disappearing act on him. And why she gave him the cold shoulder in the alley.

Drew got up and put on his street clothes. He needed to take his mind off her. So he went below and watched people drive Dawson City's dirt streets and clomp along the boardwalks. The nocturnal tourists prowling for excitement reminded him of a Red Baron robbery party, everybody intent on good times. Everyone except him. Betsy didn't trust him. That was obvious, he thought. Of course, no one else trusted him, either. Certainly not the Mounties.

And he was angry at Harsted for being so pushy about getting his big story. Especially earlier at Yukon Lights right after Betsy got called away. Harsted had even asked Drew to persuade Betsy to give an interview. Drew had tried to be friendly with him, but saw now that it was pointless. He just wished the reporter would get wind of an even bigger story someplace else and move on.

After a few minutes, Drew tired of the street spectacle and went back to his room. Just where the Mounties could expect to find him, he thought. They'd probably checked the hotel's registration book already. The more Drew thought about Sergeant Randall the more insulted he felt. The police had no right to suspect him of wanting the Red Baron loot. Wasn't it clear to Randall that he only wanted to find his father, dead or alive, and clear Sam's name?

Drew got back in bed and thankfully felt sleep coming on. As he closed his eyes, his determination grew. He would prove his father innocent. Drew realized he already had an edge on the police. He believed in his dad.

If Randall wanted him to hang around, fine, but Drew was going to do more than play tourist.

THE BEAM OF THE FLASHLIGHT darted around Betsy's garage, illuminating the scattering of papers and keepsakes on the dirt floor. Then the light went searching through the rafters.

"No electricity?" Selkirk asked.

"No," Betsy said.

"And this is just the way you found the garage?"

His face was obscured by darkness—besides the flashlight, there was only faint light from the single window—so Betsy couldn't read anything more into his voice. "I haven't touched a thing," she told him.

"Good. In a minute, we'll try to find out what's missing. But first, let me ask about the locks." Selkirk turned the flashlight toward the front of the garage.

"The one on the big doors is broken," Betsy said. "You can't swing them back unless you slide the bolt from inside. The side door we came through was open when I got home. That's how I knew something was wrong. It was locked before I left for work."

Selkirk walked over to the door and directed a beam of light to the knob and lock. "Dead bolt. Looks pretty substantial, but it could have been picked. There's no sign of forced entry. No splinters or anything." He tried the inside knob on the dead bolt, locking and unlocking the door several times. "Are you sure you had this fastened?"

"Positive."

"And no one else has a key?"

"No one."

Selkirk's flashlight scanned the rest of the garage and stopped on the window. He walked over to it. "You use this window?"

Betsy followed. "No, it was painted shut years ago."

"Hmm. Hold the flashlight a minute."

He put his hands on the top of the lower sash and pushed. The window slid up with ease.

Betsy was embarrassed. "I was sure—"

"Put the light over here," Selkirk told her.

She did and quickly saw gouges and splinters in the outside wood.

"Pried open," Selkirk said, taking back the flashlight. "Whoever did it crawled in, looked over your papers and then opened the dead bolt from the inside and strolled out the side door."

"Who do you think did it?" Betsy asked.

"Hard to say. Either somebody who knew what he was looking for or maybe just a vandal. Probably the latter. If the guy wanted something valuable, he would have broken into your house."

Betsy recalled Selkirk's earlier warning about strangers. She couldn't help voicing her fear. "You don't think it has something to do with my finding the plane, do you?"

"I doubt it," Selkirk said quickly. "After all, no one except you and the Mounties know you're the one who found it."

But other people know, Betsy thought. Drew McKay and Greg Harsted. "Can I use your flashlight again?" she asked.

Selkirk gave it to her. She hunched over the papers on the floor and began sifting through them with her free hand, trying to figure out what might be missing. Then it came to her. There had been an old shoe box. "Grandpa's letters," she said.

"What?"

"That's what's missing. A box of old letters my grandfather had saved. I should have taken more care with them."

"Don't be too hard on yourself. Maybe your grand-father won't mind," Selkirk said.

Betsy looked at him oddly a moment and stood up. She gave him back his flashlight. "No, he probably doesn't mind. You're new in town, Constable, so I wouldn't expect you to know. My grandfather died last year. Conrad Parks was one of the finest men Dawson City ever saw."

"Sorry," Selkirk said. "I didn't know."

Betsy rubbed at her chin a moment, then began talking as if Selkirk weren't there. "A year. It's been that long and I've barely looked at those letters." Her voice quivered as fond memories of the old man swept through her. "I'm not even sure what was in them. But I know they were in that box."

"Doesn't sound like anything a burglar would want," Selkirk said absently. "Sentimental value, I suppose."

"I guess." She couldn't really blame Selkirk. If the letters had no monetary value, she couldn't expect a Mountie to get excited about a minor break-in.

"Well, you'd better get some sleep, Miss Archer. In the morning, you can look over the garage and give me a call if you think anything really valuable is missing."

"All right."

"Good night, then."

Betsy went into the house and as she got ready for bed she kept trying to connect the break-in to the Red Baron plane. But she had no proof, only a feeling that she was overlooking something and that whatever it was, it was turning dangerous.

She got into bed, her mind whirling through the senseless possibilities. Although he would have had the opportunity, she couldn't really believe Drew would break into her garage, not after the way he'd confided in her. He had seemed warm and genuine. She also realized that if the police knew what she did, Drew would be the prime suspect. The idea unsettled her and she closed her eyes. She didn't think she could sleep, but she was too exhausted not to try.

At ten, she woke, dressed and ate a quick breakfast. Despite the break-in, she had rested fairly well. But she was still weighed down with the same questions she'd had the night before. She needed someone else's advice, and there was only one person in Dawson City she felt could set her mind at ease. She'd procrastinated long enough. It was time to see Evie Saunders.

Betsy walked the six blocks, letting herself be distracted for a few minutes by the beautiful weather. Another sunny day, temperature in the low sixties already—she couldn't have ordered it better. And she enjoyed the exercise. That was one of the advantages of Dawson City. It was small enough that you could get around fairly easily on foot.

Just about everyone in town walked, even Evie, who was seventy and looked almost too frail to support her own weight. When Betsy got to her house, she hesitated on the porch, wondering if she was doing the right thing. She'd always admired Evie. Years ago, Evie had taken care of Betsy's mother, then finally fallen in love with Conrad. Betsy never understood why the two hadn't married. She only hoped that what she wanted to know wouldn't upset the older woman.

Betsy stepped up to the door and knocked. There was no answer for a long time. Then the curtains parted at a front window and a moment later the door opened.

"Betsy." Evie gave her a hug, which was strong, considering Evie's slight frame. The top of her gray-haired head barely reached Betsy's chin.

"Oh, it's so nice to see you," Evie said. "You don't come and visit enough."

"I know," Betsy said. *Great, Evie thinks this is a social call.* "How are you doing?"

"Up and down," Evie said. "But what can you expect with an old woman? Come in. How about some coffee?"

"All right, if it's made."

"It is. And still fresh. I don't get up too early these days."

Evie went to the kitchen to pour the coffee. Betsy followed and noticed a row of prescription bottles on the windowsill above the sink. A small vial of tranquilizers stood to one side. She still wondered if questioning Evie was a good idea. She said nothing and carried the coffee cups back to the little living room. Evie's house was smaller than hers, one bedroom instead of two. Conrad had helped her buy it five years ago when Betsy had come to Dawson City and moved in with him.

When they were seated, Betsy on the green sofa and Evie in a matching overstuffed chair, Evie said, "So what really brings you over?"

Betsy sipped her coffee. "Is it that obvious?"

"I can see that you're worried. So you've come to me for advice. That's good, though," Evie said brightly. "At my age, that's probably all I can give you."

"I should have come out of friendship."

Evie drank some coffee and put the cup on a table. "You *have*. Friends are supposed to help each other. I know you're busy with the club, but I'm glad you still think of me. It makes me feel needed. Of course, I was very accustomed to giving Conrad advice. Even when he didn't want it." Evie smiled at her joke and then grew serious. "The past year hasn't been so easy without him."

Betsy thought Evie was going to cry. It was wrong, Betsy decided, to bother Evie with her troubles. "I miss him, too."

Evie nodded and bowed her head.

Reluctantly, Betsy edged into the reason for her visit. "Now, I'm missing his letters."

Evie looked up. "Letters?"

"They were stored in my garage in an old shoe box. I never thought anyone else would want them. But while I was at work last night, someone pried open the window and stole them."

Evie's face fell. Betsy knew what the older woman was feeling because it had hit her, too: even Conrad's memory wasn't inviolate—a stranger had tampered with it.

Agitated, Evie twisted her fingers together. "Stole them? But why?"

"I was hoping you could give me a clue," Betsy said. "I don't even know what was in those letters." When Evie didn't respond, Betsy said, "I called the Mounties."

"The Mounties?" Evie's appalled tone suggested that Betsy shouldn't have told the police.

"Well, a crime was committed," Betsy said. "Of course, when I called, I had no idea what was taken. I was too upset to look. But you shouldn't worry about the police. They aren't taking this seriously, anyway. The constable who came to check the garage thinks the letters are worthless and that a vandal took them for a prank."

"But you don't think so."

"I don't know what to think." Betsy had considered telling Evie about the Red Baron plane, and about Drew, but decided that Evie was under enough strain without that.

Evie smoothed her hands on her dress. "Well, I think you worry too much," she said. "I don't know what was in those letters either, but I can't imagine they would be worth anything to someone else. Whoever took them probably just dumped them in the river when they got a good look."

"Then you agree with the Mounties?"

"Why not? Now drink your coffee, like a good girl, before it gets cold."

Betsy did. Sitting back against the sofa with her hands wrapped around the warm cup, she tried to relax. It would be so nice, she thought, if Evie could just give her a simple direction to clear up the whole mess. Even if she knew nothing about the letters, maybe she could help with something else. Betsy cleared her throat. "I have another question."

"About the letters?"

"No. About a man I met yesterday. He came to Yukon Lights, asking for Conrad. His name is Jacob Talbot."

"Talbot?" Evie frowned.

"Yes. Do you know him?"

Evie hesitated. "I met him once or twice. He bought Tom Fioretti's land."

"Yes, we talked about that." Then Betsy recalled Talbot's pawing through the papers on her desk. For a moment, she wondered if he might have done the same with Conrad's letters. The prospect perplexed her. She paused, then realized Evie was waiting. She hurried on. "Talbot wanted to see Grandpa. Claimed they were old friends, but yet he didn't know . . . that he'd gone."

"They weren't friends," Evie said. "Not to my knowledge, anyhow. Talbot was always pestering Conrad to sell him the mineral rights to the property. But I don't know why. The Lost Lady Mine played out years ago. Even so, Conrad would never have sold the mineral rights. Tom wanted Conrad to keep them."

"What did you think of Talbot, as a person?"

Evie pondered the ceiling a few seconds, then gradually brought her eyes back to Betsy's. "He was an odd bird, the few times I saw him, anyhow. There was something . . . intense about him. He would laugh when there was nothing funny. Like he was a bit touched." She tapped her temple. "Did he bother you?"

"He upset me. I didn't trust him. But he seemed genuinely sorry to hear about Conrad."

"He always made me uneasy. I never knew what he did for a living, or where he came from. Though now that I think about it, he might have been from the States. Didn't talk much like a Canadian."

Betsy agreed with that. Of course, it was common to see Americans in Dawson City during the summer. People seemed to come from all over for one reason or another. Like Drew McKay. Betsy forced Drew from her mind. "Talbot wants to see me again, to talk over old times or something."

"He's probably harmless, but you never know." Evie fluttered her eyes as if she were getting sleepy.

Betsy stood up. "I'll let you rest now."

Evie slowly pushed herself onto her feet. "All right, young lady, but don't wait so long to come and see me again."

"I won't," Betsy said. "Take care of yourself."

They embraced and said goodbye. Then Betsy went out. Evie seemed even thinner now, she thought, and her skin looked translucent, like pale parchment. Betsy worried about Evie's health and wished she hadn't mentioned the stolen letters or Jacob Talbot. Obviously, hearing the news had upset Evie. On the porch, Betsy looked back through the living room window to the back of the house. Evie was at the kitchen sink, reaching for the tranquilizers.

WHEN BETSY GOT HOME, she took the precaution of gathering up the rest of Conrad's papers. They were scattered throughout the house, wedged into every bit of available space. The stuff in the garage had been overflow, and Betsy had been meaning to go through it all when she felt she was ready. Now was not the time.

After she'd swept the house clean of almost everything Conrad had left behind except kitchen utensils and furniture, Betsy had three big boxes in her living room. At first, she'd thought of taking Conrad's papers to the bank and having them locked in the vault. But there was too much for that, and she didn't have the time or the peace of mind to sit down and separate what was valuable from the rest.

She stacked the boxes by the front door and tried to decide where to put them. Yukon Lights was out of the question. Anyone could walk right in and take them from there.

Besides the bank, the only other safe storage site Betsy could think of was her grandfather's old place in the hills. She went to her jewelry box and dug out the key, though it was ridiculous to believe that a lock was worth much in the wilderness. If hunters and hikers were desperate to use the old cabin, they'd just break a window.

The cabin was miles west of the airplane crash site she wanted to forget. Conrad had built it ten years before.

Winters were hard there and from the outside it looked much like any other isolated shack, about twenty feet square with well-weathered log sides and a sagging shake roof, but it had a trapdoor and tunnels beneath.

The cabin sat atop Conrad's defunct gold mine, the Lost Lady. Betsy had no idea where the tunnels ultimately led. She had climbed down the old wooden ladder into the mouth of the tunnel a few times. But when Conrad was alive, he wouldn't let her go beyond the first turn. It was too dangerous, he had said.

She checked her watch. Yukon Lights was open for lunch now. She phoned and one of the waitresses answered.

"I won't be in for a while," Betsy said. "Just keep the soup warm."

Betsy was ready to load the boxes into her Bronco when it occurred to her with chilling clarity that if someone followed her to the cabin she'd have no way to call for help. She gritted her teeth and went to the chest of drawers in her bedroom. From the back of the bottom drawer she took out the .38-caliber Colt Conrad had left her. Until now, it had been just another one of his possessions she couldn't bring herself to make a decision about.

Kneeling down, she found the box of bullets in the drawer and loaded the gun. He'd shown her how to use it a few years ago, and she was surprised she remembered. She slipped the gun and the spare bullets into her shoulder bag. Then she went back to the living room and picked up one of the cardboard boxes and opened the front door.

An old abandoned rooming house was her neighbor across the street, and when she looked at it, she almost dropped the box. Leaning on a column supporting the porch roof was Drew. Watching her.

She pushed open the screen door and headed for her Bronco, but when Drew moved toward her, she turned around and took the box back into the house.

By the time she'd set it down on the other boxes and thought about shutting the wooden door, Drew was about ten feet away, eyeing her through the screen.

"Morning," he said. "Guess you got home okay."

"Of course." She let go of the box and straightened up. "You're the only one who thought I wouldn't."

"Forgive me for doubting." He put his hands in the back pockets of his jeans. "I'm here now because I was sorting through some maps this morning, trying to figure out exactly where my dad's plane went down. I've seen the plane, but didn't know where I was. I got tired of guessing, and then I realized you might be able to help."

He smiled at her, as a good salesman would, although Betsy wasn't in a buying mood. She went to the screen door and looked at him more closely. He appeared relaxed, anything but threatening, but she couldn't be sure. "I didn't expect to see you—here."

"You mean, how did I find your house? It wasn't hard." He shuffled his feet on the wooden step in front of the door. "Are you going to invite me in?"

Betsy thought quickly. It seemed that nothing was going to stop him. Least of all an unlocked screen door. She decided to test him. "It depends," she said. "I like to keep *pests* outside."

"Real funny." He opened the screen door, stepped inside and let the door bang shut. "I'd like to be your friend. So why don't we drop the accusations?"

"Only if you promise to leave me alone."

He stared at her. "Come on, Betsy. Forget the maps—I found you this morning because I wanted to see you again. Simple, huh?"

Betsy didn't answer. She'd turned slightly to let him by, thinking he'd walk to the middle of her living room, but instead he stopped next to her. His jaw was about a foot away directly in front of her eyes. He'd shaved again this morning, and she wondered if his skin was really as smooth as it looked. Then his mouth slanted in amusement.

Betsy realized she'd been studying him and backed into the center of the room. She felt foolish, but knew she had to stay alert not to fall into a trap. Arms crossed and with her right hand close to the gun in her shoulder bag, she waited.

Again Drew moved toward her, but stopped five or six feet away. When he spoke, she listened carefully. "Look, I spent a lot of time trying to figure out why you cooled off toward me last night. Why you left me in the alley. Why you were so damn angry. The only thing that happened between our dance and your telling me off was a chat I had with that jerk Harsted. He's no buddy of mine, I assure you. As far as I'm concerned, he's just a pest, as you would say. I've been sorry ever since I met him. Once he gets hold of you, watch out."

"Harsted does get around. But I guess that's what reporters are supposed to do." Betsy wondered what Drew would say if he knew what Harsted had said about him. It was probably best to keep quiet about that, though. Things were already complicated enough. "Anyway, I'm kind of busy right now," she said politely.

"I'll bet you are." Drew's gaze intensified and nearly cut through Betsy. Then at last he looked away. He scanned the room for a second, then turned and looked at the three cardboard boxes of Conrad's possessions. "I can help you load those," he said.

"It's all right. This stuff can wait." She couldn't very well let him load up and then leave for the cabin. He'd probably invite himself along for the ride.

"No, really," he said, "I'd like to help. Are the boxes heavy?"

He bent to lift the top one, which came up to his waist, but she pressed in front of him. Instead of picking up cardboard, he accidentally brushed her denim-covered thighs.

Betsy heard his sudden intake of breath. He let his hands fall away and straightened slowly. Her mind scrambled for something to divert him. And herself. The memory of her own excitement when he'd held her before came rushing back and even now his touch had sent a tingle up her legs. "Surely you can find more interesting things to do in Dawson City than help me load boxes," she said hurriedly. "Have you been up to Midnight Dome?"

"No. What is it? Some kind of sports arena?"

Betsy couldn't help laughing.

Drew's face turned red. "What's so funny?"

"It's not a building," she said, barely containing her amusement. "It's a hill, the big one overlooking town."

"Oh." He smiled. "I should have known. I was just thinking it sounded like a football stadium. I went to the Kingdome in Seattle once."

"How did you like it?"

"Too much noise. The game was good, but sixty thousand screaming fans can get on your nerves. I think I'd like your dome better. Sounds peaceful."

"It is," she said. "Most of the time. Tourists drive up there for the view and we have a mob scene on the summer solstice, but there shouldn't be a lot of activity right now.'' Betsy was counting on there being at least a few tourists there to give her security. She and Drew could talk privately without being alone. And she could get him away from Conrad's papers.

''You driving?'' he asked.

''I guess so.'' She stepped toward the door and added in a teasing tone, ''It's five miles by road to the top and you don't have a car.''

## Chapter Six

Betsy pointed out sights along the way, and when she and Drew arrived at the top of Midnight Dome, she parked her Bronco near three other vehicles. Scanning the top of the hill, she counted ten people. She didn't know any of them, but figured their presence alone would be enough to keep Drew from trying anything strange.

She got out of the four-wheel drive and walked with him a little way until they had a good view of Dawson City to the southwest.

"The town looks pretty small from up here," he said.

"It doesn't take long to find your way around." Betsy had good distance vision and could spot her house and Yukon Lights, but she decided not to point them out to Drew. She had brought him up here to take his focus *off* her.

"Well, there's the Yukon River," she said. "Dawson City sits right in the floodplain. In fact, the town lost a few buildings in the spring of '79."

"During the ice breakup?"

"That's right. I wasn't here then, but I saw the damage when I came up from Vancouver that summer."

"You're from Vancouver?"

"Grew up there, but Dawson's my home now." Betsy was wary of sharing even this detail with Drew and quickly tried to return the conversation to something less personal. "Anyway, the river—"

"Then you like it here," Drew interrupted. "You're going to stay?"

"Sure," she said, wondering what he was getting at. "I'm not making predictions, but I don't have any plans to move. I have my own business. Yes, I like it here."

He arched a brow. "And the long winters?"

"I'm acclimatized." She paused. "How about you?"

"I wouldn't be an outdoor guide if I couldn't stand a little cold weather." He flashed a smile and said, "Now what were you telling me about the flood?"

Betsy turned away, flustered by the look he was giving her. "The river," she finally said. "Well, with all the ice, it didn't have anyplace else to go that year except through the town. But the new levee should prevent another big flood. That smaller river you see flowing into the Yukon at the edge of town is the Klondike."

"Klondike." Drew stretched out the word, sampling its resonance. "There's a lot of magic in that name."

"You mean the gold. Most of the dredging was to the south." Betsy turned a little to her left. "Over there, along Bonanza Creek. You can still see some tailings." After almost a century, piles of dirt and rock and gravel remained a testament to the hardworking miners who had dug their ore by hand.

"Is the gold all gone?" Drew asked.

"No. Just a lot harder to find, and it's not all in that one area. There's probably a little all around."

"Any mining still going on?"

"Yes, but it's mostly big companies, and pretty unexciting compared with the gold rush. Of course, a lot of people like to try their luck at panning."

"How about you?"

"Now and then." Betsy didn't know whether she should tell him, but she saw no harm. "That's what I was doing out in the woods just before I found your father's plane."

Drew rotated slowly, taking in the full 360-degree view. "Tell me where the plane is. When I went out there yesterday with Sergeant Randall, I got my directions mixed up."

Betsy pointed north. "In the Ogilvie Mountains."

Drew looked, then shifted his gaze to the west, toward Fairbanks, then back. Betsy was almost certain that he was trying to calculate his father's flight path. Conrad's cabin was on the arc that Drew had plotted visually, but Betsy didn't mention it. If she was going to hide Conrad's things in it, the fewer strangers who knew its location the better.

She sat down on the ground and tried to direct his attention away from the plane site. "See that road there? To the west? That's the Top of the World Highway. It'll take you back to Alaska."

"Take me back?" Drew threw her a look of astonishment, which blossomed into a grin. He lowered himself close beside her, their bodies separated by little more than her shoulder bag. "I hope you're not trying to get rid of me."

"No, no, I meant . . ." What did she mean? Did she want Drew to go home? Her life might return to normal then. Assuming Harsted and Talbot left her alone, too.

"Anyway," Drew said, "I won't need the highway. I'll be flying back when I'm ready. But first I have questions. Maybe I should start with you."

Betsy gulped. *Here it comes.*

"What really happened last night?"

"What do you mean?" she responded, knowing exactly what he meant.

"Let's start with the alley."

"You scared me, that's all."

"Are you sure?"

Betsy stared out over the vista spread below Midnight Dome and tried to take the bearings of her feelings. Her emotional compass had been spinning wildly for days, but this place always seemed to give her some direction. She owed Drew an explanation, she knew. "I've walked home after work hundreds of times and never been mugged. It's perfectly safe." She thought briefly of the break in at her garage, and knew she might not be safe at all. But now wasn't the time to iron out contradictions.

"Maybe I just wanted to be with you," he said.

"You were acting like the great protector."

"Was I?"

"Yes, you were."

"I'm sorry."

Betsy paused, deciding he was sincere. "It's okay. I've always been a bit prickly about being independent."

"Now what about all that time you spent in the kitchen? You were avoiding me. Was my being with Harsted the only reason?"

"I was working," Betsy said. "And when I saw you chatting with Harsted, I wondered if, in a way, that's what you'd been doing, too. After all, I've only known you two days."

"Three," he said. "I came to your club night before last."

"Three then."

He broke into a smile again.

"What's so funny?" Betsy relaxed, unable to maintain her sternness.

"You," he said. "Your mind is working overtime trying to think of reasons not to like me."

She shrugged, refusing to admit he was close to the truth.

He put a hand on her shoulder, just above the strap of her bag. "Betsy, I'm not a criminal and I'm not a madman."

His touch seemed to dispel all that remained of her resistance. She looked off toward the Yukon River. "I never said you were."

"But the idea crossed your mind."

His fingers strayed gently from her shoulder to the back of her neck and toyed with the newly repaired chain of her medallion. The gentle pressure nearly drove her to distraction. She turned back to him and rested a hand on his thigh. "How could I sit here with you if I really thought that?"

His eyes sparkled. "I've been trying to figure it out. Maybe it's because you haven't decided what to think of me."

Betsy pulled her hand away. *He can read my mind,* she thought. "We should leave. I need to be going to work."

"All right." Drew sighed.

Despite his words, his fingers continued to brush, back and forth, mesmerizing. As they stood, Betsy began to lose her balance.

Drew reached to steady her but only bumped her shoulder bag. The strap slipped and Conrad's pistol spilled out.

She caught herself and froze with surprise, then tugged the strap back onto her shoulder.

"Are you all right?" Drew asked.

"F-fine." Embarrassed, she bent to scoop up the pistol. But Drew beat her to it.

He picked up the .38 by the handle and tested the heft of the weapon in his palm. "Do you always carry a gun?"

"No." Betsy checked Drew's face. She saw concern in it and disappointment.

"Then why now?" he asked quietly.

"I've . . . been a little nervous lately."

"About finding the plane, you mean? Do I scare you that much?"

She choked out a laugh. "You're making too much of this. Lots of people in the Yukon carry guns. It's the law of the wild."

He stared at her a moment, then said, "Okay, but you ought to find a better place to keep this thing." He carefully replaced the gun in her bag. "You don't want to give anybody the wrong idea."

Drew had patiently allowed her to lie her way out of the predicament, not believing a word she'd said. For that she was grateful, and at the same time sorry she'd brought the pistol along. She had seen the sadness return to Drew's eyes when he picked up the gun, and again she felt she had misjudged him. He'd been kind to her—and he'd been through so much. She felt inexplicably drawn to him. As she watched, his features softened, the blue in his eyes deepened. He was about to kiss her.

"Drew, I don't think..." Her voice trailed away. They'd touched before, had danced close enough to feel each other's bodies respond, but that was different. On the dance floor, you were expected to hold each other. You could pretend that nothing important was happening because you were merely dancing. But now she could almost feel his warm breath, his mouth's gentle strength.

"Betsy, please let me do this." Slowly, he tipped her face. His mouth hovered above hers briefly, then descended, pressing against hers, lightly at first, then with more intensity, as if testing her resistance.

Betsy weakened, melting against him. His kiss was all she'd imagined. Her hands slid along his waist, beneath his shirt. Warm skin and taut muscles contracted at her touch. Enough to take her breath away.

"Wonderful," he whispered. "As I knew it would be. I've waited so long for this."

"Three days," Betsy reminded him. "You didn't know me before that." She felt giddy.

"See what you do to me?" Then he kissed her again, his lips feathering her nose, her cheeks, her chin.

Betsy could tolerate his teasing no longer. Now she was eager for the taste of him. Their lips met again and she closed her eyes, oblivious to the fragrant breeze, the brilliant sunshine and the tourists scattered around the Dome. She enjoyed the rush of passion shooting through her body. Drew held her like a man who knew what he wanted. One arm circled her back, molding her breasts against him. His other hand flexed lazily across her hips. Betsy's lips parted and Drew's tongue met hers, probing, tracing the smooth outlines of her teeth.

Betsy's senses magnified. No man had ever kissed her like this before. It was a bliss she'd barely imagined. They were acting like lovers. But not yet, she thought lazily. Perhaps soon. The prospect pleased her. She moved against him, her fingers playing along his spine. Drew moaned with pleasure.

*My God! This is impossible.* The rich sound of his enjoyment prodded Betsy, dragging her back to reality. The situation was getting out of hand. This was all too sudden. She pushed away, trying to regain control. "Drew, we can't do this," she gasped.

"What are you talking about?" He looked dumbfounded. "We just did. It was great." Breathless, he reached for her again.

"No, I mean it. This isn't right." She edged backward, still feeling the moist imprint his mouth had made on hers. She was learning to trust him, but until she was sure, she knew she could not trust herself. Right now she wanted to help Drew, to ease his pain. But she knew she could not get involved in looking for Sam McKay. The Mounties thought Drew's father had killed a man; she should take a hint and stay out of it.

"Getting close to each other is right." Drew dragged his fingers through his breeze-tousled hair. "Don't you feel it, too?"

She kept silent, fidgeting with her shoulder bag. It was all she could do to squelch her overwhelming desire to fling herself back into the pleasurable circle of his arms. "I'll take you back to town," she said.

"If that's what you want," he answered softly.

Looking resigned, he walked back to the Bronco with her. The ride down the hill was strained. Betsy tried to be casual, but she knew the act was unconvincing. As she talked about how Dawson City had nearly turned into a ghost town, her voice came back to her sounding artificial and off-pitch. Drew feigned interest, but she knew he was not thinking about local history.

Betsy realized that their relationship had changed. Their paths would cross again and she would have to reassess her feelings. She longed to stop the Bronco and allow herself the delight of another wonderful embrace. Fortunately, she had to think about driving.

When they got back to town, Betsy asked, "Where do you want me to drop you off?"

She hoped he would say, "My hotel." Regardless of what had happened on Midnight Dome, she wanted to load Conrad's papers alone.

If Drew knew what she was thinking, he'd decided to be contrary. "Just go back to your place," he said. "Maybe I can help with those boxes."

"I don't have time for that now," she lied. "I have to get ready to go into the club."

"Oh." Drew seemed disappointed, and Betsy fought the urge to capitulate and cheer him up.

She parked in her driveway, and they got out. Drew stood awkwardly a moment, then said, "Well, maybe I'll see you again at Yukon Lights."

"Sure," Betsy said. He retreated up the street, and she tried to ignore a pang of regret.

As soon as he was gone, Betsy lugged the boxes out and shoved them into the back of her four-wheel drive. She would drop by Yukon Lights and tell the staff she'd be away for a few hours. There was still plenty of daylight, plenty of time to go to Conrad's cabin.

As Drew walked the five or six blocks back to his hotel, he couldn't get his mind off Betsy. He wanted her, and her intensity told him she wanted him, too. Absently, he checked his surroundings. The streets grew more crowded as he neared the Bonanza. When he walked through the lobby, he was pleased to note that

Greg Harsted was not in sight. He never knew where or when the reporter would turn up. The man was a menace, Drew thought.

He climbed the stairs to his room and unlocked it. For a moment, as he was opening the door, he had a feeling that Harsted might have picked the lock and tossed the room in search of some zinger for his story. But maps of the Yukon were laid out on the bed exactly where Drew had left them. Everything else seemed in order, too. Except his life. Drew folded the maps and stacked them on the dresser.

What should he do now, just sit and wait? He circled the room like a caged mountain lion. Then he tried sitting on the edge of the bed. Still restless, he leaned back, ordering himself to relax. But he couldn't.

A minute later, he was bounding down the stairs two at a time. Outside the lobby, he quickly fell in step with a crowd moving along the boardwalk and let himself be distracted. It might help to pretend he was a tourist on vacation.

Drew walked calmly for a few minutes. As he stepped along, he noticed empty lots and vacant old buildings mixed with the new. The foundations of some of the weathered structures were twisted at different angles, jerked around by years of melting and thawing along the permafrost. But he could see that a lot of buildings had been restored.

Sergeant Randall had suggested he enjoy the town. Maybe that was the thing to do. He glanced in store windows as he walked by, and when he passed a jewelry shop, he did a double take and stopped on the sidewalk. Nose to the glass like a little kid, he peered at the row of gold medallions. They were in a glass case for protection. Betsy had been right. They were common in the Yukon.

Beyond the jewelry was an array of maps. One was like the map he had in his room. As he focused on it, thoughts of his father rushed at him. And then Randall's words. Something about the body in the plane . . . A parachute. Yes, that was it. Why hadn't he thought of it until now? Randall had said the parachute had been strapped on.

Drew hurried away. The parachute business was beginning to make sense. As soon as Randall had told him that the dead man wasn't his father, he'd assumed that either his dad hadn't been on the plane in the first place, or that he'd gone down with the plane and then miraculously walked away from the crash. Now there was another possibility. His dad could have parachuted.

Sam wasn't an expert sky diver, but he had jumped for practice, figuring that if he flew airplanes long enough he'd eventually have to use a parachute to save his life. If the engine had failed, Drew was sure that Sam wouldn't have been afraid to bail out.

Drew looked back toward his hotel. A Mountie in his tan shirt and dark blue pants was strolling his way, so he went the opposite direction past more shops and then turned into an alley where he could be alone. Leaning against a building with his eyes closed, he tried again to imagine the final minutes of the plane's flight. Remembering the crash site and the position Betsy had pointed out from Midnight Dome, Drew calculated where his dad might have bailed out. The plane had landed virtually straight north of Dawson City, so his father would have jumped northwest of town, closer to the Alaska border.

The area was so large and after ten years there wasn't much of a chance he could find any clues, but Drew had to do something besides wait for the Mounties to make their own conclusions. He stepped back onto the sidewalk. The Mountie was moving closer, only a half block away now, seeming to look directly at Drew. The man wasn't Randall, but Drew realized that the sergeant had probably issued a warning about him to the whole RCMP force in Dawson City. *They're checking on me,* he thought, *making sure I don't leave town.* Then someone stopped the Mountie to talk, and Drew legged it to the next corner and turned out of the policeman's sight. Then he jogged a block and went up another street. He saw a restaurant and went in. The place was crowded, so he had to wait in line just to talk to the cashier. High noon, time for lunch, but he was far too keyed up to eat.

Finally, when he got to the cashier, he asked, "Where can I rent a vehicle? I want to drive out of town."

"Maybe Bernie's Garage," the cashier said. "Bernie's always got a few rigs sitting around. If you don't need anything fancy, he could probably fix you up."

The garage was only two blocks away, and within ten minutes, Drew was driving a Toyota pickup.

He headed north along the Yukon River and then northwest as the river turned toward Alaska. He wasn't sure where to go, but he had a compass to guide him. His foot stayed on the accelerator as an unfounded urgency pushed him faster along the desolate dirt road than he knew was reasonable. It was only when he saw a vehicle ahead that he slowed. His own safety was one thing, but he wouldn't take chances with other people's lives.

As his Toyota narrowed the gap, he began to sweat. He hadn't counted on this. The vehicle ahead of him was familiar. He got close enough to make sure, then dropped back to a discreet distance. He didn't want to be recognized. For the moment, he forgot about searching for the remnants of his father's parachute. He had only one choice: follow the Bronco ahead of him, because Betsy was driving off into the woods.

AFTER BETSY CROSSED the old bridge at Lost Lady Creek and turned into her cabin, she sat in the Bronco a minute, waiting to see if she'd been followed. A half hour before she'd noticed a Toyota behind her for a short time, but she thought now that it must have turned back or gone to another cabin. It was nowhere in sight.

Satisfied that she was alone, Betsy backed her vehicle close to the weathered door. The boxes of Conrad's papers were heavy, and she didn't want to carry them far.

She got out and undid the old padlock. At least it hadn't been disturbed. Immediately she crossed the plank floor to the middle of the one-room building and slid aside a small rug.

She and Evie had to be the only people alive who knew about the trapdoor and where it led. Betsy lifted the door and stared down into the darkness. Conrad had described the Lost Lady gold mine as a maze, and somewhere in a remote shaft was the cave-in that had claimed Tom Fioretti's life. The tunnel gave her the creeps. It was no wonder that Conrad had never let her venture more than a few feet past the entrance.

Betsy went back to the Bronco to get a flashlight and then climbed down the shaft, testing its old wooden ladder. Then she began lugging in the boxes. They were heavy and too awkward to carry down the ladder thirty feet to the main tunnel, so she carefully pushed them into the shaft and climbed down afterward to straighten out the mess. Fortunately, the boxes took the fall okay and contained nothing breakable.

Once the boxes were neatly stacked in the mine, Betsy lowered the trapdoor, replaced the rug and locked the cabin. As she walked to the Bronco, she heard a noise from the woods near the lake, a branch snapping. An animal? Or was it something more threatening? Fear shot through her and she stopped to listen.

But she heard nothing except the thumping of her heart. She scanned the area, checking everything from the hilltops to the brushy ravines feeding the lake fifty yards below the cabin. Everything looked normal. But she couldn't shake the feeling she was being watched.

Quickly, she climbed into the Bronco and hurried back toward town.

DUST CHURNED UP from the Bronco's tires and covered the roadside. Beyond the bridge was a knoll, and behind it was a Toyota pickup. Drew crouched beside it, coughing in the cloud of dirt. After he had given Betsy a few minutes to get well ahead, he would go directly back to Dawson City.

He'd wanted to head for the cabin and peek through a window to try to understand what was in those boxes and why Betsy had gone to such pains to keep their contents a secret. But now he didn't think it would be wise to get that close to the building.

When the branch had cracked, Drew had been watching Betsy and felt her apprehension. He thought the snap had come from the shore of the lake, but he wasn't going to go see what, or who, had caused it. He was sure that no one had followed him and just as sure that he and Betsy hadn't been alone.

The certainty plagued him all the way back to Dawson City and the rest of the afternoon. The sun had been down a couple of hours when he left his hotel and started out on foot for Yukon Lights. He didn't know if going there was wise, or even why he was doing it, but he was drawn to her for many reasons, not least of all because he was worried about her.

When Drew walked into the nightclub, his eyes shot to Betsy immediately and the nape of his neck grew warm. She was scurrying around behind the bar, mixing drinks and chatting with customers. He stood back a moment, admiring her liveliness and still relishing being so close to her on Midnight Dome. He had to talk with her again.

But as Drew stepped toward an opening at the middle of the bar where Betsy was working, a man brushed past him, throwing him off stride. Drew recovered quickly, took another step toward the bar and stopped. There was no point in rushing. The other man, distinctive at Yukon Lights in his long-sleeved white dress shirt, already had his elbows spread wide on the bar. Drew couldn't have squeezed in if he'd stood sideways.

Drew looked at the man again and blinked. A bald head reflected the room lights. Of course, it was Talbot. Tonight he wasn't wearing a jacket or tie, but he had on the same plaid suit pants. The good-looking blonde beside Talbot might explain why the man had been in such a hurry. Still watching the older man, Drew edged to an empty spot at the far end of the bar.

BETSY HAD NOTICED Drew come in. She was torn between ignoring him and throwing her arms around him. Thankfully, she was busy making drinks so had a reason not to talk to him just yet. But their eyes caught, and when he smiled she couldn't help smiling back. As the other bartender went to Drew and served him a beer, she turned to Talbot. She would have to take his order. He'd burst to the middle of the bar as if he'd been denied a drink for years. It would really be his third one tonight.

"Hello again, Mr. Talbot," she said. "What can I get you this time?"

"Make it a whiskey, Betsy. On the rocks. And please call me Jacob." He winked at the blonde to his left and then at Betsy. "Remember?"

"Jacob," she said and bent to fill a tumbler with ice.

Talbot *was* an odd bird, Betsy thought, as she poured his drink. He seemed harmless enough, as Evie had said, but his hucksterism was certainly off-putting. It was making Betsy edgy. If he hung around much longer, she thought, she'd need to borrow a tranquilizer from Evie.

Drew had taken advantage of a fresh opening toward the middle of the bar and moved closer to Talbot. As Betsy handed Talbot his drink, she glanced at Drew again. He was staring at the older man.

"So, Jacob, what have you been doing in Dawson?" she asked.

He drank deeply from the tumbler and then flipped a hand from side to side. "Little of this, little of that."

"Are you staying in town?"

"The Double River Inn," he said, wrinkling his nose. "Nice place, real nice." He grinned at the blonde and she left the bar.

Betsy paused to pour two white wines for a waitress and then went back to Talbot. "How long will you be here?"

He gave her a glassy stare and then sipped his drink. "Hard to say. Depends on…circumstances." He turned to the man at his right and laughed for no reason.

Betsy remembered Evie's mentioning Talbot's inexplicable bursts of laughter. Alcohol seemed to amplify the problem. Drew was obviously listening to her conversation with Talbot and, strangely, that seemed to make her bold. She pressed on, determined to find out something about the man. "So where did you say you were from?"

"Did I say? No, I don't believe I did." Talbot wrinkled his nose. "Whitehorse, that's where I'm from. I have a new practice there."

"What?"

"I'm a GP. General practitioner."

"You're a doctor?"

"That's me. Old Doc Talbot."

"I didn't know you were a doctor," Betsy said, almost in apology for not recognizing his status earlier. But she was still uneasy. Why hadn't Talbot introduced himself as a doctor when they'd met in her office?

She glanced at Drew, partly in question and partly for support, but he only shrugged.

"Thanks for nothing," she silently mouthed.

Drew shook his head.

Between making drinks for other customers, Betsy continued to quiz Talbot. Though he answered freely, his responses were often vague. Betsy thought he might be playing a game with her. Or maybe even putting on a show for Drew, who occasionally grimaced at something Talbot said. Odd laughs and non sequiturs punctuated Talbot's conversation, but Betsy eventually had to conclude that he knew a lot about the Dawson City area. And from what he said, she had no doubt that he had walked every square foot of his acreage. Still, she couldn't shake what Evie had told her that morning about how he had pestered Conrad.

Betsy sighed. There was just too much to think about, including Constable Selkirk's call an hour before. He had obviously been trying to make up for not keeping her informed of developments earlier. By tomorrow, everybody in Dawson City would know the news, but for the moment she was probably the only one in the club who'd heard. At first the turn of events had played on her nerves, but then she had decided to take advantage of the situation. Midnight. There was no better way to start a new day than stirring up a little excitement.

She went to her office, knowing Drew and Talbot were watching her. In a moment, the tables would be switched. She jotted down a short announcement, then took the paper back out to the lounge pianist. "Turn on your mike and read this," she told him. "And make it loud. I want everybody to hear."

When the pianist threw her a quizzical look, she just said, "Go ahead," and walked to the bar. She leaned back where she could observe Drew and Talbot.

"Ladies and gentlemen," the pianist barked. "Could I have your attention please. I have an important message."

A hush fell over the nightclub, and only the clatter of dishes in the kitchen could be heard. All eyes except Betsy's turned to the pianist.

He cleared his throat and read the message. "The armored car company in Fairbanks, Alaska, that lost two million dollars to the Red Baron robbers ten years ago is now offering a reward of twenty-five thousand dollars to anyone finding the Red Baron loot."

The crowd roared with delight, but Drew and Talbot stood impassively at the bar, deadly serious.

"Wait!" the pianist hollered. "There's more." The crowd quieted again and he went on. "The armored car company is also offering twenty-five thousand dollars for information leading to a conviction of one or both of the Red Baron robbers.''

Hoots of joy sprang up all over the nightclub, but Talbot only took a long swig of whiskey and wiped his mouth with the back of a hand. Betsy filed his reaction and concentrated on Drew. Sadness showed in his eyes. Betsy hadn't wanted to hurt him, but she had to know how he felt about the reward.

Talbot finished his drink and muttered a hasty good-night to Betsy, and then Drew moved down the bar. He looked her in the eye and said, "This whole thing sickens me. There was a time when the money interested me. Now I don't want anything to do with it.

Betsy leaned forward, the bar between them. "I know," she said sincerely. "I'm sorry."

"There's something I *do* want, though. I want to take you home tonight. No more disappearing acts. No more arguments or excuses."

Betsy hesitated as her old defensiveness about being independent sparked then died as she thought about the previous night's break-in. Then she said, "All right." She would be grateful for the security of a companion. When she'd come home from the cabin she had found more of Conrad's things buried in the back of a closet, and now that was preying on her mind. But it was more than that. She wanted to be with Drew.

"Let's go now then, but wait here," she said. "I have to tell a couple of my employees I'm leaving."

In two minutes they left by the main door. Betsy and Drew walked close together, saying little. About a block from her house, she slid her hand into the crook of his arm. Her touch appeared to surprise him. He laid one hand on top of hers and squeezed. The gesture was comforting. She saw nothing unusual at the garage and relaxed a bit as she unlocked the front door of her house.

Then she felt a crinkling underfoot. A folded sheet of white paper lay by the door. She opened it and held it under the porch light, trying to make out the typewritten message.

When the full import of the words filtered through, Betsy sagged against the doorjamb. "Oh my God," she said. "This is crazy."

The threat was clear, speaking volumes in five little words: *Back off—the legend lives!*

# *Chapter Seven*

"Let me see the note." Drew tugged the paper from Betsy's trembling fingers. The characters looked smudged, uneven. He had a hunch the typewriter that made them was old.

"What does this mean?" Betsy's eyes were imploring, frightened. "I'm not bothering anyone. I've never had anything like this happen before. I'm afraid."

Drew tensed. Betsy was confiding in him, something he'd nearly given up hope she'd ever do. He couldn't let her see his own bewilderment and concern.

"Don't be scared," he whispered. He reached with his free hand to lace a wayward lock of hair behind her ear. His thumb lingered for a second on her neck. He felt her pounding pulse. "It's probably just a stupid joke."

"No." She twisted away and glared at the note. "That's more than a prank. *The legend lives.* Whoever wrote that means the Red Baron robbery."

Drew's shoulders stiffened. Betsy was right. They were both sinking into a horrible mess.

"The Mounties warned me that there would be a rash of fortune hunters in town, but they didn't say anything that prepared me for this."

The accusing way she stared at him made Drew realize she'd been unsure about his motives. He lowered his voice. "I'm not one of them, Betsy. I'm not after that money. All I want to do is clear my dad's name." He held up the note. "I couldn't have done this. Think about it."

Betsy stared at him, then at the crinkled piece of paper. "I don't know what to think."

"Come on. Let's go to the police." Drew reached for her arm. Perhaps the Mounties could ease her mind.

Betsy ignored his gesture and, taking the note from him, moved ahead of him down the steps to her Bronco. He followed, hurrying to keep up. She still didn't believe him, Drew thought grimly. He could see her agitation, could feel her distrust. He wanted to gather her to him and tell her everything would be all right. But he couldn't. She would certainly push him away. And besides, he knew that assurance would be empty, a lie.

THE RCMP OFFICE WAS QUIET when they went in. It was almost one o'clock in the morning, and a solitary young officer sat at Constable Selkirk's desk.

Betsy placed the note on the counter and looked at him. "I found this at my front door. Tell me what it means."

The Mountie stood and came toward them. Holding the note by the edges, he studied it, then placed it carefully in a plastic bag. "I don't know," he said, shaking his head. "You'll have to leave this, Miss Archer. Sergeant Randall won't be in until eight. There's been a break-in in town, and most of the men are over there questioning the victim."

"But I need help now." Betsy made fists on the counter. "Look, it might be a threat. I feel unsafe."

"I know. I've talked with Constable Selkirk. It's just that I can't do anything about it tonight, ma'am." The officer looked tired and eager to end his shift. He grabbed a pencil and paper. "Give me your phone number again and I'll tell the sergeant. He'll get back to you. Better yet, check back here after eight this morning."

The policeman jotted down Betsy's information, but Drew could see they would get no answers now. He stepped forward. "I'll see that she gets home okay."

"Good," the officer answered. He smiled at Betsy. "Don't worry. It could turn out to be nothing."

In silence, Drew rode with Betsy back to her home. He could sense her fatigue and worry. She climbed the steps to the porch. Patiently, he waited by the fence, longing to follow, but not wanting to push. She stopped several steps above him and turned. Rays from the porch light glistened on moisture brimming in her eyes.

"Come inside," she whispered. "Please."

"You really want me to?"

Betsy nodded. She fumbled in her purse for the house key. Drew took it from her, unlocked the latch, then pushed the door open. They went inside and he closed the door behind them.

"Have a seat." Betsy headed for the kitchen, flicking on a couple of lamps along the way. The entry was empty, the boxes were gone. He knew she'd shunted him off to Midnight Dome that afternoon to get him away from the boxes. He thought of asking her why she'd taken them to the cabin in the woods. But he didn't want her to know he'd followed her.

And now wasn't the time for more questions. Suddenly, he felt self-conscious. He halted and looked at her living room. It was small, cozy. Flowered cushions were plumped on the furniture. Bright, modern pictures lined the walls. He especially liked the photograph of Mount Logan. Everything was tidy. Very feminine. Pleasing.

"Want something to drink?" Betsy pulled open the refrigerator door. "Whiskey or a glass of wine?"

"Whiskey, I guess," Drew answered. He could see her in the kitchen. Light from the refrigerator made a nimbus around her hair. She looked nervous and unbelievably beautiful.

"Please . . . sit down. The bartender isn't quite as fast at home. I'll have it for you in a minute."

"Thanks." Drew went into the living room and dropped onto an overstuffed sofa, struck by his unexplained good fortune. Betsy's mercurial moods amazed him. She'd already made her distrust of him clear. Now he was sitting in her living room in the wee hours of the morning while she was fixing him a drink.

Maybe Betsy really needed him, he thought. Maybe she even wanted him. Or maybe fear was the bond. She could be so edgy that almost anyone would be welcome tonight. It was a sobering thought. Was he more than just company? This was not the time to test that theory. She'd been through enough tonight.

"Here. I hope it's all right." Betsy handed him a glass. "I'm out of mixers, but I figured you probably took it straight anyway."

"Just the way I like it." Their hands brushed when he took the glass from her. She had long, slim fingers, Drew noticed. Graceful, perfect. He sipped the whiskey and waited, hoping she'd give him some sign that would make it clear how welcome he was.

She sat down on a chair opposite him, took a swallow of her own drink, then placed it on the coffee table. "Thanks for staying."

"I wasn't going anywhere important." Drew couldn't take his eyes off her. Her skin looked like velvet in the lamplight. And her lips were full and gentle. "Actually, I'm glad you asked me. A little surprised, though."

"I know." She rubbed at her temple. "Drew, I'm so mixed up. I need someone..."

He put down his drink and leaned forward, elbows on his thighs. "Someone to count on, someone who cares about you," he finished.

She nodded.

"We both need that." He opened his arms. "Come here, Betsy. Let me hold you."

She stared at him for what seemed to Drew an eternity, then came over to sit beside him.

He pulled her to him, savoring the scent of her, fresh and pure like an alpine meadow. Her hair was soft and he buried his chin in it.

"I don't know if we should be doing this," she whispered.

With his thumb, Drew traced the line of her chin. "It feels right to me. I don't know any more than you about what's going on around us, but I have a feeling we're in this together."

"Will you stay with me tonight? I don't want...to be alone."

Drew felt his belly tighten. Betsy's eyes had deepened to a mesmerizing shade of emerald. My God, he thought, she was seducing him. Of course, he could make love to her. But not like this. She was too vulnerable now. He couldn't take advantage of her. Somehow, he would have to get out of this. Gently.

"I'll stay as long as you want," he answered.

Betsy half closed her eyes. She curled one arm around his neck and pulled him down to her. "Maybe I'm crazy, but I'm glad you're here," she whispered. "You don't know how hard these past few days have been." Her lips parted as she began to feather them, back and forth, against his own.

For several seconds, Drew kissed her back. Her touch was like satin, smooth and intoxicating. Enough to drive a man mad. He tried to restrain himself, but the sweetness of her breath, the softness of her breasts against his chest made his head spin. Reluctantly, he pulled away.

"It's late. You're tired." He began to ease her arm from his neck. Then he exposed her palm and lifted it to his lips. "Don't get me wrong, lady. Lord knows I love all of this. But tomorrow you may be sorry. I don't want you to do anything you really aren't sure about."

Betsy stared at her open hand as if he'd branded it. "You're right. I don't know what came over me."

"I'm not abandoning you," Drew said. "I'd be happy to sleep on the sofa."

She was still a moment, then squeezed his hands. "I'll get you a blanket." She stood, walked rigidly across the living room and disappeared into what Drew thought must be her bedroom. She returned carrying two quilts and a pillow.

He got up and she arranged them on the sofa. "I hope you'll be comfortable," she said. "I don't have an extra toothbrush, but there're fresh towels and soap in the bathroom."

"Great," Drew said. "I'll be fine. Don't worry about anything out there." He made a mock fist and shook it at the front door. "I'm here." He smiled. "Whoever wants you will have to get me first."

Betsy stood on tiptoe and kissed his cheek. "Thanks, Drew... for everything." Then she went back inside the bedroom, but didn't quite close the door.

Drew got ready to sleep and turned off the lights. He peeled down to T-shirt and briefs, then stretched out on the sofa with a quilt wrapped around him. He heard Betsy get in bed and turn off her light. Then the house was silent.

He rolled over and stared at the ceiling. What a night. The street outside was quiet. Nightlife in Dawson City had finally come to a standstill. He thought of all the people in town and wondered which one had left the threat on Betsy's porch. It angered him that someone would want to harm or frighten her. Beneath the quilt, his hands tensed. *Damn it.* None of this would be happening if it hadn't been for Sam and the robbery.

Well, Drew thought, at least he had been noble, after a fashion. Slim consolation, but he knew it was not the right time for either of them. It was too soon. She needed to know him better, to understand what drove him. For now, he would try to content himself with imagining. And Lord, how he hoped she'd offer him another chance.

Drew bunched the pillow and tried to sleep. Seconds turned into minutes, which turned into quarter hours. Finally, he got up, pulled on his jeans and went to Betsy's room. He hoped she was sleeping, but he wanted to check on her anyway and assure himself she was all right.

The bedroom door swung when he pushed it. Moonlight shone through blinds, slanting lines across the bed. Drew leaned against the jamb and studied Betsy's slender form. A comforter barely concealed her. She was like a dream, her auburn hair splayed wildly over the pillow. She wore a filmy kind of gown, feminine and sexy. Creamy white skin shone on her neck and bare arms. He smiled at her relaxed face. She was having pleasant dreams. If only reality could be as good.

He started to close the door.

Betsy shifted. "Drew?"

"Yeah?" Her voice gave him a start. "I didn't mean to wake you."

"I've been awake," she answered.

Drew didn't respond. He felt slightly embarrassed.

"There's something I want to tell you." She pushed onto her elbow.

"It's very late, Betsy. You need to rest now. Can it wait until we've had a little sleep?"

"Sleep? We haven't done much of that, have we? No, I'd like to say this now. That note tonight scared me so much because last night, while I was at the club, my garage was broken into."

"Broken into?" Drew repeated. "What was taken?"

"Nothing, really." Betsy tugged the comforters more tightly around her. "Just a shoebox of my grandfather's. It was filled with some of his letters. Personal stuff, I guess. I'm not really sure."

"You reported the theft, didn't you?" Drew's voice was low.

"Of course. Constable Selkirk was here. He said it was probably vandalism. Now I'm not so sure...."

Drew crossed the room and sat down on the edge of her bed. "I'm sorry, Betsy. We will get through all this. I promise."

"Think so? Yesterday, I really got paranoid. I loaded up all Grandpa's things, from the house and garage. You saw the boxes, remember? You wanted to help me. I took them to his cabin in the hills. Pretty silly, huh?"

"Nope." He shook his head. "Sensible." There was nothing to be gained now.

Betsy sighed. "I thought I'd gathered up everything, but after I got home I found more of his stuff in the back of a closet. Just some ledgers and books that I was going to leave here, but since the note . . . I don't want any of his things around."

"I agree," said Drew. "I'li help you take them later. If you want me to."

"I do." Betsy dropped her eyes and seemed to be struggling with a decision. Finally, she looked up at him. "Drew, I have a confession to make. All that's happened has been so confusing and upsetting that I've tried to protect myself by being wary and suspicious. I'm afraid that I've suspected you of having had some part in all of this. But now I know I was wrong."

Drew looked relieved. "Well, at least *you* have some faith in me. I sure haven't earned any points with the Mounties. They don't want me to leave town." He held up one hand. "But don't worry that my going with you to the cabin is going to break any rules. It was a request the Mounties gave me, not an order. I'll do whatever it takes to help you."

"Drew, I want to tell you something else." Betsy fingered the edge of the comforter. "I know the police asked you to stay in town. I know a lot of things about you."

Drew squinted. "I don't understand."

"Sergeant Randall had quite a conversation with you that morning at the station. I was there too, remember. In the office next door, with Constable Selkirk. The walls are pretty thin. I'm sorry."

"Hey, you couldn't help it. That saves me having to explain everything to you all over again." Drew twisted and pulled her to him. "Betsy, I've put you through hell."

"Not you . . ."

"Shh. I have." He nuzzled the top of her head and waited for her body to relax. Then he eased her back under the covers. "Sleep, Betsy. I won't be far away."

EARLY-MORNING LIGHT FILTERED through scrub trees as Betsy and Drew jostled along the pitted road in her Bronco. The road skirted the mountains, and the land dropped steeply on one side.

Drew glanced at her from the passenger seat. "We've been out an hour. Are we close yet?"

"Almost." She nodded ahead to rounded hills dotted with trees. "That little peak is part of Grandpa's land. That one there belongs to Jacob Talbot. The bridge in front of us goes over Lost Lady Creek. A lot of gold's been taken out of her. Too bad my grandfather and his partner didn't get much of it."

"This is really in the wilderness." Drew gripped the seat as Betsy swung the Bronco onto the bridge. Beneath them the creek bubbled and dropped, disappearing down the hill in a small waterfall.

"It sure is. Grandpa loved it. I did, too. As a child, I used to visit him often." Betsy glanced furtively at open areas as they passed, checking for vehicle tracks in clearings. Constant wind had shifted the dust, wiping out any sign of human activity. Maybe yesterday she'd imagined she'd had company.

"Something wrong?" Drew asked.

"Just looking for game. Plenty of bear and moose live in these woods." That was what she'd nearly convinced herself she'd heard the day before. She tried to smile, not wanting Drew to see how edgy she was. She'd already made a fool of herself by coming on to him too strong late last night, perhaps confiding a little too much. She'd overreacted. But she'd promised herself, from now on, she would stay in control.

"I don't believe you." He stared straight ahead. "I've spent enough time in the woods to know creatures like that would be afraid of *us*. Wildlife isn't what's giving you the jitters."

Betsy eyed him, trying to read his thoughts. But he continued to face the road.

Silently, she drove onto the bridge. Timbers creaked below them. On the other side, Betsy turned onto an overgrown trail. Along the road, fireweed bloomed in spiky blankets of mauve. Although it was still early, the air held a promise of heat. When they reached the clearing, Betsy pointed ahead. "There's the cabin." The familiar wooden structure stood to one side. Beyond, the lake shimmered through the trees.

"Water too, huh?" Drew asked.

Betsy stopped the Bronco in front of the cabin. "All the amenities. Lost Lady Creek goes into it. Some of the land you see on the other side of the lake was Tom Fioretti's. He was Grandpa's mining partner. Now that land belongs to Jacob Talbot. You know, the bald guy at Yukon Lights."

Drew frowned and Betsy could tell he was confused. As they waited for the dust to settle, she explained about her inherited mineral rights. "The land beneath us is combed with mine shafts. I have no idea where they all lead. But some stretch onto Talbot's land. In fact, almost directly across the lake from us was the opening to Tom's end of the Lost Lady Mine. He died there in an accident. Losing Tom nearly killed Grandpa, too. They were as close as brothers."

Drew squinted. "I don't see any mine entrance over there. Just a huge pile of loose boulders."

Betsy nodded. "It's still there, but buried under half that mountainside. I was in Vancouver when the landslide happened, but I'm told a massive snowmelt weakened the mountain. The mine played out years ago," Betsy went on. "Grandpa always warned me the tunnels were dangerous. It's just as well that one of the entrances is sealed off." Betsy climbed out of the Bronco. Drew followed.

"There's more than one entrance?"

"You'll see." Betsy tugged an old key from her jeans pocket and opened the heavy door. They went inside, stopping briefly for their eyes to adjust to the dimness.

Drew pivoted. "Hey, this place looks like a museum."

Betsy strode to the center of the cabin. "I haven't done much with it." The room was filled with old things: a pick, a shovel, an ax, the small outboard motor Conrad had used for his skiff—all reminders of a time when gold was sought with much more abandon.

She swiped at a thick layer of dust on the chimney of a kerosene lamp. "I doubt this old lamp will work. There's a flashlight in the Bronco. You know, it must have been pretty wild out here in the hills once. Might have been fun to be part of all that Klondike gold rush stuff." She brushed her dirty fingers against her thigh.

"Probably. But times haven't really changed much. If there were another strike in these hills, everyone would turn loco all over again." Drew looked around. "Well, where shall I put those boxes?"

"Down here." Betsy had been standing on the faded throw rug. Now she stepped off it, stooped and tossed it aside.

"What's that?" Drew stared at the extra lines in the planked floor. "An opening?"

Betsy crouched. "You wanted to know if there were any other entrances to the mine?" She gripped the edge of the trapdoor and lifted. Blackness fell away beneath it. The room was, instantly, filled with cold and the smell of damp earth. "This is Grandpa's entrance," she said, throwing the door wide open.

Drew hunkered down beside her. "Under his cabin?"

"Tom died at the other side of this mine, remember?" Betsy peered down the narrow ladder into deepest ebony. "Apparently, a support beam at the other entrance collapsed while he was under it. Crushed him. He probably died instantly. Tom and Grandpa had dreamed of striking it rich here. With one blow all that was wiped out.

"Later Grandpa lost his craving for gold," she continued. "He built this cabin himself ten years ago on top of the only other entrance to Lost Lady. He swore no one would work it again. As far as I know, there are no maps of the tunnels. Grandpa said the only chart he needed was in his head."

"Fascinating." Drew got to his feet, then pulled Betsy up beside him. "Creepy, too. You want the boxes put down there?"

Betsy nodded. "At the bottom of this ladder. That's where I hid the stuff yesterday. I figure even if a hunter broke into the cabin, he'd never look for a trapdoor."

"Well, whatever you think. I'd better get that flashlight." He started back outside, but stopped in the doorway.

"Something wrong?" Betsy stared after him.

"In a way. Betsy, you've been honest with me, so now it's my turn."

"You have been honest."

"Except in one area. I haven't told you what I did yesterday after we went up to Midnight Dome."

"Drew, you don't have to give me a minute-by-minute report. I know you have things to do on your own."

He looked at the floor, then up at her. "I was preoccupied with my dad. I just had a crazy idea he might have bailed out of his plane for some reason. And I sort of figured out that, if he did parachute, he might have landed around here."

"But you didn't even know where my cabin was then."

"Right." Drew went back to Betsy and took her hands. "What I'm saying is that I rented a pickup to drive around and look because it seemed like the best idea at the time. And what I did was accidentally end up following you."

"Really?" She was amused. "I saw a pickup behind me, but I thought it turned off the road. That was you?"

"Yep." Drew went back to the door and looked out. "When I realized you were ahead of me, I dropped back. I didn't want you to think I was following you."

Betsy was touched by Drew's confession. It was a relief to know that he understood the need to knock down the barriers that had been thrown up between them by the events of the past few days.

He turned to face her. "I didn't mean to follow you, but by then I was so curious about those boxes you didn't want me to see that I had to keep going."

"I could have used some help getting them down the tunnel," she joked.

"Well, you turned me down once. I didn't figure you'd care to see me pop up at your cabin uninvited. So I just hung back and watched. I'm sorry about all this.

I couldn't bring myself to tell you last night, but now I don't want to keep anything from you.''

"Drew, I'm glad you told me.'' She went over and gave him a hug. "You know, I thought I heard something in the bushes when I was leaving yesterday. So it was you.''

"No, it wasn't.'' They walked outside together. "I heard the same sound, like a twig snapping. I saw you glance up. But the sound didn't come from me.''

"Then what was it? An animal?''

"I had a strange feeling it was a person.''

"Drew, you're making me nervous.''

"I'm sorry.'' He squeezed her around the shoulders and scanned the horizon. Then he frowned and leveled one palm across his brow. "Then again, maybe we have reason to be concerned.''

"Why?'' Betsy peered across the lake.

"Maybe our visitors were hiding yesterday, but today they're out in the open. Look over there.'' He pointed to the hills.

"Where?'' Apprehension filled her. She should have known better than to think they'd be safe.

"Across the lake, farther down. On the other side of that landslide,'' Drew said.

Betsy narrowed her eyes. Two figures scurried along the shoreline. "But that's my land. Do you suppose it's Talbot? The dividing line between our properties is very close to there. If it is Talbot, he's trespassing.''

"Listen.''

Angry male voices wafted across the water. The men shouted at each other, then disappeared into the woods.

"Well, at least there's a lake between us.'' Drew started again for the Bronco, still watching the hillside.

Betsy hurried after him. She could tell that seeing the trespassers had also disturbed Drew. As they opened the trunk and slid out several boxes, an engine revved in the distance.

Drew was instantly alert. "A floatplane."

"So that's how they got here." Betsy scanned the lake. "I should have guessed."

Seconds later, a pontooned white plane taxied from a partially hidden cove. They watched as it gained momentum in the distance, became airborne and circled over them.

Drew shaded his brow with one hand. "Damn it. I can't make out the numbers, but I think it's a Stinson."

"Let's stow Conrad's stuff and go over there," Betsy urged. "I want to find out what they were doing."

"It might take a while."

"We've got a boat. And a motor. Think you can start a twenty-year-old Evinrude?"

Drew started to answer, but Betsy interrupted. "Never mind, I know you can. Come on," she said, pulling at his shirtsleeve. "Grandpa's boat is hidden in those trees. The motor's inside the cabin. I'll go alone if you don't want to join me."

"I can't believe this," Drew muttered as he followed Betsy back to the cabin. "You're crazy."

They stored the boxes in the tunnel, then fastened the motor to the barely floating, wooden skiff. Soon they were crossing the lake. They beached the skiff on the far side and jumped out. Betsy jogged ahead, checking the shoreline.

"Tracks," she pointed. "There...and there. They disappear into the brush." She took off in the direction of the footprints.

Drew followed, then angled in another direction. "Betsy, check this." He hadn't gone ten feet. "Someone's been doing a lot of digging." He looked at the ground more closely. "It seems as if they've been trying to rearrange the forest." He raised an uprooted huckleberry bush.

Betsy folded her arms. "Why dig here?"

"I don't know. If this is Talbot's work, what could he have been searching for?" Drew dropped the bush.

"And who was with him?" Betsy added.

As Drew followed the path of the footprints into the brush, Betsy squatted on her heels at the site of the digging. It was a puzzle, she thought, idly sifting the sandy soil between her fingers. There was no reason for anyone to have been digging in this spot.

She shifted position to forestall the cramp that was building in her calves and froze. The sunlight that streamed over her shoulder blazed back at her from the mound of dirt at her feet. Carefully, she brushed more soil away from the pinpoint of reflected light until she had uncovered its source.

Recognition stabbed through her as she stared down at the yellow metal in her palm. It was a perfectly wrought miniature pickax—the skill and precision, the loving attention to detail, Frank Saunders's signature.

Where had it come from? Had the men she and Drew had seen dropped it while digging or... The other possibility was poisonous. Had it been dropped mere minutes ago? Did Drew have another confession to make?

The pickax might mean nothing, just an innocent purchase, but finding it in the woods was so unsettling that the prospect of asking Drew about it seemed more frightening than not knowing at all.

UNANSWERED QUESTIONS continued to build as they re-crossed the lake, locked up Conrad's cabin and headed back to Dawson City. By the time they reached town, they both felt rummy and out of sorts. As they waited for the light to turn at an intersection, another four-wheel drive pulled up beside them. Sergeant Randall leaned across the seat and rolled down the passenger window.

"Betsy," he called. "Seems you two left town for a while." Randall looked beyond Betsy at Drew.

Betsy recalled the Mountie's request that Drew stay close and she scrambled to cover for him. "Not really," she lied. "Just sight-seeing. The Bronco needs an oil change. I'd be afraid to drive it too far."

Randall studied them for what seemed an eternity. Betsy wound her fingers more tightly around the steering wheel. Now, because of Drew, she was telling white lies to the police. And she didn't think Randall believed her.

Finally, the officer spoke. "I've been looking for you. Frank Saunders had a break-in at the shop last night just after midnight. The place was ripped apart though nothing of consequence was taken—just a couple of small things from that display case he keeps for the tourists. Frank's okay. He's over at his sister's but she isn't doing very well. I thought you'd want to know."

Betsy felt a new conflict well up in her. Her concern for Frank and Evie and the sense of violation she felt for them was tempered by relief. Drew had been with her last night, so whoever had dropped the small gold charm at the digging site had either bought it or had stolen it, but at least she knew that it hadn't been Drew.

Randall was speaking again before Betsy could respond.

"What I'm really concerned about is that typed note you brought in this morning," he said.

"Were you able to tell who left it, Sergeant?"

"No." The Mountie glanced meaningfully at Drew, then back at Betsy. "We're baffled. I don't want to alarm you, Betsy, but that warning and your break-in might be linked."

"What should I do?" Betsy asked.

"Be cautious," Randall advised. "Keep your doors locked and watch the people around you."

"I understand." Betsy cringed. It was clear that Randall was including Drew in the warning. "And thank you for letting me know about Frank. I'll call when I get back."

When Randall said goodbye and drove on, Drew finally spoke. "Who are Frank and Evie? Does this have anything to do with you?"

Betsy shoved the transmission into gear. "Evie lived with my grandfather, and Frank, her brother, owns the jewelry store on Front Street. The three of them were very close, especially during Grandpa's mining days. Frank is a gifted goldsmith—this is a sample of his work." Betsy rummaged in a pocket and extended her palm to Drew, showing him the small pickax charm. "Drew, I found this across the lake where the men were digging. It could be a coincidence. Frank sells lots of these. Or it could be that my break-in, Frank's and the note are linked in some way. If that's the case, then I feel awful that I'm dragging everyone down into this nightmare and I don't even know why."

"Randall seemed to think that I'm doing the dragging," Drew said, "and that you are the primary victim."

"Randall didn't say that." Betsy tried to concentrate on the street.

"Good Lord, he didn't have to." Drew's voice rasped. "Will you park this thing? I can't talk to you like this." She spotted an empty space near the curb and slid the Bronco into it.

Drew waited until she had flicked off the engine, then he grabbed her forearm. "Betsy, I want you to trust me. I'm tired of trying to prove myself, to you and to them. Jacob Talbot's the man we should *really* be checking out. I'm sure of it. He was probably trespassing, digging on your land. Remember?"

"We can't jump to conclusions," Betsy said. "We don't have any proof." She could still see Talbot snooping in her office.

"Then let's find some." Drew's eyes glittered. "Where do they keep property records in this town?"

Betsy blinked. "At the city office on Front Street, I guess."

"That's only a few blocks away. Let's walk. You can make your call and then we'll see if there is anything in the books on our friend Talbot."

Fifteen minutes later, Betsy had been reassured that Frank was irritable but fine and that Evie was upset but being cared for, and she turned her attention to the task Drew had set them. The city office receptionist knew Betsy and was helpful, and soon they were poring over a microfilm reader.

"There." Betsy stabbed an index finger at the screen. "Talbot, Jacob..."

Drew read the end of the entry aloud. "Fairbanks, Alaska..." His brows shot up. "That's where I saw Talbot before. He was in Fairbanks the night Harsted interviewed me for his newspaper story. The night we were notified about Dad."

"But Talbot told me he lived in Whitehorse. That he was a doctor."

"Maybe he *is* a doctor," said Drew. "But I don't think he's been truthful about his address."

Betsy sighed and flicked off the viewer. Her head had begun to ache and she could barely think.

"Enough of this. You're tired." Drew dropped his voice. Then he touched her shoulder. "I'll take you home so you can catch a few winks. Besides, I could use a change of clothes myself, and all my stuff's at the hotel. We'll get together later, at the club. Maybe after we've rested, we can figure this out."

Betsy agreed. "You don't need to go with me. I can make it on my own." Exhausted as she was, the pressure of his fingers sent a prickling charge down her spine.

"But . . ." Drew started to protest, then thought better of it. "You win. Tonight, then."

MINUTES LATER, Betsy headed down the boardwalk alone. Nothing made sense at the moment—Frank's robbery, Talbot's discrepancies, Randall's suspicions. Most certainly not her escalating attraction to Drew McKay. It was already midafternoon. When she got home she would take some aspirin and have a shower, then crawl into bed. With luck a nap would clear her head.

Her house seemed even more comforting than usual when she pulled into the driveway. Sunlight dappled lavender sage blossoms in Conrad's herb garden. A bird chirped in the old spruce tree. This time, thank goodness, everything seemed in order.

Then Betsy spotted it. Paper poking out of her ornamental mailbox. There shouldn't have been anything in it. Everyone in Dawson City had a post office box. Slowly, she opened the lid. The paper inside had lines on it and colors. It appeared to be a sketch.

Betsy cried out. Her fingers became like rubber and the paper floated to the ground. Some maniac had left a felt-marker drawing of Conrad's medallion. Not the front of it, but the back. It was perfect in every detail—except one.

The rendering was dribbled with blazing red blood.

# Chapter Eight

Betsy fell to her knees. Her weary mind was reeling. The drawing lay on the lawn, its crimson lines glowing like fire. Betsy felt sick. What maniac would torment her like this? Someone was trying to frighten her, but she didn't know why.

Gingerly, she picked up the sketch. If there were fingerprints on it, she didn't want to smudge them. Her legs felt paralyzed, but she had to move. She had no idea when the warning had been left, but sensed the culprit was nearby, watching her squirm.

Betsy scrambled to her feet and went inside her house. She needed the medallion. Today she hadn't worn it. And she needed Drew. More than ever, she longed for his understanding and his strength. She snatched the pendant from the top dresser drawer and drove to the Bonanza Hotel.

"Who is it?" Drew's muffled voice answered her third knock on his door.

"Betsy," she whispered. "It's important. Please, let me in."

"Just a second."

Betsy anxiously waited to get out of the vacant hallway. Scuffling sounds filtered beneath the door. When

Drew finally released the latch, she realized what had delayed him. He'd been taking a shower.

"Sorry I was so long. What's wrong?" He tugged a towel across his bare shoulders.

Betsy's gaze traveled unabashedly down his muscular body, from the curling black hair behind his ears, to the smooth jeans he'd obviously just pulled on. Moisture still clung to the mat of dark curls tapering down his chest to his unfastened belt buckle. For a second, she almost forgot the sketch she was pressing to her breast.

She blinked. "This is what's wrong." She held the paper out. "I just found it. I think that's blood on it. Drew, this is really too much."

"Let me see." He guided her inside the room, then quickly shut the door. Frowning, he took the sketch and examined it. "This looks like your medallion." His face had turned pale.

"Compare." She pulled the charm from her jeans pocket and handed it to him. "It's the etching on the back. Someone knows what they're doing."

"I don't like this." Drew laid the necklace against the paper and eyed the wild red smears. "What is this design, Betsy? The police will want to know."

"Conrad never told me. Oh, what's the point in going to the police with this? They still haven't found out who left the first note, or who broke into my garage." Tears began to brim in her eyes.

"I know." Drew reached to comfort her. He fastened the medallion around her neck, then rested his hands on her stiff shoulders, lightly moving his fingers back and forth. "But you have to report it. I'll go with you as soon as I finish dressing."

Exhaustion closed in on Betsy. She stared at the muscle flexing in Drew's forearm and pressed her cheek against his open palm. His soothing voice seemed to come from far away.

"Sit down over here," he urged. "I'll be back in a minute."

Drew directed Betsy to a chair in the corner. She slumped into it. She felt safe now. Drew was close by. No one could find her here. For a little while, she would be secure.

Betsy's eyelids drooped as she watched Drew lay the sketch on the bed, grab a shirt and disappear into the bathroom. How strong his body was, she thought, how capable. Male and sexy. Every move solid, fine-tuned, like an athlete's. Despite her apprehension about the sketch, she'd nearly forgotten it when he'd come to the door. She'd wanted to brush her fingers across his chest, bury her face against his bare shoulder.

The daydream made Betsy smile. She couldn't think anymore. The room around her was…growing fuzzy….

"BETSY?" DREW'S VOICE CUT through the darkness. "Wake up."

She half opened her eyes. Drew knelt beside her. Nothing looked familiar. Then she knew where she was. The Bonanza Hotel. The sketch. They had to get to the Mounties.

"Did I fall asleep?" She jolted upright on the edge of the chair. Drew was dressed now. The shadows in the room had lengthened. "I'm sorry. I was able to relax here and . . ."

Drew sighed. "It's okay. You obviously needed rest. Too much has happened too soon. You're in a better frame of mind now to deal with that sketch."

Betsy pushed to her feet and straightened her blouse. "Okay, let's get it over with."

Ten minutes later, they were inside the police station showing the drawing to Constable Selkirk.

"I don't know what to make of this," he told Betsy. "What is this drawing supposed to mean?"

"I don't know, Constable. It's a reproduction of the design etched onto the back of this medallion that belonged to my grandfather. He never told me what it represented."

Selkirk sighed and handed her back the pendant. "Well, Miss Archer, with so little to go on I can only warn you again to be careful. As it stands, we have nothing concrete to link the threats and the burglary together yet, so I can't do much about this."

"Come on, Constable," Drew interrupted. "You know they're tied in."

Selkirk stared at Drew. "We have no proof—about anything."

Betsy noted the unspoken message in the constable's words. Drew was still under suspicion. There was too much going on, she thought helplessly. All she wanted was to uncover the truth—simply. She'd already decided not to tell Selkirk about the trespassers at the Lost Lady Mine and the pickax charm. Explaining Talbot now would be far too complicated. She didn't want the Mounties to find out that Drew had been with her in the woods. His leaving town, against their request, would only make matters worse.

"McKay, I've been trying to find you." Sergeant Randall stepped from his office. "Don't stay in your hotel much, do you?" Betsy flinched as Randall came to stand beside Selkirk.

Drew leveled his chin. "You told me to see the sights of Dawson, Sergeant. So that's what I've been doing."

Randall paused a second. "Good." Then he glanced at Betsy. "Everything all right?"

"Not really." She bit her lip and Drew stepped closer.

Selkirk showed Randall the sketch and explained the new threat.

The older man looked at it, then picked up a memo from the desk behind him. "Sounds like someone out there has a few loose screws. Probably means nothing, Betsy, but we'll try to keep a closer eye on your place. You watch, too. Tell us if you see anyone suspicious hanging around. I've got some news for you though, McKay." He waggled the memo. "Do you mind if Betsy hears this?"

Drew shook his head. "Anything you have to say to me she can hear, too."

"I figured as much." Randall cleared his throat. "The Fairbanks police called us a while ago. We finally have positive identification on the body that was in your father's plane. It was a man named Ed Sherburne." Randall checked Drew's face, but Drew showed no sign he'd recognized the name. Randall went on. "He was a former pipeline worker on the North Slope. Didn't have a family and no one seems to know where he went after he was laid off up there eleven years ago. Ever heard of the guy?"

"Nope," Drew said grimly.

"Did your father ever work with him, take him out in the bush?" Randall asked.

"How should I know who my dad did business with ten years ago?" Drew's jaw clenched.

"Easy, McKay. Just checking."

"Fine, I just don't understand how any of this is helping you find my father."

"You don't have to," Randall said. "That's our job."

Betsy could see that Drew was puzzled about the identity of the body. She wanted to help him somehow, to ease his anxiety, but didn't dare do it now. The police had already noticed she was spending time with Drew. Her better judgment told her that was all they needed to know.

The sun was dropping to the west when Betsy and Drew headed out of the Mounties' office. It was almost time for Betsy to put in an appearance at Yukon Lights.

"Why don't you wait a little while before you go to work?" Drew urged. "Let's grab a bite to eat at that snack bar across the street and forget our problems. It's been a long time since breakfast."

"A little food does sound good." Betsy lifted her hand to wave at the waiting proprietor. The tiny fast-food restaurant was flamboyant with neon and green-striped awnings. "Johnnie makes the best hot dogs this side of Toronto, I'm told."

They placed their order, then found seats beneath a fluttering Cinzano umbrella, Johnnie's latest acquisition. The red umbrella looked slightly out of place in front of the vintage buildings.

Betsy laid her shoulder bag on the table. She was silent a moment. "One more thing, Drew, about the crash . . . I've had a thought."

"Can't we forget about all that for now, Betsy? There's so much more we can talk about."

"I know, but this might be important. Wasn't your dad's plane a four-seater?"

"Yes." Drew stretched back in his chair, looking a little more interested.

Betsy frowned. "Maybe I'm way off base, but since there was room for four, couldn't someone else besides your father and the pipeline worker have been aboard?"

Drew shifted uncomfortably. "Of course. But don't get any wild ideas that I was along, because I wasn't."

"I know."

"Let's hope the Mounties believe that, too."

A waitress appeared with their hot dogs and Cokes. They waited until the girl had gone before speaking again.

Drew leaned toward Betsy. "You do have a point, though. Whoever killed that pipeline worker might have been sitting behind him. And if my dad was flying the plane, he'd be in the clear. Surely the police have already figured out that possibility."

"Probably. But maybe they wouldn't tell you if they had." Betsy stared at him above the rim of her Coke glass and tried to read his mind. Their thoughts had to be traveling the same line—that the Mounties were trying their best to prove Drew was implicated in the Red Baron robbery and murder. She stifled a shiver as she sipped the drink. It wasn't the ice in it that chilled her, but the feeling they were both sinking deeper into this nightmare.

Quietly, they finished their meal. Finally, Betsy asked, "Will you come to the club later and take me home again tonight?" She could barely believe that she'd asked, but a longing had been building in her, one unfamiliar to a woman who'd long taken pride in her independence. It was not a need for protection, although she was sure that Drew would chalk it up to that. No, it was a need to be near him, to care for him.

Drew's response was her answer. His mouth slanted into his familiar lopsided grin. It sent a warm tingle to the tips of Betsy's toes.

"Of course I will," he said, his eyes sparkling. "That's the best invitation I've had all day."

DREW SHOVED ANOTHER LOG into the fire and turned back to Betsy. "That ought to do it." Flames lapped against the wood, replacing the shadows in Betsy's living room with flickering light.

Betsy pulled her knees up under her chin and snuggled back into the sofa. "The fire's lovely. Are we silly to build one in August, in the middle of the night?"

"What we do is nobody's business but our own." Drew sat down beside Betsy and slid one arm about her. "And I think your idea was great." His fingers made slow swirls against her forearm. "There's no place in the world I'd rather be right now than here—with you."

"This seems impossible . . . you and me . . . like this," Betsy murmured as she stared into the fire.

"I'm not complaining." Drew pressed his chin into the softness of Betsy's hair. He was grateful to be alone with her. He'd watched her work, as usual, at Yukon Lights and had felt buoyed up by the sight of her. He'd also been on the alert for Talbot and Harsted to turn up. Neither had appeared, and their absence bothered him.

Betsy shifted, giving Drew the chance to pull her even closer. "At least we didn't find any more messages tonight," she said.

"Thank goodness." Drew tried to sound reassuring, but knew it was probably just a matter a time before something less harmless than a note turned up.

"I'm so tired," Betsy whispered. "And so glad you're here."

"Then close your eyes. I don't intend to leave."

Drew stretched his legs on top of the coffee table and, watched the crackling fire almost as if he were hypnotised by it. He was tired, too. He would wait, patiently, and hold Betsy until she fell asleep. Then he would carry her to bed and spend the night, as he did before, on the sofa. He knew where she stored the bedding.

Betsy's even breathing soon told Drew that she was dozing. Her slim body was curled like a cat, soft and sleek, against him. He ached to devour her, absorb every beautiful inch of her into himself. Firelight colored her bare arms, her blouse, her jeans in coppery light. Her breasts rose, then fell, evenly, sexily.

*Lord!* Drew sighed, and tossed his head back against the cushions. He'd felt the tautness below his belly, the rush of warmth through his veins. Now he wondered how much patience he really had. This woman nestled beside him was like no other. Yes, he longed to be part of her, to touch her, to know every intimate detail about her. He imagined himself making love to her, giving her pleasure, showing her what it meant to be valued above all else.

Drew also knew his feelings coursed even deeper, that since he'd met Betsy, his life could never be the same. He stared briefly at the dim ceiling, then pressed his eyes shut. Betsy was a new world to him, an undeserved haven. He wanted more than mere physical satisfaction. He needed her love. Because he'd fallen unshakably in love with her.

SUNLIGHT STREAMED into Betsy's bedroom. She awakened slowly, her mind coming hazily into focus. It was late, well after ten. The heady aromas of fresh-brewed coffee, toast and bacon filtered from the kitchen, making her sit up. Drew was fixing breakfast and it smelled divine.

Betsy tossed away the covers. She was wearing only her underwear. Her blouse and jeans lay neatly on an armchair in the corner. Hurriedly, she flung on a bathrobe. The night before, she and Drew had watched the fire, and she'd been so sleepy. She didn't remember removing her clothes. Now she realized Drew had done it for her. But instead of being embarrassed, she found the idea provocative. *What was getting into her?* Agitated, she went into the bathroom, straightened her hair and tossed cold water onto her face. Then she walked, as nonchalantly as she could, into the kitchen.

"Morning." Drew began to pour coffee into a mug. "I hope you like your eggs scrambled. They're ready."

"This is incredible." Betsy stared at the table, set for breakfast.

"I had to do a little poking around your kitchen to find what I needed." Drew placed the steaming mug on the table. "I've gotten kind of used to taking care of myself. You know, cooking instant stuff on a camp stove. Of course, this ought to taste a little better."

Betsy pulled her robe closer. "The food looks good," she murmured. Drew looked natural in her kitchen, even though he nearly filled the tiny space. He noticed her fidgeting fingers, though she dropped her hands to her sides. Like her, he'd probably been thinking about the previous night.

Drew smiled vaguely, then swung back to the stove, busying himself dishing eggs and bacon onto plates. "I need to go back to the hotel for some fresh clothes. Do you want to go with me?"

Betsy sipped her coffee. He might as well bring his bags over here, she thought. Because of her urging, he'd practically become a permanent fixture on her sofa. The awareness both startled and pleased her. Yes, she *did* want to go with him, more than anything else. This was all so crazy and wonderful. "Sure," she answered. "I'd love to go with you."

Drew didn't answer when he turned around. But Betsy was pleased. She wasn't sure if it was what she'd said, or the way she'd said it, that made Drew look so satisfied.

They dawdled over their meal, enjoying the simple food and the pleasure of each other's company. It was nearly noon when Drew and Betsy crossed the lobby of the Bonanza. An employee behind the checkout desk looked up from a group of travelers paying their bills. "Mr. McKay? Excuse me, you have a message," he said.

Drew glanced at Betsy, then went to the desk. The man pulled a paper from a slot and handed it to him. Drew read it as he walked back to her.

"It's from Pete," he said. "My brother in Fairbanks. He phoned about the business this morning. It looks like he needs help."

"Do you want to call him?" Betsy could see that Drew was concerned. "I'm sure everything will be all right. You haven't been away that long."

"It's more than that." Drew folded the message and stuck it in his shirt pocket. "Let's go over there where it's more private." He led her to an empty alcove in a far corner. When he was sure they were out of earshot, he took out the note and looked at it again. "I've been half expecting to hear from Pete. I've always taken care of the bookkeeping and scheduling...at least since Dad left. Now Pete feels swamped. And I feel guilty. He can't handle NorthStar alone."

"What are you going to do?" Betsy steeled herself for what she knew was inevitable.

Drew studied her. His eyes softened as he brushed an index finger along her cheek. "I have to go back."

"But you can't.... What about the Mounties?"

Drew lowered his hand. "They won't do anything to me. I've nothing to worry about. It's you I don't want to be without. You're not safe here. Betsy, come with me. I'll only stay in Fairbanks long enough to get Pete on the right track. I'd like you to meet my family...see my home."

"Drew...it sounds so good," Betsy stammered. She wanted to go with him more than anything. "But I can't. Who would run Yukon Lights?"

"You're the boss, Betsy. You've got employees you can count on. We'll find out where Jacob Talbot really lives. Couldn't you use a vacation?" Drew rocked back on his heels. "Besides, I'm a great pilot."

Betsy's face suddenly clouded. The only plane she could envision now was crumpled and horrible, stranded in the hills. It upset her to think of Drew in a similar cockpit, although he was undoubtedly competent.

Drew grabbed her shoulders. "Hey, relax. I know what you're thinking, but I'm at my best when I'm up in the sky." He laughed. "I want to stay around a long time and enjoy being with you."

Drew's humor was contagious and she had to smile. Even so, she couldn't leave the club. Not during the busiest month of the year. She would be safe alone at home—she had to be. She stepped away and his hands slid down her arms. "I'm sorry, Drew. But I can't go with you. Just promise you'll hurry back to me."

In the evening, when Betsy stood on the tarmac at the airstrip, she finally admitted the truth. She'd wrapped her sweater around her and swiped away tears, while Drew McKay, the man who'd become so incredibly important to her, had climbed into his plane. They'd spent the entire day together, sight-seeing, talking, becoming closer than two people had a right to be. Now she waved at Drew as he gave her a high sign and started the engine. He couldn't know that her soul and heart were being wrenched away.

Betsy solemnly watched while the Piper lifted and circled. Finally its navigation lights disappeared among the still-faint stars. She was alone, just as she'd been before Drew came into her life. But she wasn't the same person. Now she was a woman in love.

# Chapter Nine

Betsy joined the line of cancan dancers, letting the music carry her. *One, two, three, kick!* Activity kept her from constantly reminding herself that Drew wouldn't be dropping in tonight. *One, two, three, kick!*

Since coming to Dawson City, she'd had remarkably few problems in living independently, but now, hundreds of miles from the endearing American pilot who'd flown into her life, she felt an infinite loneliness.

*One, two, three, kick!* Suddenly the audience was clapping and Betsy bowed with the rest of the cancan line.

She went down to the bar, poured herself a glass of ice water and drank half of it. Then she wandered away and began looking around for a customer to visit with. Within seconds, Jacob Talbot had motioned her to his table. Reluctantly she went over to him.

He stood up. "Great dancing, Betsy."

"Thank you."

"Say, I'm sorry for not getting together with you like I planned. I've been pretty busy." He grinned.

Busy at what, Betsy wondered. "Don't worry about it."

"Let's sit," he told her, stepping around to her side of the round oak table to pull out a chair. "Take a load off. You must be tired after jumping around like that."

She sat down and let Talbot scoot her chair forward. "Not really. Just thirsty." She drank more of her ice water as he reseated himself and picked up his own glass. He had whiskey again.

After a few awkward seconds, Talbot clanked his ice cubes together and put down the glass. "Well," he said, rubbing his hands together, "what do you know about panning for gold?"

Betsy's mind zoomed back to what she'd been doing minutes before she'd found the airplane crash. Was Talbot leading her on? Surely he didn't know that she was the one who'd discovered the plane. For her own peace of mind, she had to pretend he didn't. "Panning? I've done my share."

"No doubt." He squinted and almost broke into a laugh. "But not rich yet. Naturally, I don't have any hope of collecting this fifty-thousand-dollar Red Baron reward your piano player sprang on us the other night, but I would like to take home a little gold dust." He arched his brows. "It's just that I don't know any good spots around here."

Betsy couldn't believe that. "After all your visits, I'm surprised you don't know where to go," she told him. She still wondered if Talbot had been poking around her land. "Panning for gold in Dawson City is like riding a cable car in San Francisco," she went on. "It's pretty hard to avoid. I'm sure your hotel can set you up with an organized outing."

"Oh, I know about those tourist things. But that's not what I had in mind. I was thinking of something... more remote. You know, out in the woods." There was a twinkling in Talbot's eyes for a moment, but it stopped when he noticed Greg Harsted standing at the table, beer in hand.

"This chair taken?" Harsted asked, then sat down between Betsy and Talbot before anyone could answer. He set his beer glass on the polished table and looked at Betsy. "Now what's this about going out in the woods?"

Betsy wanted to sneak away. Being with these two men only intensified her longing for Drew. She wasn't any more comfortable with Harsted than Talbot. For a moment, she did consider leaving. There was always work to do at the club, so she could have offered a dozen plausible excuses. Instead, she decided it might be to her advantage to ride out her uneasiness. She could play one man off the other—and learn something more about both of them.

After introducing them, she looked at Harsted and said, "Dr. Talbot was just proposing a gold-panning expedition."

"Really?" Harsted turned to Talbot.

"Sort of a private trip," the older man responded.

Betsy didn't especially relish the thought, but this panning trip might be an opportunity for her to get some insight into Talbot's real reasons for being there. If he was an innocent eccentric, she could listen to his stories about Conrad and assuage her conscience. If he wasn't... "Maybe Greg would like to go along," she said.

"You're inviting me?" Harsted asked. "That's hard to believe, coming from a lady who refuses to be interviewed."

"Interviewed?" Talbot said, his eyes widening.

"Greg is a reporter," Betsy explained to Talbot. "He's covering the Red Baron story and thinks that asking a lot of questions of a Dawson City nightclub owner is going to put him in line for a Pulitzer." Then, turning to Harsted, she smiled and said, "Of course, he's wrong."

"Could be," Harsted said evenly. "Any time you change your mind..."

"No chance," Betsy said. "But I am willing to pan for gold with you—and Dr. Talbot. How about tomorrow?"

"I'm game," Harsted said.

Betsy looked at Talbot. "Doctor?"

"Tomorrow's great. Couldn't be better. But since it's not going to be just the two of us, why not make it a foursome, bring along one of your girlfriends?"

Betsy thought a moment, remembering the adage about safety in numbers. "I could get Laura...."

"Laura?" Talbot asked.

"She works here," Betsy said. "My best waitress. Stay here a minute. I'll go ask her."

Betsy spotted Laura waiting on a table by the stage and went over to her. As soon as Laura had taken the order, Betsy took her aside and said, "I need a favor."

"Sure, Boss."

Betsy laid out the gold-panning proposition. Thankfully, the chatter of customers packing Yukon Lights let her speak in a normal voice. Talbot and Harsted couldn't possibly hear anything fifty feet away, not that she was divulging secrets.

For Laura's peace of mind, Betsy thought it was best not to tell her too much. Laura was a friend and a loyal worker, but not so close that Betsy had shared with her any of the strange events of the past few days. There would be plenty of time to do that after everything had quieted down. So Betsy kept her request casual and told

Laura she knew Talbot and Harsted, but didn't mention how.

To Betsy's relief, Laura didn't ask. She only glanced at the two men and said, "Panning for gold sounds great. I've been wanting to try it. You'll teach me?"

"Sure."

"Good. I should go out in the sticks more often. Where do we meet?"

"Out in front of the club, I was thinking. Free sandwiches for the two of us from the Yukon Lights kitchen, and I'll drive and bring the panning gear."

"An irresistible offer. What time?"

"How about nine? Or is that too early?"

"Not if I can get out of here in an hour," Laura said with a grin. "My feet are *killing* me."

Betsy broke out laughing. "What a negotiator. Make it a half hour. But remind me to cut your pay next week."

"Oh, no—" Laura deadpanned "—not again."

Laura went back to work in high spirits, and Betsy returned to the table feeling good herself. Harsted and Talbot were apparently doing well, too. In the couple of minutes she'd been away, they'd managed to acquire fresh drinks. Briefly, she wondered what they'd talked about, but she wasn't going to hang around to find out.

"Okay," she said, leaning her hands against the table. "Laura's in. I have to get back to work now, but you two be out front at nine in the morning. Pack your own lunches and I'll handle the equipment and transportation."

Then Betsy turned and headed toward the kitchen. If she didn't get busy on those sandwiches she'd promised Laura, she'd probably forget.

But before she even got to the kitchen, she noticed Talbot head for the front door. She stopped and looked back at Harsted. He was up now, leaving his full glass of beer, apparently following Talbot. Harsted caught up and the two men talked briefly near the door. Betsy wandered over to the bouncer and asked him to keep an eye on them.

She went to the kitchen to make the sandwiches, and when she came out a few minutes later, the bouncer had news about Harsted and Talbot. "They talked in low voices—I couldn't hear what they said—and then they walked down the street together like old friends."

She thanked the bouncer, but she didn't understand. Hadn't the two men just met?

IN FAIRBANKS the next morning, Drew slept in. He'd been tired from the flight over and not getting enough sleep the night before. But he knew he'd stay up seven nights a week for Betsy.

After fixing his breakfast, he went to NorthStar Expeditions. He'd left a message on Pete's answering machine that he probably wouldn't be in first thing. When he did get there, he had to step aside as three fishermen took their time walking out. They were joking and their laughter gave Drew a lift. Despite Pete's accounting problems, the business appeared to be in good shape.

Drew went in. His brother was behind the counter, making notes in the appointment book.

"Hey," Pete said, looking up, "the wandering brother has returned."

"I wasn't that far away," Drew said. He went over next to Pete and chucked him on the shoulder.

"I know." Pete was somber now. "Anything new on Dad?"

"Yes and no. Come on in to the office and I'll tell you." Pete followed Drew in. They sat down at opposite ends of the sofa. The no-nonsense quarters of NorthStar Expeditions looked like an old friend to Drew. "It's good to be back," he said, searching for a way to begin. "But things are still a mess in Dawson City, maybe more of a mess. Dad's plane, the body in it, the Mounties' suspicions—all that's just like I told you on the phone."

Pete nodded. "They can't prove a thing."

"Maybe not," Drew said. "But I hope I can."

"Then you're going back?"

"Yes. For a couple of reasons."

"Hmm." Pete grew pensive. "Those three guys who left just before you got here? They flew in from Los Angeles and only have four days in Alaska. But they've got money and want to do some fishing. So I'm taking them up north—probably on the Porcupine River. They liked the name."

"Nice going," Drew said.

"Yeah. Except I had to schedule them on Sunday and I was hoping to do some work in the office this weekend. I'm having a little trouble with the books."

"You hired another temporary guide?"

"Yeah," Pete said. "He's out now. He has a little experience and I think he'll be good. His flying record is excellent. We may want to use him again."

"Great." Anything that took the pressure off the business sounded good to Drew. As much as he wanted to pull his weight with Pete, his mind was back in Dawson City. "Look, keep the guy on. Tell him he can work until October. Maybe longer, maybe even next summer. As for the books, I'll show you a few ways to cut down on the drudgery. I want you to be able to handle the numbers."

"But—"

Drew raised his hand. "No, let me finish. I appreciate everything you're doing, I really do. I know you're already carrying the load of two men. I feel bad about this and if you weren't my brother, I wouldn't be leaning on you. But you may have to get by without me a few more days."

Pete blinked. "I don't like the sound of this."

"I have to go back." Drew got up and went to the Alaska-Yukon map on the wall. "It isn't just Dad. It's me now. I wasn't even supposed to leave Dawson City. The Mounties suspect me. Maybe both of us."

Pete looked shocked. "Suspect us of what?"

"Of being accomplices in the Red Baron robbery."

"That's ridiculous."

"To us," Drew said. "But to the police..." Drew shrugged. "Look at the evidence. A pilot disappears in his plane the same day two guys in aviator outfits steal two million dollars. The police questioned us then—remember? Then the Mounties find the goggles and part of the money in our dad's plane. And a body with a dent in the back of its skull."

"Why can't they let it go?" Pete said. "Don't you think Dad is dead now?"

"Yes, I do. But I want to know it all. Every damned detail." Drew crossed the room and leaned heavily against his desk. "If somebody killed him, I want the killer taken in. And that's not the only problem."

"I don't know, I might not want to hear about it."

"Yes you do. It's your business, too. NorthStar. Pretty soon, word about Dad is going to get out—whether the Mounties have a case or not. And unless

Dad's name is clear, then it's going to hurt Northstar. A few bad rumors, and it could be down the tube for both of us.''

Pete swallowed hard. "All right. Then I'll go to Dawson City next time. You're getting too emotional about this. You need to relax. I'll go to the Yukon and you fly those California guys up to the Porcupine River.''

"No.'' Drew shook his head and sat down at the desk. He'd thought of mentioning Betsy, but not now. If he did, Pete really would think he was too emotional. Well, maybe he was. But he liked to think that love was an emotion that couldn't hurt him. He'd gone to Dawson City with the aim of doing the right thing for his father. Now his feelings for Betsy were just as strong. He didn't see any conflict at all. "I have a better sense of what's going on over there,'' Drew told his brother. "It would take you too much time just to get established. Besides, the Mounties might be disappointed if I don't show up again.''

"Okay, okay.''

"Good, now let's get to work. After I finish here I have to do another thing or two while I'm in town.''

In the afternoon, with the books in order and Pete back on the right track, Drew drove to another part of Fairbanks. He had an address in his pocket. He wanted to see where Jacob Talbot lived.

When he got to his destination, he parked out front and double-checked the address. He'd made a mistake, he thought. He must have written down the wrong number or street when he and Betsy checked the property records.

Still, on the odd chance he was right, he got out of his car and went up the sidewalk. Wait till Betsy hears this, he thought, half chuckling to himself. Who would believe that Talbot lived in a nursing home?

Inside, he saw what he'd expected. Several old people were sitting in the lobby, two of them in wheelchairs. Was putting down this address Talbot's idea of a joke? Drew thought the man was even wackier than he had seemed at first.

Drew decided to go through the motions. He'd come this far. He stepped up to the front desk.

Behind it, a man in a beard wearing a white hospital-type uniform looked up. "May I help you?" he asked.

"I probably have the wrong address," Drew said softly, "but I was wondering if a Jacob Talbot lives here."

"Talbot?" the bearded man barked. "Sorry. No one here by that name."

Drew forced out a weak smile. "Thanks anyway." He'd known from the start that there was no hope.

As he began to walk out of the nursing home, a cane tapped loudly on the floor. "Young man," a woman called after him. "Young man."

Drew turned. A gray-haired woman about eighty years old sat nearby, leaning against her cane, scrutinizing him. "Did I hear someone say Talbot?" she asked.

"Pardon?"

"You'll have to come closer. I can't hear you."

Drew walked back to her. She was wearing a hearing aid. "I was asking about a man named Talbot," Drew said.

"My name used to be Talbot," the woman told him. "Before I was married."

"Really I—"

"I have a famous son," the woman interrupted, scanning Drew from head to foot. "A little taller than you. Very famous. He won lots of awards. I can show you his trophies. Pictures, too, nice pictures.''

Drew was wondering how to extricate himself when the woman got to her feet and scuttled around a corner. "Let me get you a photograph," she shouted back to him.

Seeing no civil alternative, he followed her and waited in an open doorway. Her room was close by, facing the front desk. The bearded man behind it was ignoring him.

The old woman came back to him with a framed eight-by-ten photo. "Here we are. That's my son. The best sky diver in Alaska."

Drew accepted the frame from her. In the old black and white photo a man about Drew's age proudly held up a trophy. He had a parachute strapped on. Great, Drew thought. Another guy who jumped from airplanes. Just what he needed to cloud his mind. But something about the man's face intrigued him. Drew stared at the picture a few seconds before the realization hit.

"This is your son?" Drew asked.

"Oh, yes," the woman said. "My one and only. Very good boy."

"He looks familiar...what's his name now?" Drew tried to keep the excitement from his voice. "Jacob Talbot?"

"Talbot? Of course not," she snapped. "That was mine before I got married. He's Kalen Trent. I'm his mother, Abigail Trent. I named him. I ought to know."

"I can see that you're proud of him," Drew said, trying to calm her.

"Very famous," th woman went on. "I thought you might have heard of Kalen."

"No, I guess I haven't." Drew backed off. "I must have been too little." He checked the photo again. The trophy winner was much younger and had a full head of hair, but there was no doubt in Drew's mind. "It's a good picture," he said. "Thank you very much for showing it to me."

Drew left the nursing home in astonishment. He stopped outside for fresh air and leaned on an iron railing, still absorbing the shock. To his mother the man in the picture was Kalen Trent, but to Drew the sky diver was undeniably Jacob Talbot.

Drew got back into his car and headed to his apartment. He needed to pack more clothes before going back to Dawson City. There was still so much to do for his father. And so much more confusion, so many questions.

Why did Kalen Trent buy the land next to Betsy's under an assumed name? And why did he use his mother's address rather than his own?

On a hunch, Drew stopped at a phone booth and found Kalen Trent's name in the directory. He drove to Trent's place. It was a modest little white house with the curtains shut tight, certainly not the home of a doctor. Drew got out of his car and rang the doorbell.

Of course, there was no answer. Trent was still in Dawson City—with Betsy. Thinking that only made Drew more nervous. He had to get back to Betsy and fast.

Back in his apartment, Drew hurriedly threw together fresh clothes. Maybe he was worrying over nothing, but he couldn't fight off the feeling that he'd left Betsy at the wrong time. He'd finally found the connection he'd been looking for, and he was in no position to do anything about it. And the Mounties couldn't help.

First, he was a suspect, so they wouldn't believe him. And second, the evidence was far from ironclad.

But it was enough for Drew. Trent must be concealing his identity for a good reason, Drew thought. And what better reason than the Red Baron robbery? If Sam had jumped from the plane, it would have been natural for Trent to jump, too. *If* Trent had been on the plane. It was a big *if*. Still, people didn't lie about their names without a cause.

Drew stalked around his apartment, unsure what to conclude and what to do. Trent's appearance at a Red Baron party and his presence now in Dawson City wouldn't mean a thing to the police, Drew realized. They would just see it as an attempt to divert suspicion away from his father, and himself, if he was to go to them with so little.

Drew went to the phone and started to dial his mother, but hung up. This call would only upset her unnecessarily. He'd wait a few more days. Somehow he had faith there would be better news.

But first he had to warn Betsy. She'd already been threatened several times. Drew didn't know if Trent was behind any of it, but he couldn't ignore the possibility.

After phoning Betsy's home and getting no answer, Drew called Yukon Lights. She wasn't there, either, and wasn't expected for hours.

With a gnawing in his gut, Drew drove to the airport and filed a flight plan to Dawson City. Betsy would be waiting for him. If Trent hadn't already done something to her.

WITH THE OTHER THREE LOOKING ON, Betsy crouched beside the stream and scooped up a sample of gravel and water. She was using one of the four worn half-size steel pans she'd brought. They were each two inches deep with a diameter of twelve inches at the top and seven and a half at the bottom. Some people liked the modern plastic pans, but Betsy preferred the traditional steel, which Conrad had used.

She stirred the material in the pan with her hand, breaking up the lumps of rock and dirt. Then she lowered the pan into the stream and let the current carry away the muddy water. The larger rocks she washed, picked out and threw aside. Keeping the pan level and still slightly under water, she moved it vigorously several times left to right and then right to left.

"What I'm doing is stratifying the rocks," she told Laura, Talbot and Harsted. She plucked out more large pieces of gravel and discarded them. "The principle," she said, "is that gold is heavier than the gravel around it and a lot heavier than water. So if the particles are separated, the gold will sink to the bottom."

She rotated her pan, tipping the front edge down to flush lighter bits of gravel back into the stream.

Talbot leaned over her left shoulder. "It could take a long time to get rich this way."

"Well, most people pan for fun now. If you're a serious prospector, you'd probably just do enough panning to find where the gold is, then move in some bigger equipment for the major work."

Talbot dipped a hand into the stream. "It's cold."

Betsy chuckled. It was hard to imagine Talbot trespassing on her land now. He seemed so harmless. "Think about where the water's coming from—the mountains. You'll get more accustomed to the cold, but don't overdo it. Remember to keep water in your pan until you're done, or else the gold can't settle."

"Seems like a lot to keep track of," Greg said.

"I know," Betsy told him. "You won't learn how to do it in five minutes, so just take your time."

She demonstrated some of the finer points of separating ordinary rock from gold and said, "Try working in the eddies and backwaters, where the current slows. There's a good chance that's where the gold settled after being carried downstream. If you find gold here, most of it's likely to be flakes or dust—'color,' it's called. When you get down to a couple of tablespoons of sand, stop and let it dry in the sun. Then you can dump it out on those pieces of cardboard we brought and gently blow away the sand." Betsy reached into a pocket. "Here are some vials and tweezers if you want to pick out the gold flakes. If you think you've found a nugget, sing out and we'll all have a look."

"Finders keepers," Laura joked.

"Hey," Greg said, "if there are any nuggets in this stream, they've got my name on them."

Betsy had to laugh. She turned and looked at Laura and Greg standing on her right. They were as eager as kids.

Too bad Drew wasn't here too, Betsy thought. She wanted to teach him how to pan for gold, to show him more of the Yukon, to share a lot of things. But she had to put him out of her mind for a while. Thinking about him hour after hour wouldn't bring him back any sooner.

"Okay," Betsy said, "let's spread out and see if anyone can strike it rich."

They were on a stream south of Dawson City that fed into the Yukon River. A friend owned the land and let her look for gold whenever she liked. Even so, it wasn't her favorite panning spot, although she had taken a few nuggets there. If she'd been alone, she would have headed north. But she'd wanted to take her gold-panning crew *away* from the Lost Lady Mine and the ravine where Sam McKay's plane had crashed.

Betsy put down her own pan a moment and watched the others. Talbot proved to be such a quick study she had to compliment him. "Nice technique, Jacob. Keep this up and you'll be a pro."

He let out a high-pitched laugh. "Not really. Haven't seen any gold yet."

"Don't worry. It'll come in time."

Betsy turned downstream to Laura and Harsted. Out in the woods, Greg didn't seem so intense or threatening. He was even smiling. Apparently Laura had diverted him, which was good. Whatever Harsted's intentions were, Betsy still didn't want to be interviewed.

Laura and Greg were panning like the novices they were, splashing water almost at random, but Betsy didn't see any point in correcting them and making work of their efforts. As long as they were having fun, she was satisfied.

"How are you two doing?" Betsy shouted to Laura.

"Great. At this rate, we ought to find gold just before Christmas."

"Ho, ho, ho," Greg hollered.

Gradually, at Talbot's suggestion, he and Betsy moved upstream, leaving the area eighty yards below to the other two. An hour passed uneventfully and then Talbot stopped and opened his thermos. "How about some coffee, Betsy?"

"Sure. You go ahead and pour. I want to finish this pan first." Her back to Talbot, Betsy carefully swirled the gravel. She thought she'd found a nugget, but when she picked out the tiny rock in question, she was mistaken. "No luck yet," she said as she dumped the pan out. "Hey, that coffee smells great."

"It's pretty strong," Talbot replied. "Of course, I like it when it's crawling over the sides. Here, try it."

Talbot handed Betsy a steaming cup. She took a sip and shook her head. "Whew, that is strong. How long have you been aging this stuff?"

"It was fresh this morning. I got it at breakfast."

Betsy took another sip. "Must be your thermos then." She glanced at it. Its metal casing was as scratched as her panning gear. "You ought to try some baking soda. Put in a couple of spoonfuls, fill it with water and let it soak overnight. That should freshen things up."

"Good idea," Talbot said. He drank coffee from his cup. "Guess I'm just used to the taste. Do the same thing often enough and you overlook your options."

"Hmm." Betsy tried more coffee and found it just as strong as before, almost bitter. But she drank anyway. There was nothing like a cup of fresh coffee in the woods, the brew's aroma mixing with the clean scent of the trees.

"Options," Talbot continued. "Yes, indeed. Best thing, keep moving, find those options." He looked down the stream at Laura and Harsted. "I like to move around."

"But you keep coming back to Dawson," Betsy said.

"True. You got me there, Betsy. Of course, I am a landowner now. Actually, that forty-acre parcel is about the only thing of value that I do own."

"You're a doctor," she said. "Surely you've been able to make a few investments."

"No, spent almost every penny I've made." He drank more coffee. "Probably moved around too much. I've only been in Whitehorse a few months."

Betsy nodded, remembering part of Drew's mission in Fairbanks, to check out Talbot's address on the property records. "Where were you before?"

"Prince Rupert," he said. "And Kelowna."

"British Columbia?" Betsy brightened. "I grew up in Vancouver. Or did I tell you?"

"I think Conrad did. Anyway, I wasn't there too long, either. Before that it was Montana. Only two things constant in my life. I've always stayed close to mountains and I've always moved north. Started in Colorado."

"I thought you had an American accent," Betsy said.

"No point in hiding it. Coffee any better now?"

"Not really," Betsy said. "I think I'll leave it to you." She tossed out two-thirds of a cup, splashing it on the rocks. "Sorry."

"Well, whatever."

They went back to panning for gold. Laura and Harsted were still below but seemed to be working their way toward her. If they'd found any gold, they were keeping quiet about it. Greg was probably too busy quizzing Laura about her "boss," Betsy thought. It was a good thing she'd found time this morning to warn Laura about what to expect.

Fortunately, Laura had seen no problem. "I've been fending off advances from beer drinkers for years. I can handle a sober reporter with my eyes closed."

Betsy worked steadily without any success. Talbot was panning about ten yards upstream with his head down, not talking. The day was warming and Betsy felt drowsy. She'd skipped breakfast and cut her sleep short to meet the other three early, and now she was paying for it. Talbot's coffee hadn't helped. In another hour, she'd go back to her Bronco and have lunch. After that, they'd pan maybe one more hour and then go home. She could doze a little before work. If she was sleepy on the way to town, Laura could drive.

Betsy swirled gravel around her pan, then stopped, slightly dizzy. She wet a hand in the stream and wiped her brow with the cold water. Maybe she'd have that nap now. But that was ridiculous, she told herself. If you got up at eight-thirty, you didn't nod off at eleven.

She started swirling the pan again, and this time everything swirled with it. She heard her pan bang to the rocks, but her head was still spinning. The pan was right in front of her. Why had she dropped it? She stood up and looked for it. Sighting it, she bent over and reached for it, but it moved away. She reached again, and then there were two pans. Then three, farther out in the stream. She waded out into the cold water and reached again, for all the pans, and lost her balance. She tried to straighten up but her body wouldn't cooperate. *So dizzy, feet so cold. Just want to sleep. Forget the gold. Going to sleep.*

And then she fell into the stream.

Immediately, her head began to ache. She kept it underwater. The cold was a shock, but at least it was reviving her, she thought, bringing her back to her senses. The stream was much deeper than she'd imagined. And so fast. She'd have to get up. What would the others think? She was supposed to be the guide, showing them how to do things.

She raised her head above the water and gasped for air. Talbot was beside her.

"Pull me out," she yelled.

He gripped her around the waist and then, inexplicably, let go. Her head went back into the water and she panicked. She was going to drown in a little stream and never see Drew again. She flailed in the water and brought her head up one more time. Talbot was still there, somehow unable to save her. She managed to work herself onto a rock, but her legs were cold and limp, holding her down. Again she was dizzy. And nauseous. She was going to pass out.

Betsy heard voices: "Damn it, help her," a man said. Then another man said, "I tried. Couldn't hang on."

Then suddenly she was out of the water and being hoisted to dry ground. Talbot—no, it was Harsted. He laid her down and Laura threw a jacket over her.

"Betsy," Laura said. "Are you okay?"

"Got so dizzy..."

"No water in the lungs," Talbot said, "but she's got a bad bump on her head."

"I can see that," Harsted snapped. "Why didn't you pull her out?"

"Like I said, I tried," Talbot said, "but I've got a bad back. It just froze up the moment I got a hold. I—"

"Never mind," Greg said. "Your bad back won't keep you from checking her out, will it, Doctor?"

"No, of course not."

"Then go to it."

Betsy shivered.

"She has a blanket in the truck," Laura said. "I'll go get it."

Harsted stood by while Talbot checked Betsy's head, pressing various spots and peering into her eyes and mouth. "Just the one bump," Talbot said. "You feeling better now?"

Betsy looked up and brought his face into focus. "Some." She paused. "What happened?"

"I don't know yet. Do you hurt anywhere else?"

"No, I'm...stomach sick...weak, sleepy."

"Did you eat breakfast this morning?"

Betsy had trouble thinking. "Didn't . . . have time."

"That's probably it then," Talbot said. "Blood sugar got too low. Without any medical equipment here, I couldn't say for sure, but I can't find anything else wrong."

"Well, no more gold panning today," Harsted said.

"Right," Talbot said. "She needs to rest."

Betsy agreed with that but was too weak to say so.

Laura came running back. "Here's the blanket."

"Good." Talbot took it and wrapped it around Betsy. "We've got to keep her warm."

Betsy was still wet but the chill was wearing off. She usually took a blanket when she went panning, as a precaution. She'd put it in the Bronco only that morning.

"Where's her lunch?" Harsted asked Laura.

"In the truck."

"She's got to eat a little," Harsted said.

"I can go get the food," Laura volunteered.

"Take me home," Betsy said.

"What do you think, Doc?" Harsted looked at Talbot. "Can she move?"

"She shouldn't walk. Not yet."

"Then I'll carry her."

"No," Betsy said.

"Betsy." Laura took her hand. "Don't argue."

Too weak to protest further, Betsy let Harsted carry her to the Bronco. She wished he were Drew.

Once there, Harsted made her eat a few bites of her sandwich and drink a little juice. Afterward, she felt slightly better but still woozy. She gave Laura the ignition key, and sat in the back with Talbot.

Laura drove fast and straight to Betsy's house.

"No offense to Dr. Talbot," Harsted said when they got there, "but I think you should see a local MD, Betsy. Have a few tests, an X ray or something."

"I agree," Laura said. "You look pretty shaken up." Betsy got out of the Bronco on her own and unlocked her front door. "I'll be okay. It's probably what Dr. Talbot said about my skipping breakfast. I just need to eat."

"All right, but only if you promise to call the doctor," Laura said. "But why not take the night off. Rest up. I'll tell the crew they'll have to get along without you."

"Thanks, Laura."

"Okay, talk to you later."

Betsy waved goodbye to Laura, Talbot and Harsted and then went inside. She poured milk and got out crackers. That would ease her stomach, she thought. But as she tried to eat, she only got dizzy and nauseous again.

Betsy decided she was too cold so she went into the bedroom to change out of her wet clothes. She sat on the bed, fighting to keep her balance. Reaching for the buttons of her blouse, her fingers fumbled and fell away. She dropped back on the bed, her body at an angle. *So sleepy. Just a few minutes' rest before* . . .

## Chapter Ten

Drew banked his plane between the mountains. Dawson City spread below him, a colorful patchwork. The Klondike and Yukon rivers wound around it like glistening snakes. Somewhere down there was the loveliest woman he'd ever seen. And not far away was Kalen Trent, a chameleon who gave Drew a sick, suspicious feeling in the pit of his gut.

A crisscross of streets and buildings, and finally the airstrip, lifted to meet Drew. Within seconds, the plane touched pavement. He taxied to a parking spot, secured the plane and got a ride into town. Soon he was in front of Betsy's home. The tiny wooden building already seemed like a refuge to him. But it wasn't the house, it was the woman who lived inside. *She* was the shelter, the love in his life, the excitement. He'd missed Betsy even more than he'd imagined. One night alone in Fairbanks had been too long.

Drew climbed the steps, knocked on the front door, then waited for Betsy to answer. It was almost evening. If she wasn't home, she was probably at Yukon Lights. When she didn't respond, he rapped once more. He was ready to head for the club when shuffling noises told him she was home. Finally, the door cracked open.

"Drew." Betsy peeked outside, then opened the door more. "I'm so glad you're back," she said sleepily. "Was everything all right in Fairbanks? What did you find out about Talbot?"

"My God, what's happened to you?" Drew ignored her questions. He was stunned. Betsy's hair was flattened against her head, her jeans and blouse were dirty and damp, and she'd draped a blanket haphazardly around her shoulders.

"I'm all right. I've been taking a nap," she said softly. Her shoulders quivered.

"No, somethings's wrong." Drew quickly pulled her inside and shut the door. Betsy's normally glowing skin was pale, the whites of her eyes a glassy pink.

"It's all so weird." Betsy leaned back against the wall. She threaded one hand through her hair. "It was quite an afternoon. I feel a little dizzy now, that's all. I was lying down and got up too fast. I'll be better in a minute."

Drew frowned. He could see that Betsy was chilled and needed dry clothes, but that would have to wait. She was about to collapse. "Let's sit down." He guided her onto the living room sofa and tucked the blanket around her. When he was sure she was comfortable, he knelt on the floor beside her. "Better?"

She nodded, but he wasn't sure he believed her. He studied her several seconds, then said. "You're sick and exhausted. What did you do today?"

Betsy sighed. "Nothing much, really. I went gold panning—with Jacob Talbot, Greg Harsted and Laura Bertino, one of my waitresses. Talbot has been pestering me to go, then Harsted decided to join us. I invited Laura so I wouldn't be alone. We didn't find gold. All I got was a little wet." She lifted one leg and brushed her hand against clammy denim. "I slipped into the stream. Guess I was too tired to get out of my wet things when I got home."

"I see." As Drew thought about Kalen Trent with Betsy in the woods, his skin began to crawl. Harsted being along didn't please him much, either. A real cozy party. And he was out of town. Drew tried hard to stay calm. "Tell me how you slipped."

Betsy tightened the blanket. "It was so silly. I've panned there before. I know those rapids, those boulders. We had coffee. Then I got light-headed. Probably because I didn't eat any breakfast this morning. That's what Talbot diagnosed anyway. For once, I was glad to have a doctor close by."

*If he really is a doctor,* Drew thought. He could still see Trent's shabby house in Fairbanks, and the old woman in the nursing home who was so proud of her sky diver son. As far as Drew was concerned, Trent was a fraud. Drew touched Betsy's cheek. "I should never have left you."

Betsy pushed upright. "I'm all right. Really." She paused. "I missed you though."

"Not as much as I missed you." He gathered both her hands in his. Her palms were cold and he rubbed them, trying to transfer some of his own warmth. "Betsy, this probably won't make much sense to you, but please try to recall the entire day. I want to know everything that happened out at the stream. Can you do that?"

"Hey, stop worrying," she said firmly, exhibiting more strength. "I've already lived through a totally miserable afternoon. The last thing I want to do is rehash it. Let's do something special—celebrate your return to Dawson." She started to get up, but paused when Drew tightened his hold on her fingers.

"Listen to me, Betsy. You don't know what I do. Your accident might have been...planned." There, Drew thought, he'd said it. He waited for her reaction.

"What are you talking about?" Betsy yanked her hands away. "Of course it was an accident. How could it have been anything else? I fell in. Harsted fished me out."

"Humor me," Drew said softly. "Please. Tell me what happened."

Betsy finally agreed. When she told him how she'd refused to see a local doctor and then how she'd apparently, collapsed on her bed, Drew felt even more convinced that Trent was up to no good. He also knew he should be grateful to Harsted for saving her, but somehow he couldn't muster much appreciation for him, either. He just didn't care for the guy. His real concern was for Betsy. *I could have lost her today,* he thought. The close call made his blood almost freeze.

Betsy tipped her face. "It's Talbot you're worried about, isn't it? Enough of my problems. What did you find out in Fairbanks?"

Drew swallowed. "Well, for starters I don't think he's been honest with you. This is going to be a shock, but his name isn't Jacob Talbot. It's Kalen Trent. And I don't think he's a doctor." Drew told Betsy about the nursing home, and about the house he'd found at Trent's listed Fairbanks address. When he'd finished, Betsy slumped back against the sofa cushions. She looked even more pale and Drew wondered if he'd been wise to tell her.

"Jacob Talbot lied to me...and to Grandpa," she whispered. "As far as I know, he's always gone by Talbot. Why would he change his name? And what does any of this have to do with this afternoon?"

Drew shrugged. "I just don't trust him, that's all. He turns up and you have trouble. Maybe he's the one responsible for those threats, too. And your break-in."

"I can't believe this. It's just too farfetched. I really don't even know the man." Betsy stared beyond Drew, at the far wall, and he could see the horror of the implication slowly sink in. Finally, she turned her gaze back to him. "Drew, I'm worried. If you're right, the only thing he could be after is the mineral rights to his land. But why, after all these years? They're probably worthless."

"I wish I knew." Drew was solemn. "But he's far more complicated than we realize, and I don't like you being with him. He could be dangerous."

Betsy sighed. "Nothing seemed unusual today until I got dizzy and slipped. I'm a strong swimmer. Lord, if it weren't for Harsted, I might not even be here right now."

"I know." Drew's voice was low. "And that scares the hell out of me."

Betsy hadn't been part of his life very long, but Drew already couldn't imagine that life without her. Even now she was like a vision to him, soft and vulnerable. He couldn't help smiling. Betsy was studying him. She had to know how he felt about her, and to sense how much he wanted her. He laid one hand on her blanket-wrapped leg. He longed for their world to be perfect, but how could he make that world for her when his own was in such a shambles? "If Trent really is dangerous," he finally said, "I think the police have to be told. Not that they've done much to help us so far."

Betsy gripped his wrists. "No, we have to keep this to ourselves. Think how crazy we'd sound to them. Flinging around accusations like matchsticks. We haven't any proof. And they already suspect you of God knows what. We have to let the Mounties work this out on their own. She crossed her arms and a shiver coursed down her body.

Drew felt her legs tremble. "Betsy, I've been a fool to keep you here. I'll run you a warm bath. You have to get out of those clothes or you'll catch your death. I'll go back to my hotel if you want."

Betsy suddenly leaned forward and brushed her lips seductively against his. "I need you now, more than ever. Don't you dare leave."

Drew's mouth went dry. The emerald of her eyes was deepening even as he watched. Slowly, she rose and walked across the room to her bedroom. The languid, loving look she cast over her shoulder answered at least one of his myriad questions. That night they would really be together.

BETSY WRAPPED A FLUFFY TOWEL around herself. The warm bath had been just what she needed. She felt revived and excited, the dizziness and the memory of the horrid events of the day quickly melting into haze. The man she loved was beyond the bedroom door. How many times she'd longed for him, hungered for the taste, the scent, the feel, the very sight of him. She wanted him and had realized, time after time, how patient and kind he really was. Loving him now would be her gift. She prayed he would accept it.

She slipped into her silken bathrobe and, filled with determination, entered the living room. Drew was sitting on the sofa with his back to her. She dropped down behind him and threaded her arms about his neck. His hair was fine behind his ears and she touched it with her cheek.

Drew grasped her wrist, then turned her palm upward and kissed it. "Feel better now?"

"Much better." The warmth of Drew's breath, the tenderness of his lips made her heart skip. She leaned closer and brushed his ear with the tip of her nose.

His grip on her arm tightened. "I want you, Betsy. You know that, don't you?"

"I know that I want you to love me."

"Betsy... Betsy." He stood, then moved around the sofa to stand in front of her. "Think about what you're asking. I need you in my life. I love you. But I never do anything halfway."

She lifted her chin. "Hey, mister, neither do I." Her breath quickened when she saw the adoring, exciting way his gaze glided over her body. She'd probably known that he loved her. He'd shown her many times. But hearing him say it now warmed her soul.

"Lady, you're lovely." He opened his arms and gathered her to him. "Too lovely for words," he whispered into her hair.

"Then don't talk. Listen to me." With one finger, she slowly traced each button on his shirt, then unfastened it. "I...love...you," she murmured. Then Drew's shirt was open. Betsy trailed her fingertips across fine black curls and firm muscle. When she lifted her face, Drew's eyes were half-closed, but the look of pure pleasure on his features made her blood surge.

"What you do to me," he whispered. His eyes had darkened to glittering navy. When he brought his mouth to hers, his lips were firm and demanding. Betsy leaned into him, savoring his strength and his desire. She could feel her own excitement building, like an arrow tightening on a bowstring.

Then Drew pulled back, and Betsy felt suddenly cheated, as if part of her had just been snatched away. Before she could respond, Drew bent and easily lifted her. He carried her into the bedroom and placed her on the bed. Knowing that this was her moment, Betsy wanted to cherish it. She settled into the soft comforter. Light, from the rapidly setting sun, filtered from the living room, silhouetting Drew as he stood above her. She'd imagined him like this, masculine and gentle. He would love her and she would return that love a hundredfold.

Silently, he undid his shirt. Taut muscles flexed in the subdued light. A few more tugs and Drew stood bare before her. He was strong and solid, and the sight of his need for her sent a charge of molten warmth through her. Without taking her eyes from his, she slowly undid the belt of her robe. The shimmering fabric fell away and she heard Drew's intake of breath at her own nakedness.

"You're a dream," he murmured. He lowered himself beside her. "A treasure. Let me love you the way you deserve to be loved."

Betsy sighed with pleasure when Drew kissed first one breast, then the other. He ignited every inch of her, teasing each hardened nipple. Delight rippled through her as his fingers and tongue played a circular rhythm across her body. She strained to meet him, wonderfully aware of the tingling warmth quickly building below her belly.

"You're pretty good at this," Betsy whispered. His flesh was clean-smelling, warm and smooth, like velvety steel. She was ready for him now, knowing instinctively that he would lift her even higher.

Drew smiled. "I'm inspired, lady. Truly inspired." With one finger he caressed her forehead, her nose, her upturned chin. Then he followed with his lips, first hovering, then searing, dropping across her breasts, to her abdomen, then lower still, fine-tuning Betsy's excitement like the strings of a violin.

Betsy cried out in ecstasy. Drew wasn't the first man who'd ever touched her, but she'd never known such rapture before. Wave after electrical wave broke across her body until she thought she could bear no more. Almost blindly, she reached for Drew, reveling in his hardness.

Drew groaned and paused above her, his facial expression a wonderful fusion of love and passion. Betsy shifted beneath him and he entered her...slowly...tenderly...maddeningly. Betsy closed her eyes and moved with this man she loved, his excitement fueling her own. Higher and higher they both soared, until Drew tensed, then cried out; until something like the sun exploded in Betsy's head. Her body shivered with satisfaction while the sun's fragments shimmered and fell around her.

When Drew gently kissed her lips, Betsy half opened her eyes. "I'm in heaven," he whispered. "Thanks to you."

Betsy smiled and nuzzled into Drew, and his arm came protectively around her. She felt good with him, her body and spirit warm and sheltered. He'd made her forget the crazy world beyond her front door. Her fulfillment was absolute, and she knew she needed this man more than life itself.

BETSY ROLLED ONTO HER BACK and gazed at Drew sleeping on the bed beside her. The room was almost dark. Several hours must have passed since they'd made love and she had dozed. She studied Drew's peaceful, upturned face as moonlight cast his nose and cheekbones into shadowy angles. She couldn't remember ever being this happy. As she watched, his mouth slanted into a blissful smile, and she wondered at her own good fortune.

Drew shifted lazily and half opened his eyes. "Hi."

"Hi."

"What are you thinking?"

"About us," she murmured. "And about how good I feel."

"That's what it's all about, lady." He ran his thumb along the curve of her cheek. "You're so beautiful. I'm a lucky man."

Betsy languidly stretched beside him. Then the doorbell rang, startling her.

"Wonderful timing." Drew slid across the mattress and hurriedly dressed. "I'll get it. Maybe it's one of your employees. Or Trent, with another of his schemes."

Betsy bundled the comforter around her and watched Drew disappear into the living room. She heard him open the door, then the sound of a familiar male voice. It was Constable Selkirk. She jumped up, shrugged into her bathrobe and went to meet him.

"Miss Archer." Selkirk stepped around Drew. "I want to talk with you. I was out on my beat and thought it would be better to see you in person. Someone at your club told me you would probably be at home. Sorry if I've come at a bad time." He assessed Betsy's bathrobe.

"No problem." The stiff expression on the Mountie's face told Betsy he knew her relationship with Drew had escalated and that he didn't approve. And that made her mad. What she did, and with whom, was none of

Selkirk's business, but she forced herself to be civil. "What can I help you with? Have you found out anything about my burglary or those threats?"

Selkirk cleared his throat. "Yes. The test results have come back on the stains on that sketch you brought in. We thought you'd sleep better tonight if you knew it wasn't real blood. It was stage makeup."

Betsy's eyes widened.

"As you know," Selkirk said, "there aren't too many places around Dawson City that use that stuff."

Betsy shifted nervously. She didn't have to be told that Yukon Lights was one of them. "I see. You don't have any idea who left the sketch? That's the scary part."

Selkirk shook his head. "Not yet. But we will get to the bottom of it, too."

"What about the Red Baron case?" Drew asked.

Selkirk turned to him. "We're still looking for more money, or any other evidence...or remains. But we don't have any leads on your father."

Drew was silent. Betsy could see that Selkirk's mention of Sam McKay had upset him. "I've never seen so many people in town," she said quickly. "Some of them must be trying to claim the reward. If they're out in the hills, they're probably hampering your search, Constable." Now Selkirk seemed uncomfortable, Betsy thought.

"We try to do our best no matter what the conditions, Miss Archer," he said. "A lot of townspeople are helping us. But sometimes it does get wild out there. Considering what's already happened to you, Miss Archer, you should still be careful." He eyed Drew again.

"She *is* being careful," Drew answered. "She's doing the best she can. Sometimes events are beyond control."

Selkirk blinked. "You're right about that. By the way, hope you had a good flight to Fairbanks."

Betsy's pulse jumped. Here was more proof that the Mounties were still keeping track of Drew.

"It was fair," Drew answered. "Business obligations needed to be settled."

"I see. Well, that's about it." Before Selkirk turned toward the door, he gave Drew one more meaningful glance. "I'll let you two get back to your evening."

Selkirk left the door open and Drew slid one arm, protectively, around Betsy's waist as they watched the constable disappear down the street. Drew closed the door, then softly kissed her forehead. "Don't worry, Betsy," he said. "No one can hurt us. Not when we have each other."

Betsy smiled halfheartedly. Drew seemed so strong, so sure of himself. But she was anything but sure.

"THIS PLACE IS CROWDED." Drew scanned the busy restaurant. "There must be somewhere else close by still serving breakfast."

Betsy looked around at scurrying waitresses and boisterous customers. Madeline's Café wasn't usually this busy at ten on Sunday morning, and few of the patrons were regulars. Betsy hadn't slept well after Selkirk had left, so breakfast out had sounded appealing. Now she didn't think so.

"Hey, Betsy, Drew. Over here."

A familiar voice from the far side of the room made Betsy spin around. Greg Harsted, alone at a table near a window, was waving to attract their attention.

"Not Harsted," Drew moaned. "I don't think I can face him on an empty stomach."

Betsy nudged his waist. "I know, but he did pull me out of the stream yesterday."

Drew looked resigned. "All right. But only because he's hoarding the only vacant seats in the place."

They crossed the restaurant. Greg pulled out a chair for Betsy as they approached.

"Morning, both of you. I'm almost finished. There's no reason why you shouldn't have this table." He nodded at Drew, then turned to Betsy. "How are you feeling?" he asked. "Since we dropped you off yesterday, I've been worried as hell. You gave me quite a scare."

Betsy sat down and smiled. "I'm fine now. No more dizziness. Guess it'll teach me to eat three square meals, right? I really can't thank you enough for what you did."

Greg waved one hand. "Don't give it another thought. Just remember when you're ready to talk about the plane crash, I'm the man you want to see. Room 210, the Double River Inn. Don't forget. That goes for both of you." He looked at Drew. "I'm sorry about your father. The cops are working so hard that things are bound to crack soon. And there must be personal things about your father you'd like to share, stuff I can't get from the police. Don't rush into anything, but my series of stories on the Red Baron robbery could land us a Pulitzer."

"Forget it, Harsted. I have nothing to say about my dad to you...or anyone." Drew's blue eyes cooled to ice. "By the way, have you seen Jacob Talbot this morning?"

"No, I haven't." Greg's face went blank, as if a curtain had been drawn across it. He carefully folded his napkin. "I mean, how should I know where he is? I don't keep track of him."

"No, of course you don't." Drew said flatly. "I just thought since you two were together yesterday... gold panning... you might have seen him today."

"Sorry, can't help you there." Greg seemed agitated. He looked at his watch. "Hey, I've got to get to the Mounties. Hanging out in front of their station, waiting for crumbs, seems to be all I ever do. See you around." He stood, threw down a tip, grabbed his camera gadget bag and walked off. He paid the cashier quickly and hurried outside without looking back.

Betsy peered after him, wondering why he'd acted so oddly when Drew had mentioned Talbot, or Trent, or whatever name the other man was going by today. Harsted and Trent had gotten along so well the day before.

"Coffee?" A waitress with a steaming pot interrupted Betsy's speculation. She nodded at the woman.

"Make it two," Drew said. He waited until the waitress had filled their cups and left, then shifted forward. "There's really something about Harsted I don't like. And it's not just because he's a pushy reporter." He frowned. "It's something else. I wish I could put my finger on it."

Betsy lifted her coffee cup. "I know. You were testing him about Trent." She took a sip, then absently looked though the window. People were beginning to fill the sidewalks. She drank more coffee and put the cup down. Then she saw Harsted and frowned.

"Drew, look what's happening now," she whispered. A small car pulled alongside Harsted, then stopped. Kalen Trent sat behind the wheel and Harsted hurried to the car, as if he'd been expecting the older man.

As they watched, the men gestured and appeared to argue. Several cars backed up behind them and honked. Harsted hesitated, then climbed into the car's front seat beside Trent. Trent gunned the engine and the car sped away.

"What was that all about?" Betsy asked. Drew was sitting stone-still, his face an unreadable mask. The gentle, sensitive man she'd held in her arms and made love with mere hours before had disappeared.

"I don't know what we just saw," he finally said. "But I don't think Harsted was asking Trent for a lift to the police station. Something's going on between them. And since we already know Trent's a two-bit phony, where does that put our reporter friend?"

Betsy swallowed. "I don't know."

After breakfast, she said, "Drew, I have to look at a phone book. I should have done it a long time ago."

"What is it?" Drew was already on his feet.

"I want to check the list of doctors in Whitehorse."

"You already know Trent won't be in there."

"We have to be sure." Betsy grabbed her purse and headed to the phone at the back of the café.

Two minutes later, they walked outside. Drew had been right, Betsy thought. Kalen Trent wasn't listed as a doctor. Neither was Jacob Talbot. There was only one phone book for the entire Yukon Territory, and neither name was in it anywhere. Of course, he'd said he hadn't lived in Whitehorse long. She leaned against a building, her mind whirling. Who was this man who had bought Tom Fioretti's land? What did he want with her? And what kind of business was he doing in Dawson City?

Drew edged behind Betsy and pulled her against him. "This whole business makes me mad." His voice was strained. "How can the Mounties suspect me when a fool like Trent is running around free as a bird?"

Betsy spun around. "We're not going to take it anymore. We're going to do something. How brave do you feel?"

"It depends. Why?"

She flattened her lips. "We know Harsted's room number. Maybe Trent's staying in the same hotel. It's obvious they're together now. Let's search their rooms. I'd like to know what kind of notes Harsted's been taking, and what Trent's occupation really is. Are you game?"

"I like the sound of it. But I've never been good at breaking and entering." Drew grinned. "It *is* against the law, you know."

Betsy touched his arm. "Just think of it as helping the police. Come on."

Together, Betsy and Drew walked the four blocks to the Double River Inn. They asked at the desk for Talbot's room number and got it. He was three doors down from Harsted's room, which they had no trouble finding. They were even luckier when they discovered a maid working on the floor—a woman Betsy didn't know. Summer help probably. Drew pretended that he was the room's occupant and that he'd misplaced his key. Only after the maid had unlocked Greg's door, and Betsy and Drew were safely inside, did they relax a bit and look around.

"I can't believe we're doing this," Drew muttered. He wiped his hands on his jeans, then pulled open the nightstand drawer. "Nothing in here but the Gideon."

Betsy turned in a slow circle. Greg's suitcase was closed on the bed. Several shirts and a jacket hung in the closet. The desk was covered with the tools of his trade—

notebooks, film, tape cassettes, a street map of Dawson City. She headed for the dresser and slid open a drawer. Greg had placed a couple of pairs of trousers inside and she ran her fingers between them.

"Drew," she whispered. "Something's here." A small, but heavy, cardboard box was in the back. She pulled it out.

Drew was instantly beside her. The box was clearly labeled as .45-caliber bullets. He took it from her and flipped open the lid. "Eight or nine are missing, I'd say." He fished through the rest of the drawer. "But no gun. Our friend Harsted probably has it on him."

Betsy stared at the bullets, unable to stop her shoulders from shaking. "Why would he need a gun?"

Drew returned the ammo to its hiding place. "Maybe for the same reason you carry one. What was that? The law of the wild?"

"Drew, don't tease. Not about that." Betsy wrapped her arms around her waist. "I have a horrible feeling that someone might really get hurt."

Drew didn't answer. He'd taken a small packet of envelopes from another part of the drawer. They were secured with a rubber band and he slowly thumbed through them. When he spoke his voice was taut. "Betsy, what was your grandfather's name again?"

Betsy's spine stiffened. "Conrad Parks. Why?"

"Take a look at these." Drew handed her the packet.

Betsy's heart hammered. The letter on top was addressed to Conrad.

"Oh, my God," she said slowly. She lifted her face, her eyes wide. "Grandpa's letters. It was Harsted who broke into my garage."

# Chapter Eleven

"Incredible," Betsy said, dropping into a chair and shaking her head. "The man will go to any length to get his newspaper story."

Drew bent in front of her and squeezed her knees. "At least we won't have any more illusions about Harsted."

"The typed note. Do you think he did that, too?" Betsy pushed back her hair and stood up. "He's an idiot if he thinks I can be scared into giving him an interview."

"You're not going to be scared into anything," Drew said.

Betsy wound her arms around his neck. How good he felt. If only this Red Baron mess would disappear so she could really enjoy this wonderful man. Despite her vision of a tranquil future, Betsy couldn't ignore these repeated threats. Harsted obviously was a Red Baron expert, but something about laying all the blame on him troubled her. She spoke softly. "Harsted couldn't have drawn the sketch of the medallion, though. He's never seen the back of it."

"I was wondering about that," Drew said.

Betsy sighed. And there's the stage makeup. Where could he have found that?"

"He broke into your garage," Drew said. "Why couldn't he have gone into Yukon Lights when no one was looking and swiped the stuff from one of the dressing rooms? If some of your actors came up missing a little makeup, they might just think it had been misplaced and never mention it."

"You could be right." She stood and went to the window. The rest of Dawson City seemed vibrant, unaware of their problems. "Maybe he did steal some makeup. But he *did* save my life yesterday. He can't be all bad."

"He's trying to persuade you."

Betsy turned away from the window. "Then his tactics are way off base. I've never done anything to him. And why does a reporter in search of the so-called truth hang around with Trent? That man's a proven liar."

"I don't know," Drew said. "But we can't stay here debating the issue. Harsted could have seen you in the window just now." Drew quickly began replacing the letters in the drawer. "We can't let him know we've been here. Burglary's a serious offense. He took these letters because he was looking for something specific."

"But what?"

"I'm not sure. But I've made some calculations on the flight path of Dad's Cessna. If I'm right, then it went directly over your cabin. And if Trent parachuted, with or without Dad, then the two million bucks could be near there."

Betsy's jaw dropped. Trent had bought Tom's land nine years ago. The timing was right. "Are you telling me Kalen Trent was one of the Red Baron robbers, and that he's stashed the loot near Lost Lady?"

Drew shrugged. "It's speculation, I know, but it makes perfect sense to me. There's something out there important enough to make Harsted desperate enough to steal your grandfather's letters. He could have made the same calculations I did. And if he knows about your grandfather and the cabin, then he probably thinks your grandfather knew about the money."

Betsy could think of little else but Trent. "Kalen Trent—a Red Baron robber. Oh, Drew, it makes perfect sense. But it's ridiculous to think Grandpa knew anything about it. He certainly would have gone to the police."

"You know that, but Harsted doesn't. So he decided to investigate. Harsted doesn't care about your grandpa. All he wants is a great story."

"That still doesn't explain the threats."

"Look, I wouldn't be surprised at anything Harsted would do." Drew pushed the dresser drawer shut and studied the room. "Okay. Everything in place?"

Betsy smoothed the bedspread. "I think so."

"We can't be too careful," Drew said. "As far as I'm concerned, Harsted's as dangerous as Trent. He's got a gun and he's no fool. Damn it, Betsy, I'm tired of playing games with your life. And I'm getting nervous. Come on, let's get out of here."

They stepped into the hall. As they rushed down the stairs, Betsy felt safer. Until she got to the lobby.

A man was standing with his back to them, and they almost bumped into him.

Betsy said, "Excuse me," and he turned around. It was Greg Harsted.

She murmured a greeting, then they hurried toward the street. Drew stopped at the entrance and looked over her shoulder. Harsted was bolting up the stairs.

"That was close," Betsy said.

"He's going to his room," Drew told her. "He shouldn't notice a thing. Let's just walk and act natural."

Betsy's legs went rubbery, but she kept pace with Drew. "I think it's too late. We weren't very *natural* just now. He knew something was up."

"You're right," Drew said. "And we can't go to Trent's room now. If Harsted's hanging around, Trent could be close by."

Betsy glanced down the block. They were nearing the RCMP station. "More reporters," Betsy muttered. "Let's cross the street."

Drew took her hand and they walked in silence until they were out of sight of Harsted's hotel and the RCMP station. "What if your grandfather knew more than he thought? He could have made a note about a parachute or plane or something without understanding what it meant. Maybe that's what Harsted was looking for in the letters."

"There's a chance, I guess. And we've stashed everything else at the cabin. Maybe we should drive out. If there's anything vital there, I'd like to find it before Harsted or Trent does."

Drew agreed. They jogged back to Betsy's house. She went inside alone a moment and opened her nightstand drawer. Underneath her lacy nightgown was Conrad's .38. She'd taken it out of her shoulder bag after the incident with Drew on Midnight Dome, but the situation was different now. She picked up the gun and hesitated, thinking Drew might object. Finally, she stuffed it into her bag and went out to the Bronco.

When she started the engine, the fuel gauge didn't budge. Despite their impatience, they had to get gas.

A little more than an hour later, they arrived at the cabin. But Betsy was afraid they were already too late. They'd wasted so much time. The front door was ajar. She looked around for a car but saw nothing. She didn't see a plane on the lake, either. They would have to be very, very careful.

"It might be a hunter," she whispered to Drew as they quietly got out of the Bronco.

"I doubt it."

At the front of the cabin, they stopped and Betsy pointed to the old padlock. It had been blown apart. Drew grimaced, but crept inside anyhow. The trapdoor yawned open. Drew put a finger to his lips, motioning Betsy to stay quiet as they converged on the hole in the old wooden floor.

Light emerged from the tunnel. Compelled to find out who was there, Betsy suppressed the pounding in her chest and peeked over the edge. Harsted was kneeling beside the boxes Betsy had taken so much care to hide, riffling through Conrad's papers, scattering them carelessly in the dirt. She reached out and took Drew's hand, but was too late to prevent her gasp.

Startled, Harsted jerked up his head. His receding hairline emphasized the wideness of his eyes. He froze for an instant, like a badger caught in the headlights of a car, then jumped to his feet and grabbed a pistol from the floor.

Drew lunged forward, as if to jump down the tunnel on top of Harsted, but Betsy grabbed him. "Drew, don't!"

Drew stopped and glared at Harsted, who'd doused his flashlight and stuck it in his pocket. He was beginning to climb up the ladder, one hand still aiming the gun at them. "That's right, McKay," he said. "Do what the lady tells you. No point in getting yourself shot up."

Betsy and Drew backed away as Harsted rose through the trapdoor hole.

"What are you doing with my grandfather's letters?" Betsy asked. She was so angry she didn't know what to say. "You're trespassing—you have no right to be here."

Harsted stood tall above the tunnel now, wagging the long nose of his pistol at Betsy and Drew. The gun was an automatic, bigger than her .38. She figured it had to use the .45-caliber bullets they'd found in Harsted's room. "No right?" he snorted. "Is that all you care about?"

"No, I—"

"Forget the stupid letters," Harsted told her, then spit down the tunnel on them. "They're worthless. Nothing but sentimental garbage."

Betsy wanted to punch him out. Earlier, she had restrained Drew, but this time he held her back. When she stepped toward Harsted, Drew grasped her around the shoulders, suppressing her rage until common sense prevailed. She couldn't fight an automatic .45.

"Easy, little lady." Harsted laughed. "The gold in that medallion you're wearing is a lot more valuable than any of those papers."

"You broke into my garage," Betsy said. "You stole those letters we found—"

"In *my* hotel room? Ha! Who was trespassing then?" Harsted had Betsy and Drew right where he wanted them. "I didn't steal those letters. Talbot did. I just borrowed them to see why he found them so interesting. Too bad there was nothing in them."

"Talbot stole them?" Betsy gritted her teeth. She remembered that he'd also snooped in her office.

Drew tightened his hold on Betsy and squinted at Harsted. "If the letters in Parks's shoe box were worthless, then why'd you come out here?"

"Because I drove out behind you two a couple of days ago. Hid in the woods and watched the little lady carry in those big boxes all by herself. Figured she might be stashing the important stuff."

"So it wasn't my imagination," Drew said, remembering the snap of the twig.

"You could have broken in then," Betsy said.

"Yeah, but that was before my room was searched, before I realized that you thought the papers might be important."

"And I thought you were a reporter after a hot story. Was it all just a scam?" Drew glared at him.

"I *am* a reporter," Harsted thundered. "One of the best. You don't see any of those other toadies working all the angles like me, do you? That's because Greg Harsted is always first. But nobody cares, see. Nobody but me. That's why I'm going to take this Red Baron loot. And I don't need Talbot to help me. Enough of these penny ante awards these so-called journalists win. Two million ought to set me up nicely. No more drudgery, no more articles about idiots."

"So it's going to be early retirement for you," Drew said. "Going for the last laugh?"

"You got it. Kind of makes you envious, doesn't it?"

Drew didn't answer.

"There's only one problem," Harsted said with a burst of disgust. "I can't find the money."

"Then why don't you get out of my cabin and leave us alone?" Betsy asked.

"No way." Harsted edged sideways until he was between the door and Betsy. "I can't take chances. Not with your buddy Talbot still around," he said.

"He's *not* my friend," Betsy said.

"He would be if you were smart," Harsted said. "You know why? He might not know where the money is, but he's one of the Red Baron robbers."

"Just like I thought," Drew said to Betsy.

"Did you, McKay? When did you figure it out? Just now? I noticed him in Fairbanks a couple of weeks ago, looking over library microfilm of old newspapers. He was reading the accounts of the robbery over and over, so proud of his exploits that he's gone wacky. Then you and I bumped into him outside that Red Baron party. Remember? I knew something was screwy then, but I wasn't sure until he turned up in Dawson City."

"Then he really *is* the one," Betsy said.

"Damn right he's the one," Harsted said. "I thought he would lead me to the cash, but he hasn't cooperated. I made a deal to keep his criminal identity secret if I could get a fifty-fifty split. He said the money was out here in the hills. Had me playing a silly game of buried treasure. Flying him around, poking holes in the ground. But Talbot's so loony I think he's forgotten where he put it."

Betsy had a flash of insight. "So you were digging across the lake with him. You were flying the float-plane."

"Hmmph. Yeah, I've got a pilot's license. He was pulling my strings, all right. But I figured there had to be a better way."

"Like what?" Drew asked.

"Those letters." Harsted nodded toward the tunnel. "I thought they might offer a clue about the money."

"How?" Betsy demanded.

A muscle twitched under Harsted's right eye. "I thought there would be a map to this old mine Talbot kept mumbling about. Figured that's why he wanted those letters so bad. But it's all a hoax," he said nervously.

A hoax? Betsy's mind scrambled. Trent knew about the mine. He was just trying to throw Harsted off track. She glanced at Drew to see if he was thinking what she was, but he was too busy concentrating on Harsted to look at her.

"The money's stashed someplace else," Harsted went on. "I may have gone along with the digging, but only far enough to see that he was trying to confuse me."

"You *are* confused," Betsy said, trying to divert Harsted's attention before he connected the mine below him with the one Trent had mentioned. "I bet you don't even know that Talbot's not his real name."

"What?" Harsted twisted his face. "You're joking."

"No, she isn't," Drew said. "If you bothered to check the property records, you would have found that the land next door is filed under the address of Abigail Trent."

"Who's that?" Harsted demanded.

"Talbot's mother," Drew said. "I flew back to Fairbanks yesterday and talked with her. Talbot's real name is Kalen Trent."

"And he's no Whitehorse doctor," Betsy said.

"That madman," Harsted said. "I ought to kill him."

"The law will take care of him," Betsy said. "All we need to do is go tell the Mounties everything we know. They'll sort it out and you can have the reward."

"The law," Harsted mocked. "You're telling me to wait on the police to get me a measly fifty thousand dollars? How naive can you get? I want it all. That old guy has pulled more than one trick on us. Do you realize Talbot or Trent or whatever you call him tried to *murder* you yesterday.''

"Murder me?''

"I didn't know it at the time,'' Harsted said, "but he was furious that I pulled you out of the stream. He even threatened to kill me if I didn't keep quiet. Betsy, you didn't get dizzy because you hadn't eaten. Or have you figured that out?''

Betsy couldn't speak. She wasn't sure if she really wanted to know how close she'd come to dying.

Harsted guffawed. "What did you do just before you fell into that stream?''

Betsy recalled the sequence of events. "I don't know. I was panning and I had coffee. But Trent's thermos was old and the coffee didn't taste good so I threw out half of it.''

"It didn't taste good because Trent poisoned it.''

"But he drank the same coffee,'' Betsy said.

"Not quite,'' Harsted told her. "It may have come from the same thermos, but your cup was different. You probably weren't looking when he dumped in the medicine.''

"What medicine?'' Betsy asked.

"I don't know,'' Harsted said. "He didn't tell me everything. All I know is that he had some little white pills.''

"That explains why Trent's back conveniently went out,'' Drew said to Betsy. "He had no intention of saving you.''

"He's crazy to think he could have gotten away with it,'' Harsted said. "Now he's trying to get the best of me. But he's met his match.''

Drew studied Harsted. "What makes you so sure?"

Harsted aimed the .45 at the wall and pretended to fire. "Because I'll kill the old geezer if he really *does* know where the money is and doesn't come clean."

Still agitated, Harsted turned his gun back on Betsy. "As for you..." Suddenly his left hand shot out and grabbed her gold charm.

"Hey," Betsy protested. The newly repaired chain cut into the back of her neck, then snapped.

Harsted tossed the medallion up a foot, grinned and stuffed it into a pocket.

"Give that back." Betsy took a step toward him, but too late to grab her medallion. Again, Drew restrained her.

"Nope. You owed me for snooping in my room," Harsted said smugly as he lowered the gun a little. "There's gold in this."

While Harsted's attention was on Betsy, Drew jumped forward, startling her. He hammered his fists down across Harsted's gun hand. The pistol fell to Harsted's feet, and he tried to pick it up. But Drew was too quick and pushed him back. The two men struggled. When Drew tried to kick the gun away, he failed.

Frantic now, Betsy remembered Conrad's .38 in her shoulder bag. She pulled it out and fired into the roof. The blast echoed, and bits of wood shake sprinkled down to the floor.

Both men froze, then Greg suddenly knocked Drew down and ran out the door, leaving his own gun behind.

Betsy knelt by Drew. "You okay?" she asked.

"Fine," he said, letting her pull him up. "Unless I've been shot. So you're still carrying that thing."

Betsy put her gun back in the shoulder bag. "Don't worry. I wasn't aiming at Harsted. I shot straight up. I didn't know what else to do. But you're the brave one. I can't believe you knocked that pistol out of his hand. Or do you always do that sort of thing?''

"Only when the gun's pointed at somebody I love.'' Drew hugged her. "You're the one who did great, shooting away like a cowboy.'' Then he bent and picked up Harsted's .45 automatic. "The guy means business. He probably does plan to kill Trent, or whoever else gets in his road.''

"Then we should head off his nutty scheme before somebody gets hurt.''

Drew tested the weight of the gun. "Yeah, maybe he'll listen if he's looking down the barrel of this thing. If we can still catch him.''

They hurried outside. Drew kept the automatic in his hand in case Harsted had another weapon, but there was no sign of him. The woods were deadly silent.

"He's out here somewhere," Drew said, rotating slowly as he peered between trees. "Probably watching us. Let's keep looking."

Then an engine started in the distance. Betsy stopped and listened. "It's an airplane. Damn it. He flew in like before. That's why we didn't spot a car.''

"I see it now," Drew said. "It's the Stinson again—on the lake. It was hidden in that cove.''

The single-engine plane lifted off the water and flew overhead. Betsy grabbed Drew's hand. "We've got to do something. He's going to beat us back to town and get to Trent.''

"Maybe not. We might have a chance if we hurry.'' Back at the cabin, they threw the trapdoor shut and pulled the rug over it. They closed the outside door but couldn't secure the padlock. It was apparent now that Harsted had shot it off.

"I don't know why we're doing this now," Betsy said.

"Trent might be back out here," Drew told her. "We know where your mine leads. You don't want to draw an arrow to the trapdoor."

Betsy knew he was right. She started toward the Bronco. "I just about flipped when Harsted was talking about the mine."

Drew was beside her. "I knew what you were thinking. Trent is trying to outsmart Harsted, that's all. But it doesn't seem to be working. If nothing gets in their way now, they'll both be back. You can count on that."

Betsy and Drew got into her Bronco and began the trip back to Dawson City. Betsy drove.

"Harsted lied to us," Drew said. "He complained that what Trent had told him about the mine was a hoax, but Harsted knew it wasn't. He just wanted *us* to believe it. You saw how nervous he was telling us that."

"Yeah," Betsy said, "but do you think Harsted has figured out that the trapdoor leads to Trent's mine?"

"Not yet maybe. But Harsted's no dummy. I had a feeling he was making the connection while we were talking. If we hadn't come along, he'd probably be down there right now searching for the money. It's in there, I know it."

She found it hard to believe that two million dollars had been lying in the Lost Lady Mine for ten years. Of course, Conrad *wouldn't* have known. After Tom's death, he would never have gone back inside. Or would he? After all, she didn't know his real reasons for destroying all the diagrams of the tunnels. No, she told herself. Conrad would have gone to the police.

"You think Trent hid the money in the mine and then the landslide covered it?" she asked.

"What else? He's a sky diver. Harsted claims he's a Red Baron robber. All the pieces seem to fit. With Trent's sky diving ability, he could have landed just about anywhere he wanted."

"With a bag of money."

"That he couldn't spend. At least not right away."

"Do you think he knew that then?" Betsy asked.

Drew wiped a hand through his hair. "I don't want to think. Look, if you stole two million, wouldn't you want it close by while you were waiting for the heat to blow over?"

"Under my mattress. I'd want to count it every day."

"Right. So it doesn't make sense that he'd leave the money in the mine for more than a day or two. For some reason, he couldn't get it out right away."

"Then the landslide came," Betsy said. "It still seems so incredible. Grandpa always said those tunnels were a maze. Only a fool would tackle them now without a map."

"Those two would do it," Drew said.

"We *have* to go to the Mounties now. They'll find Harsted and make him talk. Trent, too."

"I'm with you." Drew put a hand on Betsy's thigh. "After this, Randall won't be able to blame Dad."

"Or you," Betsy said.

Drew twisted and moved his hand to the back of Betsy's neck, massaging the reddened area where the chain had been. "I'm really sorry about your medallion," he said. "I know it means a lot to you. And losing it the second time in a week . . ."

"I didn't lose it the first time," Betsy said, still watching the road. "The chain just broke."

"I'm still embarrassed."

"It was an accident, a lucky break."

He grinned at her. "Yeah?"

"My best break yet. Anyhow, don't worry about the medallion" Betsy said. "At least we're both alive. The way he was waving that gun around, we had a lot more to be concerned about."

"We shouldn't have trusted either of them," Drew said. "Especially Trent. The brave and daring Red Baron robber." Drew leaned back in his seat. "To think I went to parties and helped celebrate a criminal. He tried to poison you, he probably bludgeoned his partner to death, and now I'm sure he killed Dad."

"Drew, you can't say that yet. You don't know."

"You're right," he said sadly. "But we will, soon enough."

Dwelling on Trent made Betsy nervous. Her arms began to tingle. She loosened her grip on the steering wheel and flexed her fingers, trying to relax. "Drew, I'm worried about someone in Dawson City. Remember Evie Saunders? I told you she and Grandpa lived together,"

"I was going to ask you."

"She was Grandpa's mistress for years, his common-law wife. Whatever you want to call her. Grandpa was never one to do things the respectable way. Evie practically raised my mother from age two. My real grandmother committed suicide—couldn't stand the winters here, I guess."

"I'm sorry."

"I never knew her. That's where Evie came in. She started as a kind of nanny, but things changed pretty fast, Grandpa told me. They could have got married, but I guess he thought once was enough. Anyway, even though Evie's of another generation—she's seventy now—I still consider her a dear friend. That's why I felt safe in asking her about Trent."

"When was this?"

"The day after he surprised me in my office," Betsy said. "I told you about that. It was also the day after I met you." She reached over and squeezed Drew's hand.

"A double whammy, huh. Okay. You said you were worried about Evie."

Betsy nodded. "She told me she'd met Talbot—I doubt if either she or Grandpa knew he was Kalen Trent—but she got nervous talking about him. I think now that she was holding back."

"Maybe Trent threatened her, too. We know what kind of man he is. He might have gone to her before he popped up in your office."

"That's what I'm afraid of. We know he's looking for a map—just like Harsted. I'll bet he was trying to get one from Evie, and that he was the one who broke into Frank's shop."

"But there isn't a map."

"Right," Betsy said. "But Trent's not going to take no for an answer. He's got some plan concocted to get that money. And he must be desperate."

"Desperate enough to kill again."

"I hope not. Lord, I've been blind." Betsy speeded up despite the rough road. "Evie could be in terrible danger. It's not just us anymore."

"Drive as fast as you can. Don't worry about the bumps, I'm wearing my seat belt."

Dawson City was still almost an hour away. As the road stretched on, Betsy and Drew stopped talking for a while, but her mind kept roiling with fear and possibilities.

"Drew, the note, the sketch with the phony blood—I thought at first they were left by Harsted, but maybe it was Trent."

"Well, Trent had the reasons, but whoever drew that sketch had to know what the back of the medallion looked like."

Her theory was collapsing. "I don't know if he ever had the chance to see it."

"Probably the same way he had a chance to poison your coffee," Drew said. "You can't trust him."

Betsy drove even harder. Five miles from Dawson City, her stomach was twisted like a rag. Why did it have to be so far? Their plan was to go immediately to the RCMP station and get Sergeant Randall to round up Harsted and Trent, and to have a constable posted at Evie's house if Trent couldn't be arrested right away.

But when they finally got to town and headed down Front Street to the Mounties, there was still a police 4x4 angled in the road. A siren wailed and Betsy looked down the nearest cross street. "What's going on? Look at that commotion."

"There's an ambulance," Drew said.

"And more police. They're at the Double River Inn."

"Trent's hotel."

"And Harsted's."

Betsy parked as close to the Double River Inn as she could, and she and Drew hopped out of the Bronco and pushed to the head of the crowd that had gathered around the hotel.

A man lay in front of the hotel, blood seeping from his torso into the sidewalk boards. A local doctor that Betsy knew bent over him, shaking his head.

A constable scanned the crowd, and Betsy and Drew pulled back. "Can anybody identify this man?"

The hotel manager spoke up. "I can. He was a guest here."

Betsy and Drew broke from the back of the crowd without waiting to hear the name of the dead man. They knew him as well as anybody in Dawson City. It was Greg Harsted.

# Chapter Twelve

Betsy gripped Drew's arm and looked back at the crowd around Harsted's body. "That maid who let us in," she said. "She could tell the Mounties we were in Harsted's room."

Drew glanced nervously at the hotel. Sergeant Randall was on the scene now. "We also have no alibi, and your medallion is probably in Harsted's room or still in his pocket. Even if the maid keeps quiet, the medallion will lead the police to you and me in no time."

"Drew, they could charge us with murder."

"We've got to set the record straight," he argued. "We won't have anything to be afraid of if we stick together and just tell the truth."

Betsy wanted to be persuaded, but Randall's already frosty attitude toward Drew wouldn't let her. "Let's go back to Yukon Lights for a while. We need time to think—to plan."

"All right but—"

"Drew, look." Betsy pointed. "It's Evie, the woman I told you about."

"Where?"

"Right over there. On the edge of the crowd. In the green slacks and floral blouse."

Evie didn't see them at first. She faced straight ahead, peering at the death scene as the Mounties tried to disperse the crowd and get on with their investigation.

Betsy and Drew rushed to her. "Evie, what are you doing here?"

The older woman just looked at Betsy and shook her head. She started to speak, but her jaw quivered.

"Come with us," Betsy said, guiding her to the Bronco. "We'll go down to Yukon Lights. We'll all be safe there."

Betsy parked in the alley and unlocked the back door. Because it was Sunday, the club wouldn't open until five in the afternoon. They would have time to talk in peace. Along the way, Betsy introduced Drew and Evie and told her that she was the one who'd found Sam McKay's plane and that Drew was Sam's son.

"Oh, Betsy," Evie finally said when they got inside the darkened nightclub. "I wish you hadn't become involved."

"It's too late," Betsy said. "I'm just glad *you're* all right. I've been so worried about you."

"I appreciate that."

They took a table near the bar and Betsy got Cokes for all of them.

Evie drank quickly, then said, "Betsy, this whole business has gone too far. That poor reporter fellow...." Evie choked up.

"Did you know Harsted?" Drew asked.

"Yes." Evie wiped at her clouded eyes and tried to get a grip on herself. "He came to me two days ago. He'd been following Talbot and wanted to know how I knew him."

Betsy took Evie's hand and Evie squeezed back. "Did Harsted threaten you?"

"Oh, no," Evie said. "He was very nice. He told me he was writing about the Red Baron robbery and that Talbot seemed to know a lot about the case."

"And what did you tell Harsted?" Betsy asked.

Evie started sobbing and Betsy gave her a tissue. After a while, Evie said, "I told him what I told you—that Talbot bought the land next to Conrad's and tried for years to buy the minerals rights Tom Fioretti had left him."

"And that's all?" Drew asked.

Evie nodded. "And now he's dead. Betsy, I'm sure Talbot killed him."

"Why?" Betsy asked.

"He's not normal. He tries to manipulate everybody. I watched him come around to Conrad for years, throwing tantrums and acting like a spoiled brat when he couldn't get his way with those mineral rights. If you got in his road, he'd probably kill you like I'd slap a mosquito."

Betsy looked at Drew. She could tell he was seething. She loved both Drew and Evie and couldn't keep secrets now. She turned to Evie and said, "Drew and I have learned a lot about this man in the past two days. For starters, his real name is Kalen Trent."

"Trent," Evie repeated solemnly. "I'm not surprised. You can't trust a man who needs two or three names."

"And he's from Fairbanks. He's not a doctor in Whitehorse."

"Doctor? I never heard that one before," Evie said. "He always told Conrad he was a schoolteacher from Anchorage. Oh, Betsy, he's fooled us all."

"Not anymore," Drew said. He put his elbows on the table. "We know his game now."

"So do I," Evie said. "And I might as well tell you." She looked Betsy in the eye and said, "Until a few days ago, I could never understand Talbot's—Trent's—persistence about those mineral rights. When it comes to gold, they're worthless. But Conrad was so adamant that the rights not be sold. The Lost Lady Mine was dangerous, he said."

"But did Grandpa really care about Trent's safety?" Betsy asked.

"No," Evie said. "But by destroying his maps of the Lost Lady shafts and keeping everyone out, Conrad made the mine a sort of shrine to Tom."

Betsy remembered the two men together on her childhood visits to Dawson City. "They were loyal friends."

"The closest," Evie said.

Drew pushed back from the table. "I'm going to see the police now. Every minute Trent is allowed to go free puts us all in more danger."

"Wait," Betsy said calmly. "Maybe Evie knows something else. We want to build the best case against him we can."

Drew grimaced and Evie said, "I can add something, Drew. I don't know where this puts you with your father's plane, but this Trent came to harass me the day before Betsy asked me about him." She looked at Betsy. "I was so nervous when you started talking about Jacob Talbot."

"I noticed," Betsy said.

"Well, he didn't pay a social call. He *demanded* that I give him a map of the mine. Said he needed to know where the tunnels were so he could get something out of the mine. But it wasn't gold. He told me he didn't care about the mineral rights anymore."

Betsy closed her eyes, trying to piece the horrid evidence together. "And he thought you'd have a map."

"Yes. He knew I'd lived with Conrad for years. And now that I'm old and weak he thought I'd be a pushover. He pulled a gun on me."

"Evie!" Betsy had known she had good reason to worry, but her concern had almost been too late.

"Well, it made me mad," Evie said. "Bothering me about this map. So I taunted him. I accused him of the only thing I could think of—with all the publicity. When I joked that he was a Red Baron robber, he pulled his gun and threatened my life. Yours too, Betsy. He knew all about you before he dropped into your office and pretended to be so casual. He said he was a Red Baron robber, that the stolen money was in the mine and that he would kill anybody who told the Mounties about him. I believed him."

"We've got him." Drew banged the table with his fist, knocking over his glass of Coke.

Betsy went to the bar and picked up a towel. Drew took it from her and wiped the table dry.

By now, Evie was up too, pacing around the nightclub, which seemed cavernous with only three people inside. "That maniac may have scared me," she said, "but there's one thing I didn't tell him."

Betsy looked at Drew, trying to guess. "What?"

"There *is* a map," Evie said.

Betsy couldn't believe it. "Are you sure? Where? I never knew about it."

"You've had it for a year," Evie said. "I would have told you except it didn't seem to mean anything until now."

Betsy went to Evie and gripped her shoulders. "Evie, what are you saying?"

"The map is on your gold medallion," Evie said, looking at the floor. "Those lines etched on the back—those are the tunnels."

"Oh, my God!" Betsy dropped backward and pressed her head into a wooden pillar. Drew was immediately there to comfort her. Evie didn't know that Betsy no longer had the medallion.

Evie went on. "Tom was so proud of Lost Lady that he took gold he'd mined from it and had an Athabascan metalsmith make the medallion. The back of it is the only map that survived. Conrad destroyed the ones on paper, but Tom gave him the gold charm and it was too dear to his heart to toss out. Besides, he didn't think anyone else would figure out it had a map on it."

Drew held Betsy tightly. "It's okay," he said. "It doesn't change the facts."

"It changes everything," Betsy said. "Evie, the medallion has been stolen. Harsted ripped it off my neck a couple of hours ago."

"And Trent shot him," Drew said. "If Trent saw it—"

Evie sat down, pressing a hand to her chest. "He might be able to figure out the lines. He's such an evil man."

Betsy stared at Evie. Something still didn't make sense. The red-stained sketch of the medallion. Although she usually wore the charm, it was often tucked inside her clothes. Even if Trent had got a good look at it, he would have needed a photographic memory to reproduce the design so well. She'd wanted so much to blame him that she hadn't opened her eyes. Now it was obvious that neither Trent nor Harsted had made the sketch. Besides herself, only one other person had known the medallion well enough to accurately portray the etched lines.

Betsy didn't want to be the accuser, but she was tired of having so few answers. "Evie, it was you who drew the sketch, wasn't it?"

The old woman blinked. "Yes."

"And you typed the note."

"I did. Used that old typewriter Conrad had."

"I remember it," Betsy said.

"Forgive me," Evie said. "But I had to do it. I love you, Betsy, and I was afraid for your safety. I left the note and then after Frank's break-in I panicked and did the sketch. That reporter told me you were getting too involved, that you might get hurt. So I had to do something, but in a way that wouldn't put us in jeopardy. I knew you'd never listen if I just told you straight out."

"You had makeup that looked like blood?" Betsy asked.

"It was old. Conrad took some from Yukon Lights and gave it to me as a joke. I never thought I'd use it." Evie shook her head, her fragile shoulders trembling.

Betsy knelt beside her and gently put a hand on her back. "Evie, don't worry. It's over. You tried to do the right thing and I was too stubborn to listen."

Evie raised her head, more in control now. "This man, Trent, he broke into your garage."

"Harsted told us," Drew said, approaching the table on the opposite side of Betsy.

"Betsy, he had that gun," Evie said. "He wanted to know about Conrad's papers, he forced me to tell him."

"It's okay," Betsy said.

"I tried to convince him Conrad had no maps in his papers. I told him they'd been destroyed. But he was so mean to me. He just wouldn't listen." Upset, Evie reached into her purse for something. She dug around and began to panic. "They're not here, they're gone."

"What's gone?" Betsy said.

"My tranquilizers. I keep a bottle in my kitchen and another in my purse. Maybe I left those home, too. I've been so mixed up these past few days."

"Look," Drew said. "I'll take you home. If I'm along, then Trent won't bother you."

Evie got up. "No, you stay with Betsy. Trent's crazy, but he wouldn't accost me on the street in the middle of the day. I'll just go home and get my medicine. It's not far. I can walk."

Reluctantly, Betsy and Drew let Evie go. They agreed that at this point Trent would be more concerned about the loot than about Evie.

"You think Evie will be all right?" Betsy asked.

"She'll probably settle down after she finds her tranquilizers." Drew paused. "I'm just wondering though. That coffee you had at the stream. If Trent put little white pills in it . . ."

"Evie's tranquilizers," Betsy whispered. "That's why they're missing. Trent stole them."

"He's clever," Drew said. "He probably put in just enough to make you dizzy, but not to kill you. Then it would have looked like a drowning."

"Let's hope he isn't as clever with the medallion," Betsy said. "If he reads that map, no one can stop him. Let's follow Evie and make sure she gets home okay."

"I'm with you."

Then the phone rang behind the bar.

Betsy didn't want to answer. No one should have been calling when the club wasn't open. But she had a funny feeling and picked up the receiver. "Yukon Lights."

"Betsy," a woman's voice whimpered, "he's got me."

"Evie, what's going on?"

The line was silent a moment, then Betsy got her answer. "If you want to see the old woman alive again," Trent said, "you and McKay drive over to Sixtymile. I'll hand her over there."

"But—"

"If you tell the Mounties, she'll die."

The line went dead.

Betsy hung up in tears. "Trent's kidnapped Evie. We shouldn't have let her go."

"Damn that idiot," Drew said. "What's he want, ransom?"

"We're supposed to go over to Sixtymile."

"Where's that?"

"It's a little place about ten miles from the Alaskan border, not far south of the Top of the World Highway. About an hour away." Betsy kept her voice even, trying to be strong, but she'd never faced a kidnapper before. When Drew came around the bar to her and took her in his arms, she burrowed her head against his chest. "Trent threatened to kill her if we tell the Mounties."

"He probably would," Drew said. "He must have seen us come into the club and waited outside to grab whoever he could. But it's only been a few minutes, so they can't be far away. Trent would see if we went to the RCMP station."

"We can't go there, Drew."

"But we could phone and get the police to follow us."

Betsy went back to the table where they'd first sat and picked up her shoulder bag. "It's too risky," she said. "Trent's got such a short fuse. We'll have to go alone."

Drew moved to the end of the bar and stood still a moment, thinking. "Okay, we'll do it. You still have that .38, don't you?"

"Right here," Betsy said, patting her shoulder bag.

"Good. We may need it."

Betsy couldn't imagine shooting at Trent. But she knew he had a gun, and that he'd already proved it worked. "Where's the pistol Harsted dropped?"

"In your Bronco. I stuffed it under the seat."

"Okay, let's go." They went out the back door, the way they'd come in. The Bronco was only a few feet away. They got in and Betsy put the key into the ignition. When she saw some movement out of the corner of her eye, she turned.

"How's it going, Betsy?" Trent laughed from the back seat where he held a pistol in each hand. "It was nice of you to leave me Harsted's .45. It's a beautiful gun, but so loud. Or have you had a chance to hear it?"

"Oh, my God," Betsy cried.

Drew pivoted and glared at him. "Damn it, you won't get away with this, Trent."

The older man cackled nervously. "So you know my name, huh. It's surprising how many fools never look in the property records. Unfortunately for both of you, your detective work has been amateurish. But we can discuss that later. First, we'll take care of business. I've changed my mind about Sixtymile. Some other time, maybe. Today I feel like flying. What do you say, Mr. Pilot?"

"Forget it."

"Sorry, but I can't." Trent wrinkled his nose and emitted three short laughs. "You see, my heart's set on seeing Dawson from the air."

Betsy gave Drew a look of resignation. They'd been careless and let a lunatic outsmart them again.

"Where's Evie?" Betsy asked. "What have you done with her, you animal?"

"Animal, she says." Trent laughed in rhythmic spurts. "Names don't hurt me now. I've been kicked around too long for that. I make up names, Jacob Talbot, for instance. You like that one? Jacob was the name of a real doctor I knew in Montana. And Talbot's my mother's maiden name. Did you enjoy your visit with her, McKay?"

Drew's mouth fell open. "How'd you know?"

"I call her every night," Trent said. "No matter where I am. It makes her feel wanted. Doesn't take much anymore. She's off in the head, you know."

"What about Evie?" Betsy demanded.

"Behind my seat. All you had to do was look. Of course, she's under your blanket, tied up."

They heard a moan from the back.

"And gagged," Trent said.

"Why?" Betsy pleaded. "She's an old woman. Leave her out of this."

"Hey, I'll do what I want, when I want. Understand?" He jabbed Betsy's shoulder with a pistol barrel. "Now since we're going flying and we don't have a metal detector at the airport, I'll just have to ask you to give me that little gun of yours right now."

"What gun?" Betsy said.

"The one Harsted told me about. You scared the daylights out of him, shooting like that. Hand it over."

Betsy found the gun in her shoulder bag and briefly considered going for Trent. But if she missed, a bullet could penetrate the back seat and hit Evie. And even if a stray shot didn't strike anything of importance, she wouldn't get a second chance. She gave Trent the .38.

"Very cooperative," he said. "Now, you get out, Betsy, and then I get out. Slowly. We wouldn't want an accidental shooting." When their feet were on the ground, Trent said. "Now you, McKay. Stand by Betsy." Drew came around to the driver's side of the Bronco.

"Okay," Trent said. "Your friend Evie's going back inside. I don't need her anymore. Just unlock the nightclub, Betsy, and fly-boy will help you carry the old woman in. And keep the blanket on."

Too scared to do anything else, Betsy complied. When they got inside the club, the blanket fell off. Evie's face showed pure terror. She was bound hand and foot and her mouth was sealed with wide tape circling her head. Wrenched with anger, Betsy put a palm against her cheek. "Evie, Evie."

"Enough of that," Trent barked. "Put her under the stage."

"You can't do this," Drew said.

"Why not? There's a door in the floor of the stage. I've seen it. That means there's room below for somebody. Maybe not visitors but . . ." Trent shrugged and giggled.

Betsy opened the door. The space under the stage was dirty and cramped and used for nothing except storage. With the noise of the nightclub, Evie's moans would never be heard. At her age, she might die in hours.

Under gunpoint, Drew did the heavy work of lowering Evie's deadweight into the dark little room. He put her carefully on the dirty wooden floor, but Trent yelled at him. "Facedown." Drew reluctantly turned her over and crawled out. Then Trent tossed the blanket in beside her.

"Close it up," he ordered Betsy, then laughed again.

BETSY DROVE TO THE AIRPORT. Drew sat beside her, and Trent sprawled across the back, still with two guns on them. They got out at Drew's plane. They were the only ones on the strip.

"I need to gas up," Drew said. "It's almost empty. We can't fly more than a half hour."

Trent's face filled with glee. "We're not going far."

"But it's dangerous. You never know how long you'll want to be up."

Trent only laughed and flexed his trigger fingers.

Drew set to work getting the plane ready to take off, but Betsy had to stand there and just watch, numb with fear. At least he had something to occupy his hands. All she could do was imagine using hers to strangle Trent.

Betsy sat behind Drew, who took the left side. Trent strapped himself into the co-pilot's seat on the right, a red nylon bag at his feet. It was only a minor relief to Betsy that he had put away one gun. Now he had only his.

He caught her staring at it as the plane's engine coughed and started up. "It's a 9 mm automatic," he told her. "A Mauser. Quite effective in the right hands."

A memory of Harsted's bloody body jolted through her brain. "I've seen your work."

"Good," Trent said. "Then let's be off."

Drew rolled the plane toward the runway. "Which way?"

"Forget the part about seeing Dawson from the air," Trent said. "I really want to fly north."

"How far?"

"Don't worry. I'll keep you on course. It's sunny today. We'll be able to see for miles."

The Piper sped down the runway, then gracefully lifted off. Betsy had wanted Drew to take her up, but not under these conditions. As they climbed and skirted the green and brown hills, Betsy cleared her throat and asked, "Do you really know where the two million is?"

"I've always known," Trent said, sitting sideways so he could watch both Betsy and Drew. "I hid it in that mine—on the land I bought next to yours."

"But there was a landslide the next spring after the armored car robbery."

"That's right. I didn't get it out in time."

Drew glanced away from his controls. "Why not?"

"Broke a leg when I jumped. Imagine that, best sky diver in the North and I do a silly thing like that. Naturally, I couldn't carry out the money with a bum wheel. I hobbled down to the road and eventually got a ride back to Dawson with a hunter. My leg was in about six pieces, broken above and below the knee, so I had to have this huge cast. I was in no condition to go back to the mine then."

"So you stayed in Dawson?" Betsy asked.

"No, I went home to Fairbanks and healed up. Wasn't able to get back here until after the first snowfall. But I soon realized it was hopeless. I'd been in such pain from the broken leg that I got mixed up about where the mine was. With the fresh snow, nothing looked the same."

"You must have been pretty confident to leave all that money behind," Betsy said.

"Had no choice really, but then I wasn't real worried either. Nobody had found the plane, and I knew I'd be back first thing in the spring. So I got a little job in Fairbanks and waited."

"Then the slide came," Drew said.

"Got it all figured out, huh." Trent craned his neck toward the instruments. "What's our altitude?"

"Six thousand. I don't want to hit any mountains."

Trent grunted. "Oh, good thinking, McKay. I like a bright pilot."

Betsy remembered how Evie had gotten Trent to talk. If she and Drew survived whatever Trent had in mind for them, she wanted to know his complete story. "I bet you were angry then. All that money covered up with dirt and rocks."

Trent let out a whistle. "You got it, Betsy. I was fuming. Once I had the location straightened out, I couldn't believe my luck. I was hopping around that slide on my good leg like a pogo stick. Almost broke it, too."

Betsy tried again. "How'd you buy that forty acres? I wouldn't think somebody who had to rob an armored car would have much in his piggy bank."

"I had enough," Trent said. "My last stake from my pipeline wages. Of course, the land was cheaper without the mineral rights. The people who inherited the property from the miner just wanted to unload it." Trent looked down at the Ogilvie Mountains. "We're getting close. How's your fuel, McKay?"

"We're going to be in big trouble if we don't turn back right now."

"No chance," Trent said, winking at Betsy.

Drew kept the plane going north. "What are you trying to do, Trent?"

"You'll see soon enough. Now, I know Betsy has a lot of questions. Let me guess, though." He looked her in the eye. "You want to know why I never went into the mine from your entrance."

Betsy swallowed. So he *did* know.

"Simple," he went on. "I never figured it out until Harsted got me thinking. Then he found that trapdoor. Funny, huh. But it was nice work. We were partners, did you know? We dug and dug out by the mine, but couldn't find a thing." Trent shook his head.

"We noticed the digging," Betsy said. "Along with that gold pickax charm."

Trent was startled for a second but regained his composure. "So that's where I dropped it."

"Then it was you who broke into Frank Saunders's shop. Why?"

"I was looking for a map of the mine. When I didn't find one I trashed the place to make it look like an ordinary burglary."

"And what about Halstead?" Betsy asked. "You don't kill your partner."

"He broke our deal. Threatened to turn me in. What else could I do? The fool stole letters from my hotel room, and then he saved you at the stream. But he couldn't have if you'd drunk all that coffee. I could have died when you threw it out."

"I almost did die."

"I already had the Saunders woman to contend with. You were supposed to drown."

"Thanks."

Drew looked below and Betsy followed his gaze. There was no sign of civilization. "Are we there yet?" he asked.

"Very soon." Trent ordered Drew to descend to three thousand feet and circle a few times. Then he reached into a pocket and dangled Betsy's medallion in front of her. "I thought you'd like to know that the police didn't pick this off Harsted's body."

"I'm gratified," Betsy stared at the glimmering gold. "May I have it back?"

"No, I need it. There's a map of your mine on the back. Harsted clued me in. Smart fellow—in some ways.

Too bad he couldn't hang on to his gun." Trent took it out of his jacket and held it up. "You won't be needing this, will you?" He opened his window and tossed out the .45. "And we might as well get rid of this one, too," he said, jettisoning Betsy's .38.

"The map," Betsy said. "Is that what you were looking for in my office?"

"Nice reckoning, Betsy. *Dead* reckoning." Trent cackled again.

Drew checked his fuel gauge. "Time's running out. So let's hear how you killed my dad."

"You want it all, don't you?" Trent asked smugly. "Sam was a good sport. After the robbery, my old partner, Ed Sherburne, and I headed to the airport and took the first plane we saw with a pilot on hand. Sam didn't want to go at first, but we convinced him. Then Ed opened a bottle and started celebrating too early. I was sitting in the back of the plane minding my own business when he got belligerent. Wanted a bigger cut."

"So you clubbed him in the back of the head," Drew said.

"Yeah, even had to throw out the bottle."

"The police have identified his remains, you know."

"Oh, how efficient of them. Only ten years late."

"Stop smirking, Trent. What about my dad?"

"Can't wait to hear, can you? All right. We've got a couple more minutes. Your father bailed out. Must have thought I was going to shoot him, too. That would have been silly, though. I never learned to fly. I needed a pilot."

"Then you jumped, too," Betsy said.

"Of course. But unlike old Sam, I took time to grab the money bag first. After all that trouble..."

"Get on with it," Drew snapped.

"Testy, testy. Well, we landed close together. I was injured, like I told you. I offered to cut a deal with Sam, but he just tried to run away. I couldn't allow that." Trent glanced at the ground. "Enough of this chatter. We're on top of the Lost Lady Mine."

With the 9 mm automatic on Drew, Betsy could see they had no choice but to comply. Trent hummed to himself a minute, before emptying the bag at his feet. It was a parachute. Still keeping his gun on Drew, he strapped on the chute.

Then he cracked open his door. A chill blast hit Betsy in the face. "Have a pleasant flight," Trent said. He winked at Betsy. And leaped into the sky.

## Chapter Thirteen

"We're going to die," Betsy cried. "Oh, my God. Not like this." Panic nearly strangled her. She pressed her face against the window as Drew banked the plane between the taller mountain peaks. Behind them, Trent's brilliant orange parachute drifted lower and lower. The open cockpit door still flapped in the wind.

"I've been in worse jams than this," Drew answered. His knuckles were white on the throttle. "Trent can go to hell. We're not finished yet. I'm going to put this baby down." He stretched to slam the door shut, then scouted for a landing spot. "Right there, on the lake by your cabin. In the shallows."

"In the water?"

"We've got to stop that idiot from getting the money."

"Let him have it. Drew, you can't land down there. This isn't a float plane. Evie's going to die under the stage because no one will find her, and we're going to run out of gas and crash into one of these god-awful mountains." Betsy's fingers dug into the back of Drew's vinyl seat. If only he were closer. "I'm coming up front," she said.

"No," he shouted. "Stay back. You'll be safer."

But by then she had already settled in beside him and begun to buckle her seat belt.

Then the engine sputtered. Drew mumbled something incomprehensible and Betsy closed her eyes. The engine coughed again and the plane tilted to the left. Her eyes flipped open and she looked past Drew out his window. For a moment, she saw ground. Then the plane leveled out.

Drew checked the altimeter. "A thousand feet...nine hundred..." The plane dipped into a wooded canyon. Lost Lady Lake beckoned to them, a sparkling blue mirror. "Hang on, Betsy, we're running on vapors. I'm bringing her down." Drew was like a statue, his entire body stiff with concentration.

"Dear God." Betsy flattened back against the seat, paralyzed by the deadly certainty they were about to be smashed to bits. Mountains and trees became a blur of green and brown. The lake loomed dead ahead.

When the engine finally died, an eerie silence swept over Betsy and Drew. In their few seconds of free-fall, the quiet was deceivingly peaceful, spoiled only by the knowledge that they were about to crash.

"Brace yourself," Drew ordered.

Betsy covered her face, and the plane struck the lake with a thundering smack. The seat belt slashed painfully across her body as the Piper skimmed the lake's surface like a skipping stone. She pressed her palms tight to her face, trying to shield herself against the pounding. Her head was spinning with the sounds of rushing wind and swooshing water. Reeds scraped the fuselage and the plane began to slow.

"We're going...to make it," Drew said.

Betsy lowered her hands, unable to believe they were still alive. Drew's face was covered with sweat. His shoulders trembled as he gripped the yoke. But he was landing the plane, in a marshy area, just as he'd said. Betsy's thoughts fuzzed with shock. They'd survived. For once, they'd outwitted Trent. The plane bounced along the lake, then stopped and began to settle into the water.

Drew stared at the water-blurred windshield for several seconds, then dropped his arms. "Hot damn," he sighed. "We did it." He tossed his head back and swiped at the moisture running down his forehead. "We *really* did it." He turned to Betsy. "Are you all right?"

"Yes, are you? If something had happened to us...to you." Her heart was pumping wildly. She touched his shoulder, then hunched over, exhausted and relieved.

"My landings are usually a little smoother," Drew joked. "Next time we set down on a lake, we'll take a float plane." He moistened his lips and checked outside the window. The plane was listing gently, small waves lapping against the doors. "So much for the hard part. Now we have to get out of this sinking tub and get to shore." He laid one hand on her knee. "The water probably isn't too deep, but we don't want to be inside when she goes under."

"I'm ready." Betsy unfastened her seat belt and reached for the door handle.

Drew grabbed her hand. "Not that way. Too much water against the door. Even if we could get it open, we'd just fill the cockpit with water. We'll have to break the windshield." He searched under the pilot's seat for a small fire extinguisher. "Bend down and cover your eyes."

Betsy twisted away while Drew smashed the glass. He crawled out first and then helped her through the jagged opening. They squatted on the plane's narrow nose, warmed by the engine's residual heat, and assessed their predicament. Reeds and lily pads floated on the sunlit water around them. Betsy judged the bottom to be eight to ten feet down. She steadied herself and watched the water inch higher. The Piper was sinking quickly and they were a hundred feet from shore.

"Which way?" Drew asked. "I've lost my bearings."

Betsy squinted toward the end of the lake. "The cabin's around that bluff. Trent had to have landed somewhere down there." She pointed to a nearby ridge. "The curve of the lake should have kept him from seeing the plane. The shoreline might be easier going, but if we're going to catch him, we'd better cut through those woods. We can save time and stay out of sight."

"Are you sure you want to go after him?" Drew asked.

"Drew, we're at least a day's hike from Dawson and the Mounties." Betsy pressed his arm. "We've been through too much with this joker to let him get away now."

"I was hoping you'd say that. But I had to be sure. The gun doesn't worry me. Trent's older, not as quick as he could be. I think I can handle him. Besides, we've got another advantage."

"What's that?"

"Surprise. He thinks we've crashed on one of these mountaintops—that we're dead." Drew kissed her briefly on the forehead, then said firmly, "We're going to get through this. I won't let anything happen to you."

"I know." Betsy could see Drew's concern for her, his love. She wouldn't let anything happen to *him*. "Let's go," she said, "before the plane pulls us down." She stood, then dived into the weedy water. Drew followed and they were soon staggering onto a rocky beach, their clothing hanging in sodden clumps.

Breathless, Drew laid one hand on her waist. "Look behind us."

Betsy swung around. The plane's propeller pitched forward. Foamy water cascaded around the engine. Within seconds, only the tail section protruded into the air. "I'm sorry," she murmured.

Drew sucked in his breath. "Me, too. But an airplane can be replaced. At least we got out alive. Now, let's find Trent."

They dumped the water out of their shoes and began weaving through the forest toward the cabin. Betsy's clothing felt like wet cement, but she forged ahead, leading the way along familiar ground. A half mile later they crested a rocky outcropping and stopped.

"There's the cabin," Betsy whispered. "And there's Trent. Looks like he just got here." Fifty yards ahead, a figure scurried across the clearing where they'd once parked her Bronco. "Either his parachute got tangled up, or he must not have landed as close as I thought," she told Drew.

After Trent had disappeared inside the cabin, Drew said, "Now's our chance. He didn't see us." Drew started scrambling down the ridge, and Betsy hurried after him. When rocks slipped beneath her feet, she was sure either that she'd fall or that Trent would hear them. Fortunately, she was wrong on both counts. They stopped at the base of the hill to catch their breath, then began to skirt the clearing, approaching the cabin from the rear.

Betsy crouched behind a spruce tree. "I can see through the window. No one's there. Trent must already be in the tunnel."

Stealthily, they closed ground on the cabin and went inside. Despite their pains to take care, Betsy nearly tripped on the bunched-up throw rug. Drew caught her before she fell, and when she looked down, the open tunnel was staring back at her.

She let him pull her away from the abyss. The hole reminded her of where Trent had forced them to put Evie. Betsy pushed hair out of her eyes and tried to shake off thoughts of her dear old friend. She had no idea how they could save Evie, but knew that if Trent escaped, it might not matter if she were found alive under the stage. The Red Baron robber, desperate to silence everyone who knew of his crimes, could go back to Dawson City and make sure Evie never talked again.

Betsy looked around the cabin. "Trent must have taken the kerosene lamp," she said, "but I left that flashlight we used several days ago." Betsy found it behind the wood stove and switched it on.

"Put the light on me and I'll go down first," Drew said. "Trent may be just around the corner."

Drew backed down the wooden ladder to the bottom where Conrad's papers still lay scattered in the dirt. Then Betsy climbed down.

They were thirty feet below ground. Betsy and Drew fought to avoid shivering. The flashlight revealed glistening permafrost on the walls of the tunnel, and the natural coldness of the mine heightened the effect of their still-wet clothes.

Drew took the light and rounded a corner in a horizontal shaft. It was barely high enough to walk in and ran only about twenty feet before dividing in two. "Now I wish I had explored the mine before," Betsy said. "I might have some idea where to go."

They chose a tunnel at random and edged along, stopping every few feet to listen for Trent. Hearing nothing, they moved on, but always with the thought that they might have taken a wrong turn. Or several. For all they knew, Trent had found the money and slipped out of the mine behind them. Almost every minute, the shaft they were in seemed to branch off and they had to choose another fork in the maze.

"I think we're going in circles," Betsy whispered.

"Possibly," Drew acknowledged. "But Trent may be just as confused as we are."

"At least he's got the medallion. We may need a map just to get out of here."

They kept moving. Minutes stretched on as the mine's permafrost made their wet clothes colder and colder. Finally, they heard chiseling, the scratch of metal against rock. "It's Trent," Drew whispered and doused the flashlight. He took Betsy's hand and they edged forward in the dark, unable to see even their own feet.

Gradually, the blackness melted away. A dim, flickering light began to highlight the rocks in the walls of the tunnel. The chiseling grew louder as the light increased. They turned a corner and saw Trent.

Working by the kerosene lamp about fifty feet away, Trent poked and pried at a wall of rubble with a sharp steel bar. Betsy thought she recognized the bar from the cabin. Trent obviously hadn't brought his own digging tools. Maybe he hadn't expected the money to be covered by the slide. Betsy was glad something had slowed him down. Now they really had a chance to stop him.

Trent tossed the steel bar aside and started yanking on a canvas bag. His grunts echoed through the mine shaft and then the bag broke free and a few pieces of paper fluttered out. Trent fell back against the wall. He leaned against it for a moment while he caught his breath, still unaware that he wasn't alone.

Betsy could hear his heavy breathing. He didn't seem to be in good shape. Maybe Drew could take him as he said. She didn't see the gun. She kept quiet, observing, knowing that Drew would make a move only when Trent came back toward them. Except for one side tunnel, their shaft was the only way out.

She peered at the small scattering of money beneath the lamp. She was too far away to tell what denominations the bills were, but they were all green and she knew it was American money. It had to be the Red Baron loot.

Rested, Trent bent over and carefully picked up the stray bills and put them inside the canvas bag.

Behind Trent, something caught Betsy's eye. It was dull blue and seemed to blend into the rocky debris around it. She hadn't seen it at first. But when when she realized that it was a piece of fabric, she got nervous and stumbled.

As her shoes scuffed on the floor of the tunnel, Trent turned and spotted her and Drew. Her illusion about his gun being unavailable quickly vanished. Trent seemed to pull the automatic pistol from nowhere.

He fired three times and scurried to the side tunnel with the bag of money and the lamp. A bullet sent a hot crease through Betsy's left shoulder and she fell down in amazement. Drew had grabbed her to force her to the mine's floor, but in her panic she had resisted him and made a perfect target for Trent.

"Betsy!" Drew scrambled to her and turned on the flashlight. She saw blood seeping out of her shoulder, but surprised herself by not getting queasy.

"Go after him," she told Drew. "I'll be okay."

"No," he said. "You've been shot. Nothing's worth risking your life. We shouldn't have gone this far."

Betsy clambered to her feet, cupping her wound with her right hand. "Trent is getting away." She tried to ignore the burning in her shoulder. "I can still walk," she said. "Let's follow him. Now that he has the money, there's no point in staying here."

"All right," Drew said. "You're the toughest person I've ever met."

Even though all the mine shafts seemed to look alike, Drew and Betsy tried to retreat the way they'd come in. If they'd been in sunlight, the pain in her shoulder would have blurred her vision. As it was, in near darkness even with a flashlight, all she had to do was stay close to Drew. They kept reassuring each other they were on the right path, and to Betsy's disbelief, they reached the subdued light of the entrance only ten minutes later.

"Trent must still be in the mine," Drew said. "Or else he would have shut the trapdoor on us."

"Maybe he thinks he can wait us out," Betsy said. "Or he's taken a different way back."

"Who knows. Let's get up that ladder and shut the door on him. Then we'll see about the waiting."

Betsy went up first, but Drew was close behind to prevent her from falling. Unable to use her left arm, she had to depend on him to stabilize her while he reached for higher rungs.

After they'd climbed back into the cabin and Drew had shut the trapdoor, he said, "My God, your arm." Betsy's left sleeve was soaked in blood.

"It's not as bad as it seems," she said. "I'll take care of it. You think about dealing with Trent when he tries to come up."

He looked around the cabin. The only possible weapons were a shovel, a pick and a single-bladed ax.

"Drew listen. He's coming." Noises came from under the floor. Trent was climbing the ladder.

Drew grabbed the shovel, and when the trapdoor flipped open, he swung at Trent's bald head. But he'd been too eager. Instead of knocking Trent unconscious and thirty feet down into the mine, Drew had merely stunned him. The older man fell back a rung, still hanging on to his kerosene lamp and canvas bag, then surged forward.

"You fools," Trent sputtered. "You can't stop me." He shot out a string of curses, and in one swift motion put down the lamp, took out his pistol and started firing.

Betsy crawled out the doorway, then glanced back. Drew had ducked. Now he was rolling wildly on the floor while Trent's automatic spit out bullets. Betsy could barely look. Her shoulder throbbed. She felt chilled, but she was sweating. And she was torn between wanting to help Drew and fearing that she would see him killed.

Then, as quickly as Trent had started shooting, he stopped. His gun was empty, and Drew wasn't hurt. But when Trent had been shooting, Drew had let go of the shovel. Now it was a man-to-man fight, no weapons except their muscles and their brains.

Trent crouched by the mine entrance, then rushed at Drew and tackled him. While he grappled with Drew on the floor, Betsy hurried back into the cabin and kicked the money bag into the corner behind the wood stove. Drew was holding off Trent, but not getting the edge, either. The older man was strong. She had to help Drew, even though her head was spinning.

She banged the trapdoor shut, hoping to distract Trent, but he was like a mad bull and paid no attention. Then she found the shovel. Pain nearly blinded her, but she still had one good arm. She picked up the shovel and swung it awkwardly, whacking Trent on the back. But with only one hand to catch the recoil, the wooden handle slipped away and the shovel bounced uselessly behind Trent.

Now Betsy saw she'd done the wrong thing. Trent broke free of Drew and reached for the shovel, but Drew pinned it to the floor. Then Trent rushed for the other tools in the corner and came back swinging Conrad's old ax. Betsy had used it only to split kindling, so it was still sharp. In a flash of memory, she heard Conrad say, "I like to keep an ax so sharp I can shave with it."

Drew picked up the shovel, but he would be no match for the ax, Betsy realized. She screamed, distracting Trent for a second, and then threw a small wooden chair at him. The effort made her crumple on the floor.

Trent reeled backward, swatting down the chair as if it were a fly. But in the process of repelling it, Trent kicked over the lamp. The glass chimney smashed into a hundred pieces and kerosene began pouring out. With a whoosh, the single light of the wick jetted into a small fire. Licking at the floor, the flames quickly found the kindling by the stove.

"Oh, my God," Betsy shouted. "Fire!"

Drew jumped Trent with the shovel, but Trent was alert and knocked it from his hands. Frantic, Betsy picked up the shovel and tried to pound out the flames. If the fire reached the log walls, the whole cabin might burn. She slapped the shovel at the blaze, but was just as ineffective with it as Drew had been trying to knock down Trent.

The older man was far tougher than he looked, virtually a machine holding off Drew's youth and strength. They continued to struggle, Trent swearing and grunting and laughing maniacally.

The whole pile of kindling was aflame now and the fire lapped at a stack of larger wood. Then, as if by magic, a streak of orange blazed up the wall. Betsy splayed one hand across her face to guard against the searing heat. Smoke and flames filled the cabin faster than she thought possible. The building was nothing but a tinderbox. The smoke billowed and grew so thick that Betsy could barely see the men fighting. Then Trent pushed Drew away and hurled himself into the far corner behind the stove.

Drew slumped against a wall, wheezing as he tried to catch his breath in the smoke-filled room. "Go outside, Betsy," he said, coughing. "Now."

She was choking herself but still crept to him. "No, I won't leave you."

Drew put an arm around her and they looked into the heart of the fire. A shadowy figure crouched over the money bag.

"Trent, get out while you can," Betsy shouted. "Save yourself."

Their only answer was the sizzle of flames. Betsy and Drew got on their knees and crawled outside. In the center of the clearing they stopped and fell into a pile, inhaling great volumes of fresh cool air. Behind them, the cabin crackled, but Trent's agonizing scream rose above the hissing and popping of the logs and punctured the flaming horror with hell itself.

Then he staggered onto the porch. His clothes were burning like a small bonfire and his frenzied screams seemed to shake the treetops. Drew grabbed him and rolled him onto the ground. The maneuver choked off air to Trent's clothes and smothered the fire.

"Help me, help me," Trent's voice rasped. But there was no helping him now. He was dying.

Betsy knelt beside his charred form. The man was evil, a menace to almost everyone. But her heart went out to him. She wanted to comfort him now. No one should die this terrible way.

Gasping, he looked at her and said, "Conrad was…a fool. He never knew about . . . the money."

Betsy's eyes filled with tears.

"What about my dad?" Drew dropped down beside Betsy. "What did you do with him?" he asked quietly.

"Body's in the mine . . . stuck in permafrost . . . under the slide. Been down there ten years with the money."

Betsy felt like retching. Now she remembered the blue fabric she'd glimpsed between the rubble in the shaft. Her body began to tremble uncontrollably.

Trent stared at the sky. Then he grimaced and tried to laugh, but this time there was only a gagging sound. And then he went limp.

"Dear Lord." Betsy closed her eyes and fell backward on her calves. Drew took her hands. When she looked at him and spoke, her voice cracked. "Your father... and Trent. This could have been you."

"No. If Trent hadn't dived in to try to save the loot, he would have lived. That money meant more to him than anything else."

"Even life," Betsy said.

Drew nodded. "Let's back off. The fire's getting hot." He helped her to her feet. "I worry about your arm. We've got to get help."

Betsy agreed. She still didn't think the wound was deep, but she felt so weak. They staggered a few feet and turned around, still hanging on to each other like lost children in the forest.

"When this all cools off," Drew said, "the Mounties can go in and dig out my dad's body."

Betsy swallowed hard. "I think I know where to look." She told him about the blue fabric. "Drew, I feel so bad about him."

"It's over now. I just want his body out. I'm used to the idea that he's gone." A moment later, Drew said, "I'm sorry about your cabin."

Unaccountably, she smiled. Remembering what Drew had remarked about his sinking plane, she said, "Cabins can be replaced."

He looked down at her. "But the two million dollars is gone. You know, this is the most expensive fire I've ever seen."

"I don't think there's going to be any reward, either," Betsy said. "The armored car company won't get its money back."

"Didn't want the reward anyhow," Drew said.

"Me neither."

"Look, we'll get you settled in the woods, then I'll trek out of here and send help."

"I'm holding up all right. I can go with you."

"Betsy, there's no way I'm going to let you hike out with me in your condition." He paused. "But I hate to leave you here alone. Damn, we have so little time."

"I know." Betsy felt a wave of anxiety sweep over her. "Do you think someone will find Evie? She'll never make it until you get back to town."

Then they heard it—the whap-whap of helicopter blades.

"I don't believe it," Betsy said in amazement as the helicopter began to land near the lake.

"It's the Mounties," Drew said, when he saw two uniformed men aboard with the pilot. He and Betsy hurried toward the helicopter and the policemen met them by the still-burning cabin.

"Randall," Drew said, "how'd you know to come up here?"

"Evie Saunders," the sergeant said. He looked at Betsy. "One of your employees, Laura Bertino, went to work early and heard something under the stage."

"Oh, thank God," Betsy said. "Evie's all right then?"

"She's a little shaken up, but otherwise fine. And she was able to tell us everything about Trent." His gaze dropped to her bloodstained blouse. "Looks like you got in the way of a bullet."

Betsy nodded. Randall gently tugged away part of the sleeve and inspected the wound. "It's just a surface crease. You're a very lucky lady."

He turned back to Drew. "I'm sorry I had to suspect you, McKay. I had to consider every possibility."

"It's all right," Drew said. "I have my answers now."

"Where's Trent?" Randall asked.

"Over there." Drew pointed to the blackened form near the cabin. "He kicked over a kerosene lamp and died in his own fire. The two million dollars burned, too."

Randall checked the scene and Drew and Betsy told him how Trent had pulled the money bag from the mine. Drew asked Randall to bring out his father's body and Randall agreed. Randall talked on his two-way radio a few minutes, and then put Betsy and Drew on the copter with the pilot. "We'll get together later," the sergeant said. "You two go back to Dawson now and rest. Get that arm taken care of, Betsy. I've got a couple of rigs on the way to take care of things here."

"Thanks, Sergeant," Betsy said. "I'm sorry we've been so much trouble."

"Trent was the trouble," Randall said. "And that reporter Harsted. I'm sorry if we seemed to be uncooperative but Harsted had an uncanny knack for picking up information and the best security tactic seemed to be stonewalling everyone."

Drew extended his hand in a gesture of absolution. "That's okay, Sergeant. I guess we did some stonewalling of our own," he said, with a wink for Betsy.

BETSY SAT ON HER FRONT STEP and studied the indigo sky. The northern lights were playing above Dawson City tonight, like shimmering, moving streaks of gauze. She felt excited, as electrically charged as the fingers of color shooting across the sky. She was waiting for Drew. He'd had business after lunch and had refused to tell her where, or with whom.

Car headlights turned the corner and Betsy recognized the Toyota pickup Drew had rented. She straightened and pain zipped along her shoulder. Two weeks had passed since the shooting in the mine. Although the wound was healing well, she still had to be careful.

Drew stopped the little truck in front of her house and jogged the short distance to the porch. "Sorry I was gone so long this afternoon. I missed you." He took her hand in his and lifted her gently to her feet.

"Whatever you did must have turned out well." She smiled up at him. Rays from the streetlight outlined his face. "You look pleased with yourself."

"Well pleased. I've been looking at land." Drew tapped a packet of paper stuffed in his back jeans pocket. "This is our future, Betsy. I'll explain it all to you, but not here." He threaded the fingers of one hand through her billowing hair. "Do you feel like a ride? With a light show like this above us, there's only one place around here we should be."

Betsy knew he meant Midnight Dome. The hilltop had quickly become their special place, and they'd spent several evenings there. Its serenity had been a balm to ease their pain. So much had happened since she'd discovered Sam McKay's plane and its grisly cargo. The Fairbanks police had searched Trent's house and found a few thousand dollars of the incriminating Red Baron money he'd apparently packed out after he'd broken his leg. The robbery of the decade had finally been solved, but the horrors of Harsted's and Trent's deaths, and the destruction of the cabin would be indelibly marked in both Drew and Betsy's minds.

"I'm ready as soon as I lock the door." She reached behind him and secured the latch. Then they climbed into the Toyota and headed for the Dome. Moonlight washed the hilltop and Betsy could quickly see they would have the spot to themselves. They got out of the car and headed for a wide boulder where the land seemed to roll away to nothing. Dawson City spread beneath them, its lights scattering in the darkness.

"It's so beautiful here," Betsy sighed. She leaned against the rock, absorbing the cool mountain air, the brilliant borealis, the happiness of being alone with the man she loved.

"And you're part of it." Drew climbed behind her on the rock and pulled her against him. "You belong here. It's in your blood—the lure of the land, the gold panning, your nightclub."

"It's the 'spell of the Yukon.'" She moved her head back onto his chest, enjoying the way his arms tightened. "Everyone who comes here feels it, but I love you more."

"Enough to marry me?"

Betsy twisted around. She'd been waiting for him to bring up the subject. "What do you think?"

Drew smiled. "I want to hear you say yes."

"Yes, yes." Betsy laughed with pleasure. "Of course, I'll marry you. I've always wanted to see Fairbanks."

Drew traced her lower lip with the edge of his thumb. "I'll be happy to show you Fairbanks, sweet lady, but later. We're not going to live there. I want to stay here where you belong—where I belong now."

Betsy frowned. "What about NorthStar Expeditions?"

"Pete will run it." Drew spread out an arm. "We're going to expand. The office of NorthStar 2 will be located about right...there." He pointed to a vacant piece of land below them, near the Dawson City airstrip.

"What are you talking about?" Betsy could feel happiness welling within her.

"I bought a little acreage today," Drew said. "I hope you don't mind. The agreement's in my pocket. Hunters and fishermen love the Yukon. It won't take me long to size up the region, and then we'll be in business. Thank goodness my plane was insured. It'll be replaced in a few weeks. And we'll buy more."

"Will you mind staying here, Drew?" Betsy searched his moonlit face. "So much has happened here—the plane crash, the fire...your father." She sighed. The Mounties had reopened Tom's old entrance to the Lost Lady Mine and had finally recovered Sam McKay's still frozen bullet-ridden body. Sam's own Athabascan gold charm was still around his neck.

Drew wrapped his arm, once more, about Betsy. "I'm just glad he was finally found. It's a relief to my family. I knew he was a good man, that he'd never desert us, that he wasn't a criminal. Now the rest of the world knows it, too. I'm satisfied. And I have his medallion."

"It did look a lot like this one." Absently, she fingered her own charm. Trent had dropped it in the tunnel, and the Mounties had returned it to her. "Who would have believed the etchings on this would have caused so much heartache?"

Drew brushed his lips against the top of her head. "Don't forget that charm helped bring us together. If I hadn't yanked it off, you might never have noticed me."

"You're wrong." Betsy swiveled around to him. "I noticed you the minute you walked into Yukon Lights. I knew then that I wanted you."

"And I love a woman who knows what she wants."

"It's the 'spell of the Yukon.'" Betsy couldn't help teasing him. "Once you've experienced it, you're never the same."

"You can say that again." Drew tossed back his head and laughed. "But yours is the only spell that's captured me, lovely lady, and I wouldn't have it any other way."

# PAMELA BROWNING

... is fireworks on the green at the Fourth of July and prayers said around the Thanksgiving table. It is the dream of freedom realized in thousands of small towns across this great nation.

But mostly, the Heartland is its people. People who care about and help one another. People who cherish traditional values and give to their children the greatest gift, the gift of love.

American Romance presents HEARTLAND, an emotional trilogy about people whose memories, hopes and dreams are bound up in the acres they farm.

HEARTLAND ... the story of America.

Don't miss these heartfelt stories: American Romance #237 SIMPLE GIFTS (March), #241 FLY AWAY (April), and #245 HARVEST HOME (May).

HRT-1

# ATTRACTIVE, SPACE SAVING BOOK RACK

Display your most prized novels on this handsome and sturdy book rack. The hand-rubbed walnut finish will blend into your library decor with quiet elegance, providing a practical organizer for your favorite hard-or soft-covered books.

**Only $9.95**

**Approximately 16" x 8" when assembled**

**Assembles in seconds!**

---

To order, rush your name, address and zip code, along with a check or money order for $10.70* ($9.95 plus 75¢ postage and handling) payable to *Harlequin Reader Service*:

Harlequin Reader Service
Book Rack Offer
901 Fuhrmann Blvd.
P.O. Box 1396
Buffalo, NY 14269-1396

BKR-1A

*Offer not available in Canada.*

*New York and Iowa residents add appropriate sales tax.

**Deep in the heart of Africa lay mankind's most
awesome secret. Could they find Eden . . .
and the grave of Eve?**

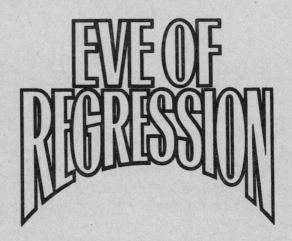

# JOHN ARTHUR LONG

A spellbinding novel that combines a fascinating
premise with all the ingredients of an edge-of-the-seat
read: passion, adventure, suspense and danger.

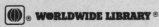